HARVE

BODY PARTS

David J. Brown

Published by David J. Brown Books LLC

HARVEST SEASON
BODY PARTS
All Rights Reserved
Copyright © 2020 David J. Brown

DAVID J. BROWN BOOKS LLC
http://www.davidjbrownbooks.com

Paperback ISBN:
Library of Congress Control Number:

Cover photography and design by:
Lisa and Brad Christenson, Northland Photo

This book may not be reproduced, transmitted, or stored in whole or in part by any means, including graphic, electronic, or mechanical without the express written consent of the publisher except in the case of brief quotations embodied in critical articles and reviews.

PRINTED IN THE UNITED STATES OF AMERICA

GOD BLESS AMERICA

Readers Praise and Well Wishes of David Brown's works and the announcement of his retirement as an Author

"Profoundly honest.....Painfully direct"
You gave me more hope, understanding, and you taught me what forgiveness is truly all about!
    Gail Phillips   Wenatchee, Washington

"Fertile ground for introspection"
With new growth comes change. Your truths resonate at a frequency that connects you with me and others.
    Brian Cook   Longmont, Colorado

"Your style is straight up with a side of pain!"
Wow. For each there is a season to work, and a season to rest. Take some rest you deserve it. Thank you for honestly sharing your heart, pain, and your endurance and love. You are a profoundly unique human. It is an honor sir.
    Nelson Glaze   LaCenter, Washington

"Wonderful my friend"
Now tie up the details and relax like you deserve to. Demons have been laid to rest and you will never know how many people you have helped by your Crusade. This is YOUR time now! You have earned it and deserve it.
    Susan Kiker   Interlochen, Michigan

"A storyteller for the ages."
Enjoyed your books immensely. They had me stop and think about life in someone else's time
    Barb Hardmeier   Peoria, Illinois

"Stay truthful my friend."
Truth can be as sharp as a samurai sword, and as soothing as a down pillow.
It just depends if you are ready for it.
  Anthony Davis Oak Forrest, Illinois

Mr. Brown
You are a HERO to the many of us that have been in your shoes. You are the voice for the one's that can't speak out of fear. Your First Responder years also proves that. Be proud my friend, we are survivors from the hands of evil!
  Debby Lomax Farmington, New Mexico

Mr. David Brown
For years I have felt like I had been carrying a burden…now I know I share this same burden and will never feel alone again in this path we walk. Thanks so much David!
  Tammy Williams-Lynch Brownsville, Tennessee

"Re-reading Flash of a Fraud"
Still pulls at my heart strings and brings a lot of tears. Makes me take a long and hard look at my life. Love you David!
  Penny O'Briant Longmont, Colorado

"Quite the journey"
The way David's books were written will speak to you on many levels. It will also allow you to relate and reflect not just on David's story of his life but it also allows you to pause to do the same.
  Christine Richie Duluth, Minnesota

Thank you David Brown
Now enjoy the rest of your well-deserved time off and take solace and comfort in the fact that you have helped many more people than you will ever realize. Thank you for your service and wisdom fine sir. We will take it from here.
    Christopher James   Milwaukee, Wisconsin

"A champion for the people"
Thank you Mate for both your caring and healing with your kind words. Excited to read your new book. Your friend from across the pond.
    Kevin Cudbertson   Sedgefield, UK

PUBLISHER'S NOTE

"Harvest Season" is the third in the series of novels by David J. Brown.

This book and Mr. Brown's other books, 'Daddy Had to Say Goodbye' and 'Flesh of a Fraud' are available free of charge through, "The United States Library of Congress, National Library Service for the Blind and Physically Handicapped" as well as from the State of Minnesota, Department of Health, Services for the Blind and Handicapped.

This story is a work of fiction. It is inspired in part, by true life events. In certain cases, locations, incidents, characters and timelines have been changed for dramatic purposes. Certain characters may be composites, or entirely fictitious.

HARVEST SEASON

BODY PARTS

A novel by David J. Brown
Copyright © 2020
DJBROWNBOOKS LLC
www.davidjbrownbooks.com
Duluth Minnesota
A special thank you to my website and book design artist:
Angie Simonson of Main Idea Creative Marketing and Design
www.mainideacreative.com
I couldn't have done it without you Angie. I am forever in your debt.

INTRODUCTION

The word fear has several definitions. The most agreed definitions have to do with indifference (denial), fight or flight. If you subscribe to the science of Neurobiology you need to read something else. I know fear, I ate fear and I threw it back up.

Some claim that there are only two forms of fear, the fear of not getting what you want or loosing what you currently have. Those are the 'indifferent' ones, the ones that say, "Oh it should be fine." They say, 'It should be fine' because they want to do something that is ill advised, dangerous or simply foolish. When it doesn't turn out, 'fine' they are inconsolable.

The condition of "Fight or Flight" is also fear biased but much more complicated.
The bulk of my fear comes from my personal life experiences. There is such a thing as a, 'healthy fear.' We don't lick the frosting off of electric beater blades when it is still being used. We don't clear grass from a running lawn mower blade. Common sense is not all that common and that is the, why of emergency departments and ambulances.

I was a fight rather than flight kind of fellow. I still am a fighter, even at the age of seventy-two. Of course you will never find me without a high quality handgun on my side. As a paramedic and later a police officer, I never had the luxury of running and hiding when things got scary. It wasn't just because the job description demanded it, I thrived on it!

I ran into burning houses and buildings wearing cotton/poly blend shirts and pants. I ran toward gunfire, found cover and returned fire. There were times that there was no cover, but I never let that stop me.

Was I too foolish, too arrogant or too frightened to accept fear? Is there a fear of all fears? I say yes, I have found that the greatest of all fears is self-discovery and all the truths behind our failures. Some think if they don't try, then they can't fail. If you hide and deny your failures, using the blame of others than you are held harmless. You also hold yourself captive. People do live that way, we all know people that live that way. I find that type of mentality, sadly heartbreaking. People give in to fears and quit on themselves.

Giving into fear is a dream killer. I sign all of my books;

Dreams are worth dreaming

Dare to dream

And

Dream BIG!

When I do book signings and 'meet the author' events I spend some time talking about fear. I have found that a large percentage of attendees secretly would like to, at least try to write a book. If you have read my other two books you already know how I view the word 'fear' as an acronym and not a valid word.

Fear: False …… Evidence …… Appearing …… Real

However you are about to enter a world of the deepest of all fears, the fear of dying alone, deep into the deepest crevasses of your mind. No sound, no light, no feeling, or touch. Enjoy your headfirst plunge into the bowels of hell!

DEDICATED TO MY READERS

You would not let me go, you asked for more, you demanded more. I am grateful for your allegiance and your kindness. I have completed this part of my journey.

Never let anyone tell you that you can't do it.
Never tell yourself that you can't do it.

Within all fiction, lies a bit of the truth.
Within all truth, lies a bit of fiction.
Our perceptions are the deciding factors.

David J. Brown

Chapter 1 DARK-DARK

  Where am I? How did I get here? I can't feel, hear or see anything! Am I dying or maybe already dead? Am I in some kind of a suspended animation? Am I on life support? Perhaps I'm in that terrifying 'golden hour', where only emergency surgical treatment will prevent my death? Did I have a heart attack? Was I in a traffic accident, stabbed or shot? Maybe I drowned, I do like the water. I love to trout fish in streams and lakes. If so, I must have fallen into a stream, as Heather forbids me to buy a canoe for fear of my capsizing and drowning. Once again, water injury would be the most likely reason that I'm laying here with having zero sensitivity indications. I'm baffled and bewildered. I do know that the average time for being underwater without a severe neurological disability is on average of 10 minutes. Maybe I did drown. Could I be in a hyperbaric chamber where the human body is detoxed from bubbles in the blood stream from rapid loss of nitrogen such as, 'the bends'? That might be why I have no sensory feedback. That would make sense but I don't think that they would put an unconscious patient in a sealed chamber. Back to the water thing, I'm thinking of my past water experiences which have been a cruel mistress to me my entire life.
  I witnessed two men drown at the same time, watched my childhood pals body be carried to shore and almost drowned myself, all before I was 12 years old. I can't even count the number of floaters I have recovered (drowned persons) in the bay of Lake Superior on Park Point, that came from the nursing home's prior to the days of patient alarms on the nursing home doors. Along with all of these thoughts, I am somehow hearing the song 'The Endless

Sleep', by Jody Reynolds. The song was about his girlfriend who threw herself into the sea because they quarreled, he found her body and joined her in the endless sleep. But I know I would never take my own life, I made a promise to God. God has brought me too far for that! I'm pretty sure that I'm still alive. I just don't know to what degree my injuries may be. Can I recover? Holy shit, am I on life support just to keep me alive to keep my organs fresh for a harvesting? Jesus Christ are they going to gut me like a fish or a deer? I know there are no cut off ages for donating organs. They do transplants from newborns to people in their eighties.

    I somehow remember that the internal organ, "out of body time" from removal to transport and transplant for a heart is like 4 to 6 hours. Pancreas and liver is 24 hours, kidney 72 hours, cornea 14 days, bone and skin is up to 5 years. I used to be an organ donor until a friend of mine who needed a heart was put on a recipient list. He was listed as number 407, well the next week his extraordinarily wealthy father came to town to visit with him and his doctors and low and behold, my friend had a new heart the following week. I would not say that the organ donations are a bad idea but I have to wonder how many organ donors could have survived except that someone may have already bought their organs. That kind of shit gives me the creeps and further deepens my mistrust of doctors and the medical profession.

    I remember that I wrote out a living will more than ten years ago, that was put in my medical file with a hospital in Colorado. I listed my final wishes as to my continued life support duration and medications. I wonder if hospitals have a national registry of living wills, if not my organs must stay with me. Heather and I are not married so she can't give consent and I have no living family members. Ok, I have to get out of my head and be still. I have to quiet my mind and try to hear or sense what is going on around me. I'm trying not to think but I keep seeing old memories like screen crawlers on the bottom of the TV screen. I'm seeing things like a plane crash at Salt Lake City, an oxygen bottling facility exploding, a passenger train derailing and falling down a deep canyon wall and smashing into boulders the size of army tanks.

Jeez this shit is just clogging my brain, I don't know how long I have laid in silence. I suddenly feel the hair on my arms move with someone touching me. Did someone walk by me or did a door open or a ventilation system blower come on? Is my mind playing tricks on me or did I actually feel something? I wonder if I'm alone, I wonder if Heather is with me. I wonder what time it is, what day it is and what the fuck is going on with me. I feel my body being lifted. Someone is lifting me, I think I hear muffled voices like they are wearing surgical masks but they are far, far away from me. Now, it is silence again. I have never heard this kind of silence before and it's black, black-black. I can't hear, see or feel anything. Panic is starting to overcome me. Do they know that I'm still alive, are they able to measure my brain activity? Am I in a morgue, in one of those big sliding file cabinets? Am I splayed wide open on a drain table? I can feel my inner self trying to fight to come back. How do I signal to them that I'm still alive? I have to be careful to not overexert myself. I could kill myself by pushing too hard to come to, too fast.
Then again, if I don't fight my ass off, I could die. I have always been a fight, not flight guy. Fuck it, I'm fighting! I would rather die with honor than live with the shame of a coward's heart. The only chance I currently have is to work with my mind. I have heard all my life that it's mind over matter. But this shit is way different. In most all police academy's you are taught that your mind is by far the superior weapon, more than any other weapon on your duty belt.

I've got no other options, I have to think my way out of this deal. How the fuck do I do that? I wish I could shout out in anger, make a fist and punch a hole in the fuckin wall. I can't even feel myself breathing. I won't quit but I don't know how to start!

Why is that rat bastard, Adam's in my mind suddenly? I hate that fuckin narcissistic asshole!

I wish I had a save button in my brain. Heather is relentless with her constant reminders to press 'save' as I'm writing. I hope she's doing OK with all of this whatever 'all of this' is. I hope it was not an auto accident and that she was with me. I have got to find a way to wake up, to make sure that she is OK. It's not fair to her to have to worry about me. I got to get it together, what if she needs me?

Chapter 2 DOWNSHIFT

OK, how do I settle down? I keep thinking about my friend back in Colorado who's a heart surgeon and transplant specialist. He had to leave the state to do his procedures because their instruments were so delicate that they were adversely affected due to smoke from nearby forest fires. I've got to be on some kind of heart monitor, maybe a special brain monitor measuring brainwaves. What if their instruments are faulty, how often do they calibrate or test them? How well trained is the technician and do they even give a shit, what if they hate their job? This shitty thinking is making me more than just a bit nuts. I don't know if I need to sleep to repair the damage to prove that my brain is still working, fuck I don't know what to do!

OK, OK, OK. I have to slow down with this scary shit that I have no control over. Use your head Brown, be smart. Except for the fact that you are now fighting for your very life, get focused and stay on task. You have authored two published books to your credit, a novelist for the Christ sake! Think like you write! Well shit I'm not a professional writer with an education. I don't understand or much care about all that crap on how to structure a story and lay out rough drafts or chapters. I just let the chapters write themselves. They decide when a group of pages completes the chapters. I did not start out with chapter titles or use a structured format. Fuck that bullshit. I just write, when I read over my work is when a chapter is complete and then I give it a chapter title and move on to the next. I write in my head for weeks if not months before my pen first strikes the paper.

Damn it, there I go again! Think, think, think! I must be going through nicotine withdraws. I've been a dedicated smoker since I was 14 years old. Why the hell did I just say 'dedicated' like that is something to be proud of? I'm cracking up for sure. I do remember the time that I woke up in a hospital and they told me that I had a cardiac arrest from an episode of cardiac prolapse from stress. When I came to I was craving a cigarette. I was in ICCU for four days. I had my wife give me a cigarette from my clothes locker. I held the cigarette under my nose and just kept slowly spinning it around and sniffing it. It seemed to take the edge off for a few minutes. My nurse saw me doing it and she snatched it from my fingers and got all bitchy about my trying to light a cigarette in the ICCU. When she settled down, I explained to her that I was just sniffing it and I had no matches or lighter and I had no intention of lighting it. I asked her for one of those nicotine patches to curb my craving. She said she would check with a doctor. The doctor came into my room and was laughing as he said he read in my chart about my sniffing a cigarette. He said he would write an order for the nurses to give me something for the relief of my cravings and it would be PRN. It wasn't but a few minutes later that a nurse came in with a drawn syringe and added it to my IV line. Whatever it was it worked. I immediately lost my craving. Two days later when I was being discharged I ask the doctor for a prescription for whatever they gave me in my IV line to help me to stop smoking. He laughed his ass off as he told me he would not as he said, "Buster that shit was morphine, pure morphine! That is how badly you are addicted to cigarettes, you better check yourself and stop smoking now. You have a four day head start, so it's a great time to stop. Give it some thought."

I remember walking out of the hospital and lighting a cigarette before I stepped off the sidewalk, the first drag about blue top of my head off. By the time we got to my wife's car I was stoned to the bone!

What the hell is this shit? How the living hell can I focus on anything with these nut job rants dancing in my skull? I know I have to keep up my brain activity to tell the monitors that I'm still alive but this freak show has got to stop! Damn it, what I wouldn't give for a pen and a notepad, hell I'd settle for a sticky note and a goddamn crayon! I have to make a list and stick to it. It's like I'm driving up and ice covered steep hill but I keep sliding backwards! I have to have a plan. OK, I can't let it matter as to what happened, it's a moot point. It can only be about what I'm going to do. I guess I have to accept that I have a brain injury of some sort. I need to fall back of my years of being a paramedic. The only thing that rings familiar is the on-going and constant arguments between two fellows I worked with.

    Larry, who was called "Doc Z" and Ryc Lyden. Both were smart as hell but equal royal pains in my ass! They were always bickering as to which ran the human body, the heart or the brain. There would always try to drag me into the middle of their arguments. Ryc was pro brain and Doc Z was the heart guru. I think Ryc was smarter but Doc Z was more cunning. Ryc would go to the public library (there was no google back in the day) to gather data and use it like ammo for their next shift, war zone bout. Crafty ole Doc Z was like the wolf, sitting with a herd of sheep discussing what's going to be for dinner. Doc Z was a charmer. He would go to the hospital's medical libraries in uniform on his days off. He would tell the medical librarians that he was prepping for an entrance exam for medical school. With his good looks and boyish charms the librarians all but did backflips for him. The library medical publications were all stamped everywhere that they were to be checked out only to physicians and they were not to leave the hospital campus. Slick ole Doc Z was given anything he wanted and was told to take them home if he needed to and he could bring them back any time he would like. As he walked out of the two different hospital libraries, I'm sure he got a kiss on each cheek, a cupcake and probably a lollipop.

    Larry, known as 'Doc Z', got his nickname from an emergency room doctor. When we brought in a patient we always gave a report and our observations to the receiving registered property. Watching those two was like reading mad magazine, 'Spy vs Spy'. Those two never quit. I guess the payout for me with those two clowns was that they taught me more than I had really wanted to know or learn. We ran several road trips a month. We took patients to the Mayo Clinic in Rochester Minnesota which was 226 miles and five hours of drive time. Saint Paul Minnesota was160 miles and just under four hours, depending upon whether. Most of those trips were one-ways with the patient being left at our destination. On the return trip home, whether it was Ryc or Doc Z, they would drag out their latest medical books and they would play '20 questions' and 'did you know'? Yes, I got a lot of fresh info but as some point I would look over at them to say, "I'm done learning for the day teacher. We are going 80 miles an hour and if I hear any more of this shit, I will crank on this wheel and roll this motherfucker and then you can tell us all about your autopsy."

Ryc was no slouch, he was a sly dog in his own rights. To get a leg up on Doc Z he proposed to the owner of the ambulance service that he (Ryc) become the training officer for the company, as he had a personal friendship with a director of emergency services at Saint Mary's hospital.

Well, Ryc got full access to the hospital's library and attended emergency medicine in-service meetings and brought in several doctors for our weekly in-service meetings. The guy's got college credit for in-service classes and we all became better at our jobs. But some of the guy's resented Ryc for showing them what they didn't know. Nobody likes their tiny little ego stepped on but they did become better and our patient's mortality numbers decreased significantly, in a short period of time.

Shit, I'm doing it again. I got to get back, I got to get back to the 'mouth ooze' that those two made me nuts with. There must be some information I can recall from those times. OK, Doc Z is first. He was the internal medicine, heart freak. Ryc was a brain and central nervous system guy.

OK Doc Z, let me think of what I remember from our driving sessions.

What was the number one statement he constantly threw out? "The heart is its own pacemaker independent of the brain. As long as it has oxygen it continues to beat."

The heart could actually be removed from the body, be placed in a saline solution, given oxygen and will still continue to beat. This is why although the brain is dead, the heart continues to beat." Well that was Doc Z's favorite flag to wave.

Chapter 3   COMBATIVE TEACHERS

I think that is safe to say that I'm in some sort of a coma. Was I in a medically induced coma due to an injury or did the condition arise from an injury itself? Of course it could also be some kind of psychosis from an emotional ass kicking. Could be a sensory overload or did my PTSD take me out? What is the true definition of psychosis? I guess it might follow under the 'Brainiac' Ryc's definitions. Something to the effect of, "Some kind of mental disconnect from a severe mental disorder where thought and emotions are so impaired that they lose contact with all external realities."

Am I sitting in a psychiatric hospital TV room, locked into my own mind with people moving all around me and my not seeing or hearing them? I wish I knew more about this shit. I do remember that less than 80,000 people get this condition a year nationwide. What more do I know about psychosis? What the fuck brings that shit on? I think it has something to do with a person's thoughts and perceptions as to recognize whether it is real or is it not. Some reports claim that it's not an illness in its own right but rather a symptom of a mental illness such as schizophrenia and bipolar disorder. Then you have that whole thing about hallucinations with seeing, hearing, feeling and tasting shit that's not even there. Ain't that fuckin fun, right?

I won't take the fall under any category like that. I'm nothing like those meth heads who dance crazy without music and hold conversations with trees and walls. I think I'm the complete opposite. I have no sensory perceptions, just a black void. I remember reading that chronic and severe depression will bring on symptoms of psychotic episodes where the patient withdraws from family and friends and loses interest in activities that are normally meaningful. So is this a transient situation that will at some point pass? Jesus Christ, I wish I understood more about this shit. I don't take any drugs of any kind. The only pill I take is a multi-vitamin twice a day. Once again I've reached another moot point. There is always that possibility that I attempted suicide and failed. I have danced with suicidal ideations most all of my life. I have mentally hung my toes over the edge of a diving board looking down into the Grand Canyon. No, I don't think so. I have challenged my many demons on several occasions. Yes I do get depressed at times but I refuse to let it drag me down the rabbit hole. I'm a survivor and more importantly, I'm a warrior. I carry a great deal of power from my writing and publishing my last two novels. I'm blessed to have a fan base who champions me daily with emails and messages from readers that tell me that I've made a difference in their lives. Many want to tell me of their newfound freedoms and joy they have discovered from reading my books.

I also get several questions when the next book will be published. Some even want to pre-order and pre-pay for my new book which is several months away from completion. There are a handful of readers who want to start a bidding war as to who gets to stand next to the printing press to pull the, 'First printed,' first edition off the press and to have a photograph with me signing their first edition book. I have had to tell them that I can't and I won't honor their games. This group is actually a lot of fun. They have established a website where my readers can do reviews and ask other readers their experience and opinions of my books. Some engage with banter and at times they become a bit aggressive with each other and will ask me who is right, they even argue about the meaning of just one sentence sometimes. I have to remind them that I am a novelist and not a playground monitor. I do take a bit of pride in influencing more than one reader to consider writing their own book. There are always a few that want to tell me about how I missed the mark and are glad to tell me and everyone else how a certain chapter or event should have actually been written.

I like to ask them about their books that they have written and published. If they continue with their envy fueled attacks I simply tell them to go fuck a tree.

Chapter 4   THE ODDS

Well that sure went south in a hurry. Yes I certainly drifted off topic once again but at least I'm showing some brain activity or least I hope I am. I may as well have some fun with whatever the fuck this is. Just like ole Doc Z would say, "Internal organs can't talk, we must first listen to them so we may speak for them." Doc Z, much like any legitimate physicians, play the same cancelation game. 'Well it's not this, it's not that, it might be this. They just cancel the possibilities through the process of elimination until they hit upon the most likely problem. Of course those were the days that head and body scanners along with blood proteins were in their infancy of development and not in production. But they were often times used in sci-fi movies. At this point I guess it's got to be a coma. It doesn't really matter what from, what does matter is how long it lasts. I do know that I only have three weeks at best, to come out of this deal before I'm a carrot or a head of lettuce. Most people don't survive after week four. If they do recover the prognosis is not good. I couldn't deal with being a vegetable, just locked into my own mind with that being my total world. Of course what would my options be?

OK so what do I understand about comas? Well according the boy genius Ryc Lyden, there is a fine line between unconsciousness and coma. Unconsciousness is an interruption of awareness and lack of ability to notice or respond to stimuli. Some people become unconscious due to oxygen deprivation, shock, or central nervous system interruptions from depressants such as alcohol and drugs or injury. In psychology, I think it's that part of thought and emotion that happens outside everyday awareness.

Comas are supposedly a temporary situation where they don't last more than two to four weeks. The prognosis depends upon the cause of the coma as to the severity of the brain injury for those who do recover. Recovery is usually gradual. Many patients can recover fully with a great deal of aftercare. OK, if I remember right, there's a window within the first six hours where patients that show eye opening have almost a 1 in 5 chance of achieving a good recovery, whereas if you do not have one, you have a 1 in 10 chance. Those who show no motor response have a 3% chance of making a good recovery. Well that's just fuckin lovely! There are supposedly three stages of a coma, a vegetative state, a minimally conscious state, whatever the hell that is, and I can't remember the third, I can't remember what they actually are either. Many patients require lifelong physical and occupational therapy while others may recover only basic functions. Well another cheery piece of news. There is something about a Glasgow coma scale where they grade you is to your ability to recover.

    I don't get any part of that shit and then there's that other side of the coin where some patients who awaken from a coma may also develop a so called, "locked in syndrome." Who the fuck wants to be completely conscious but paralyzed and unable to communicate except through eye blinks? Then you have the whole subconscious state when a conscious mind is at rest and the subconscious mind takes over. It's kind of like people that are sound asleep and yet they could smell smoke, wake up and find their house on fire. There is something within the inner person that reports that to the brain which saves a person's life. So we are back to playing with what causes unconsciousness. Blunt trauma, severe blood loss, substance abuse, alcohol poisoning, low blood sugar, dehydration and hyperventilation. I think I remember something about and I've seen it before where diabetics will go into a state of unconsciousness where they can only blink their eyes. Oxygen deprivation of course can be caused by a cardiac arrest with the blood flow being cut off to the brain and develop hypoxia after CPR. Survivors of cardiac arrest are often in a coma. Oxygen deprivation will also occur with drowning and choking victims. There is a ton of shit stored in my brain about this stuff but it isn't of any value at this time. Fucked is fucked.

Chapter 5   A TOTAL NOBODY

Jesus Christ, I have to get out of this medical bullshit stuff, it's not making any sense to me and I probably know a lot less than I think I do. I think I better move on as none of this is taking me anywhere. It makes me further know that medicine even today, is still a, "best guess practice" game. I have to trust that someone will give a shit about a total stranger that is only known to them by his medical chart and a wristband. They don't know who I am. If I were a man of prominence, a business or civic leader, if I was someone they knew, or who's known to a staff member, I'm sure I would get better treatment. Does a stranger receive the same level of care? Where does an absolute nobody fall in to the category of, "To the best of our abilities?" I know this answer. I've seen it too many times before, the answer is no, no they don't.

I hate this feeling of being so fuckin weak. I have no voice, I have no say on anything. I'm just a piece of meat at this time. I am nothing, nothing to no one. I'm locked within myself, I am completely powerless. I'm at the mercy of my caregivers that is, if I even have any caregivers and if they actually do care. I wonder if this is how a newborn feels.

OK, OK, OK, this fear and this rage is at a level that is unknown to me. I have to let go of all this shit. I just have to accept the fact that I am totally and completely fucked.

But I can still fight to keep my mind active. These are all but the very same feelings I have had with each of my failed marriages, each job loss and each family member's death.

I know a hell of a lot about loss, I know very little about success. I got to get out of this craziness if I am going to survive and recover from this, whatever the fuck this is. I need to start looking beyond my fears, none of this will serve me in any form.

Chapter 6   THE PROMISE

    I somehow have to find a way to move forward. I don't know what time it is, day or night, not even what day it is. Shit how long have I been this way? Has it been a long time, has it been days, weeks, months, or even years? I read somewhere sometime back, about a guy in England who came out of a coma after 18 years! He was pretty much a vegetable in a shell. That shits not for me! I would rather die with some level of dignity, even if I don't know I'm dying!
    Is Heather still with me, is she right next to me? I have to find a way to let her know that I'm OK. She has got to know that I'm fighting my ass off. Has this been going on for so long that she only comes by every few days or just on weekends, if she has time? Have I been forgotten, has she moved on? I know from my paramedic days that families don't visit the elderly very often in nursing homes. I've seen young people in comas who will probably never leave a nursing home. I brought many of those people from hospitals to those nursing homes myself. I always found it haunting, doing those hospital to nursing home transfers. Those poor souls, young and old were having their last ride of their lives, they were now being placed into permanent storage. Is that me? Is that old saying of, "What comes around goes around" happening to me? Is this the true definition of the cycle of life?
    I know in my heart of hearts that Heather would never leave me to be alone. She would never close the door on me like I'm just some unnecessary object in a storage locker. I remember the stories told to me by her and her family of her brother Kyle who had instantly become a quadriplegic from a traffic accident. His condition was touch-and-go as the medical staff battled to keep

him alive for several days. From the moment Heather got the call of Kyle's accident and his injury's she appointed herself as his medical advocate and the chief care provider for her little brother. She kept the nursing staff on their game for sure. She was going to the hospital every morning before work. She would brush his teeth for him, brush his hair and suctioned him, as he periodically had trouble swallowing and breathing. Kyle was a difficult patient and he refused to eat. Heather was the only person that could coax him to eat. He of course could not feed himself and the hospital staff was in too big of a hurry to take the time to properly feed him and he would choke. Heather took over the feeding duties. She would take a two hour lunch to go to the hospital to feed him properly and she would lose an hours pay each day. The moment she left work at the end of each day, it was straight back to the hospital to visit and feed him dinner. What is amazing was that they were most oftentimes at odds with each other. As young kids they rarely spoke before Kyle's accident.

Yeah, I know Heather is here with me. I just wish I could find a way to acknowledge her presence. I have to find a way to let her know that I'm OK and I'm not going to quit on me or her. I am fighting and I will continue to fight to come back. I won't allow myself to die or remain in this condition. I promised her that I would never leave her again, when I returned from Colorado the last time I left her.

Chapter 7 TIMELINES

I need some kind of timeline memory. What was the last date and time that I can lock onto? I don't write checks so that won't help, when is the last time I wrote down a date? I know that we've been raking leaves and that some light snow (without accumulation) was falling. I think it might be close to Halloween. I remember that I blew my diet from eating a bunch of Halloween candy. I remember there was an MzB's Halloween Podcast show on Spreaker, iHeartRadio and a bunch of those other channels. OK let me see now, her show is on Saturday night with John Solar. Let's see, every Monday night is the Piedmont Heights AA meeting and I know that I went to that. Then there is the Wednesday night meeting in Superior. I always ride with Dave Quinn and he brings me a cup of coffee from Quick Trip, so I will trade him cigarettes for coffee and gas. It's just a silly little game we play. Dave is trying to quit smoking so he is forcing himself to not buy any cigarettes. So he really looks forward to Monday and Wednesday night's meetings to get his 'smoke on' as well as lunch with the boys on Friday afternoons. Dave Quinn hates the weekends because his wife stays home both days and he can't openly smoke when she's there. Something about his life ending, nonsense heart problems that she is concerned about. He has A-fib and often times some extremely low oxygen levels.

With his multiple hospitalizations, I always say, "You are gonna die anyway, you might as well have a smoke and a smile before the final trip where you become ashes, just like what's on the end of that cigarette you're smoking!"

OK so I got Monday, Wednesday and Friday covered. And yes, then there is Eric Bomey (husband of Mz. Bomey) and his Friday night Podcast, "Locked and Loaded," broadcast on Spreaker which is again sponsored by John Solar. Eric (the poor bastard) has a ton of subscribers but no advertising sponsors because he goes after the 'Kookfuck' liberals and says fuck a lot, a lot, and then a lot more. But I love the guy, he is a great friend and is a realist with a heart much bigger than his wallet! He also does a YouTube show several days a week called "BandEBrewReviews" where he taste tests the latest craft beer releases from around the world. It's kind of a funny because as he tastes and drinks these beers he also plays with his many custom guns. What could possibly go wrong? Eric has a level of knowledge of exotic rifles, shotguns and handguns that would rival most professional gunsmiths. Eric does several custom gun builds himself. He and his wife Christine build guns with a group of likeminded folks and promote fundraisers for "Justin's Final Mission", though "The Wounded Warriors Project".

I met Eric when he was a small boy (50ish now) when he was only six or seven years old. His mother and I worked for the same ambulance company. Several nights a week his mom worked late in the office doing insurance billing. She was a single mom so where she went the kids went. I remember Eric and his Sister Pam sleeping on the couches in the squad room. Cute kids, both shy but polite.

Wait what the fuck was that? I just saw a small window like an airplane window. It moved from left to right and then came to dead center and danced up-and-down then suddenly it has been enveloped by a fog bank. It went away then everything got black again, just the same as it has been. I didn't even realize that there was a backdrop of a muted gray. As I understand it, hallucinations are common in the last minutes of life. Is this it, am I done? Do I just stop thinking and wait for it to happen? Can you really witness your own death? How do you know when you're dead? This is like when you're at a play during intermission and the lights flicker to tell you to return to your seats, once your seated the lights fade to black, just before the play resumes.

OK this shit is too crazy, even for me. I have to get back to establishing a timeline but wait, what the fuck was that airplane window thing? Are they opening my eyelids to harvest my eyes, was that the light I saw? First the window on the left, then it went to the right and then dead center, then went straight away and disappeared in a dense fog. Was my brain watching them take my eyes away? And then things went black, a solid black-black. Was the muted gray light when they open my eyelids to do the procedure and when they were done they closed my eye lids again which sent me back to the black. If I haven't had a heart attack yet, I'm sure as fuck about to!

I have to shut up with this shit. Focus God damn it! Find a way to a path in your memory. Discipline yourself you dumb fuck, you're fighting for your very life, now fight you pussy!

I don't read newspapers so I haven't seen a masthead from a newspaper which always has the date of publication. I do the family grocery shopping but I never look at the date on the receipts. Wait there's another one of those fuckin crawler screens like I see on the bottom of my TV. What the fuck is that, October 10th, Floodwood, Minnesota? What is going on October 10th in Floodwood, Minnesota? I have never even been there, what is it that I need to remember? Think, Think, Think. October 10th, what was October 10th? Wait a minute, I remember that way back in the spring, May or June I believe, was when I wrote something down for October 10th! What the hell was it? OK take a deep breath, breathe, breathe damn you. All right stop being so desperate, just let it come. You know it's there, just let it come. One more deep breath, that's it! Yeah Lori, my cousin Lori! Hell, the last time I saw her was at my cousin Rolene's funeral, three years ago. Prior to that I hadn't seen her for more than 50 years! If her brother Stephen hadn't been sitting next to her, I don't think I would have recognized her. Stephen and I have been pals on Facebook for several years. Our families were never close and family gatherings just didn't happen. As kids, the few times I did see Lori she was always sweet but quiet, maybe a bit withdrawn, but then again so was I. I do remember hearing that she was going to college and wanted to become a teacher. I didn't think her family was really the college type. My two uncles were both bartenders who later owned small greasy spoon restaurants. They both worked their guts out as I remember. They were good guys of course and I knew them from deer hunting camp and a few fishing trips.

Damn it, there I go again! Back to Lori. She told me at Rolene's funeral that she had retired from the Floodwood school system. I think she was there for something like more than 30 years. Lori had the same wide eyed look as most everyone when I told her that I had lived in Colorado for the last forty years, was a former police officer and I had written and published a novel. Lori was too much of a lady to say, "You gotta be shittin me, you were a cop and then you wrote a book?"

Well, I always bring a stack of books with me wherever I go. This day was no different, I went out to my truck and I got several copies of my books for all of my cousins. I guess it might have seemed a bit arrogant as if to say to them, "See, I'm not the loser that you all thought I was" but then again I don't think Lori or Stephen judges people that way.

When I released my second book, I emailed Lori along with all my other cousins and told him that I'd like to gift them a copy of me second book if they would just send me their mailing addresses. Lori sent me a very kind and flattering review about my books. She wrote that my books are on the top of her 'all-time favorite list' of 'real life stories.' I didn't realize that Lori was such an avid reader. She claims to read a book every three days since she's retired. A few weeks went by and Lori sent me an email asking me if I would like to speak at her semiannual ladies group business luncheon meeting and asked what my fee would be, (my standard speaking fee is $400.00 for an 80 minute appearance within 75 miles. If I have to fly it is a straight $2,000 for each engagement). I of course would not tell Lori that. I told her that if her group fed me and kept me in great volumes of coffee, we would call it good. I accepted her kind invitation. There it is! October 10th! I went to speak and sign books for Lori's ladies group in Floodwood, Minnesota! Yes, it was at the Rich Event Center in Floodwood, Minnesota!

It was a much longer drive than I realized and I arrived a bit late. I hate being late for anything, lucky for me there were still having their business meeting. After I spoke about my experience of writing books for about 80 minutes, I signed several stacks of books for the ladies. That's where the date came from that popped into my head. I always date my books as I sign them.

Yup, I wrote 10/10/2019 several times that day. Cool bunch of ladies, they are a, Ladies-aid type of group who look after people in rural areas with small household chores, they do shopping for them and make crafts and quilts for the elderly and the shut-in's. Pretty neat people, nice program.

OK that's my last documented date memory. Was I in a crash on the way home that day? It's just a two lane highway and it's spooky as hell with sharp curves, hidden side roads and has a heavy volume of lumber trucks hauling to the mills. I felt fine that day so I don't think I got sick but then again, I have seen and treated several hundred people who had heart attacks and strokes that felt fine right up until that very moment. Not everyone who has a heart attack or stroke loses consciousness and goes into a coma however. Damn it, I'm fading back again. I've got to focus on the last event before I ended up here, wherever the fuck, 'here' is.

I am bothered with these 'crawler lines' that turn me around and take away my main focus. Is my sub-conscious speaking to me because I'm unconscious? Are there layers of unconsciousness, like peeling the 'therapy onion'? Fucked if I know. I should have paid more attention to the Brainiac Ryc Lyden when he was badgering me with superfluous bullshit on our return road trips.

Chapter 8   I NEED A SMOKE

Maybe I'm entirely going at this the wrong way. I'm grasping for dates and timelines that makes no sense at all. Hell, I don't even know what day it is or date it is today. So I've got to move onto shit that actually matters. God what a dork I am! OK, I have got to try to use events and names to figure this stuff out. I need to go back to the last person I saw or spoke with. Or do I go for the last event or situation that I can recall? That's it! That would make things a lot less complicated. God damn it, what I wouldn't do for a smoke right now.

There it is again and now it is a double stack of screen crawlers going across my mind like the stock market reports, where there is two or three screen crawlers at the same time while some host is telling us the economy is fluttering and we are going in the toilet financially. OK, think of something else, this is data overload to the Max!

I'm sure those screen crawlers must be my sub conscious fucking with me. That shit isn't funny goddam it, stop it! I still need a fucking cigarette! I wonder if those multiple layer screen crawlers are like a sub-sub conscious, kind of like some building elevators with basement and subbasement floors.

There it is! I'm sure that the last thing that happen before whatever has happened was when I went to the smoke shop for my weekly visit to buy a carton of cigarettes. It's mostly a head shop but they have a full variety of cigarettes and tobacco products. I have been going there for several years now. Great staff and likable fellows. Every time I pull up they wave at me through the window and when I walk in, they already have my brand of cigarettes on the counter.

It kind of reminds me of my days of extreme drink, when my favorite bartenders we're pouring my drink as I walked in and they placed it in front of an empty bar stool. Hell, I had my drink in front of me before I could even take my coat off!

I walked into the smoke shop and Tim was there on the phone saying, "I've got good video on him and his car license plate, I will print it out and run a copy for the officer when he arrives." Tim then hung up the phone. I looked at Tim as I grinned and asked, "Trouble in river city, Lads?" Tim said a guy grabbed a big bag of smoking tobacco and run out the door with it. "I tried to grab him but he pulled away, I chased him out to his car but he got into his car and locked the doors, so I stood behind his car so he couldn't backup to leave. He gunned the motor and honked his horn. I saw his backup lights come on I had to jump out of the way so he didn't run me over!" The other employees said, "We got some really good pictures of his face and his neck tattoos!"

I shook my head and said, "I really do like you two lads but you better fuckin listen to me and listen tight! I'm a former police officer and I've seen retail clerks killed who have tried to stop a petty thief. I'm sure your company, like most any other company has a policy against attempting to stop a shoplifter. They would rather lose a few dollars then face the liability of the extreme likelihood of someone getting hurt, or be sued if you are wrong. Don't ever fuckin do that kind of shit again! I don't know if you two are strapped or have a gun under the counter or not and I don't want to know. You can't shoot a thief for stealing unless you want to spend the rest of your life being kissed awake every morning by your cell mate. Your perp having facial and neck tattoos should pretty much tell you that he's saying, "I'm dangerous, I've been to prison and I will kill anyone who fucks with me!"

Bad guys carry guns, knives and several other hidden weapons to hurt people. Felons who are on parole or probation are forbidden to carry guns or knives but that doesn't mean that they don't. Many of those bad guys carry long bladed screw drivers, bikers carry heavy adjustable wrenches and ball-peen hammers, they are legal to carry but I doubt they carry them to fix shit. So here is the deal, you grab ahold of a desperate bad guy. You are the only thing between him, his freedom and his going back to prison. He could easily thrust a screwdriver into your guts and have been casually driving away as you were laying on the floor bleeding to death. And even if you did survive, you would have lost your job for violating company policy and you would not be covered by work comp. Jesus Christ, it will cost you two months of wages just to pay for the ambulance bill. If you did survive the multiple surgeries from repeated stabs pumped into your organs, your body will never be the same. Chances are you'll be sporting a wheel chair and shitting into a bag for the rest your life. Almost as bad, is because you violated company policy you will have to pay for all of your medical bills. You'll need six full-time jobs for the rest your life, just to pay those medical bills. Think about this fellow's, is just merchandise, don't do that shit ever again! See you next week." I left those two youngsters with wide eyes and slack jaws. I will call that 'community service' and I'll call it a win.

Chapter 9 THAT BASTARD ADAMS

OK now that I've established to the best of my memory, my last known event. What comes next? I guess that I need to roll my memory backwards. I've got to remember that my only goal is to show a brain function, to stay alive. I'm still bothered by those airplane windows. Did they dig in my skull and pull my eyes out with one of those mini melon ball scoops? If they did can I still be alive? This shits just too fucking weird. Think of something funny for a while.

I can use the rest. Well at least my cell phone is not blowing up and not constantly ringing with those sales reps that want me to extend my automobile warranty which is about to expire, but I must act now! I wonder what it would cost me to extend my warranty on my twenty year old pickup truck with 207,000 miles on it. Then there are also those darlings reminding me of Medicare open enrollment from October 15 to December 7th. Wait a minute, that's a clue! So it's at least after October 15th but before December 7th. Well that's almost seven weeks. Hell, I will be well fucked if not dead after three weeks of a coma. Now that is a pleasurable thought!

What's the last activity I can remember? Why is that asshole Adam's still banging in my brain? God I hate that silly son-of-a bitch! What is it about Adam's that keeps sitting on top of my brain? Think, think, think, damn you!

The cops! It's the cops and that murderous fucking Adams. How many police interrogations have I had to sit thru because of that filthy little bastard?

I bet if you were to shine a light up my ass, you would find two smirking detectives with their little note pads.

That bastard Adams dragged me into his slimy, soulless world that I can't climb out of. Not to mention the DA's staff and of course the three week trial. I would like to gut that fucking defense lawyer.

That's it, holy shit! I met with two Duluth Police Department homicide detectives along with two homicide investigators and one District Attorney from each of the three adjoining county's. They are all working homicide, cold case files. They got information from a 'song bird' who is a county jail frequent flyer and was Adam's cell mate. He told them that Adams was bragging about putting down the downtown bully and that he and the famous Novelist, David J. Brown were writing a book about the one's that he killed that they don't know about.

They are all under the impression that Adams might be a serial killer. I sure as hell wouldn't doubt it. They want to get all the information available before they interview him. He drew two life-time sentences but they are afraid that the other inmates will kill him before they can get to him and hopefully close a number of active cold cases.

I of course was Invited as I was a material witness in his trial. Adam's fuck face lawyer tried to blame me for the murder and have me charged with complicity. His claim was that I told the audience in my seminar (that Adam's attended) that if they wanted to be remembered, if they wanted to become famous they would have to kill or be killed by someone famous in a very public way, with a large group of witnesses.

We tried to meet in the training room of the Duluth Police Department complex but the hallway and adjoining offices were too noisy and we couldn't hear each other. We moved to the Duluth City Hall building.

The upside was that there was a full menu order restaurant with fresh coffee. Cop coffee sucks, no matter what city or state, cop coffee sucks!

I had to start from day one that I met that sorry son-of-a bitch, twenty-eight months ago. I hadn't talked for more than five minutes and had already been interrupted three times with multiple questions. I had to put my hands up to stop them as I said, "If you are going to interrupt me on every third or fourth sentence, we will be here until the spring thaw. Everyone in this room is getting paid except me. Try to act like real professional cops. I talk, you listen and you take notes. That's how it's going to be. So now is the time that you all declare yourselves. Either I am a suspect or I am a witness. Which is it? I'm going to go out for a smoke, unless you want to read me my rights and book me into jail!"

I got up from my chair and walked to the door, turned back to them with their blank faces and said, "My cooperation will have everything to do with your professionalism!"

I went out for a smoke and didn't come back for thirty minutes, (to spank them). When I reentered the room, there sat eleven, well scolded cops! I sat down and said, "I will start again from the beginning. Interrupt me again and I will leave, can you dig it?"

"I met Adam's a little more than two years ago, about this time. The Minnesota Writers and Poets Society Conference was a three day event that started on, "Black Friday" after Thanksgiving. I was booked as an author/signer and seminar speaker during the day and the evening dinner guest speaker. I was paid $5,000 for the three days. Attendees paid $75 for general admission and $35 for each seminar they chose to attend. There were 30 seminar/workshops and about 200 authors or hopeful authors but only ten, "Guest Signing Author's." There were several vender tables selling writing, editing, and publishing services. Most of them were predatory with their services and pricing.

My signing table was on the main lobby floor of, "The River Convention Center" in Saint Paul, Minnesota. Adam's and his mother had two banquet tables across the aisle from me and four tables down to my left. They had six, five foot, high dollar planted tree pots, along with flowers and custom carpet with matching colored table covers for their set-up. I had one table with a white complimentary standard banquet table cover.

Adam's was dressed as a Colonial. He had on a gaudy misshaped white wig and a powdered face with red rouge on his cheek bones, an oversized black double breasted suit with Ben Franklin shoes and of course the period correct bow tie and frilly shirt.

On their two tables were three fancy, gold lettered oversized (three times the standard size) name signs, like the placard you would see on an office door or office desk. Each name tag read, John Quincy Adams. "On their tables were stacks of literature that looked amateurish with colorations. Behind their tables were banners that read, "Presidential-Royalty Social Media Experts."

His mom looked like she just picked up her face from an auto body shop. She had multiple layers of foundation on her face with eyebrows that you would only see at the circus climbing out of the clown car. She was wearing multi layers of multi lengths with multi colored chiffon or crepe material. Whatever the hell it was, she looked like a broken down ole Las Vegas 'brass pole spinner.'

As is customary and as a common courtesy, I went to all of the tables in the isle and introduced myself and welcomed them to the neighborhood. I shook the 'Adam's Family' hands and we exchange business cards. We only spoke briefly as my assistant had just arrived and I had to sign a few cases of books so she could sell them while I was doing the seminars or outside smoking. As you all know, 'Adams' is his, "stage" name. I didn't want to know his first name or anything about him. He was a straight up freak. From the very moment that he put out his cold, pork chop greasy hand, I knew that he was somebody I didn't want to have anything to do with. He partially bowed as the actors of old. Mommy curtsied, during our introductions and gushed and flittered like a ballerina. She was sporting the latest fashion of Morticians orange lipstick of the 1950's. As I signed a case of books, I noticed that Adam's and Mommy kept staring at me and they kept whispering to each other from across the way. I went on to my first session of the day.

When I returned to my table, the "Adams Family" was talking to my assistant. I couldn't help but notice that Adam's had a complete wardrobe change. Now he was wearing a white, ship captain's hat with some kind of gold threaded insignia. He had a summer weight navy blue double breasted sport coat with gold buttons. He had a family crest patch on the breast pocket and a white silk scarf sticking up. Which did nothing to help his white cotton gauze shirt with a paisley ascot. His blousy linen trousers and navy blue canvas deck shoes with rubber gum souls completed his outfit. Now I was sure the circus was in town! I think he was going for the Martha's Vineyard look where he probably saw himself as some asshole aristocrat named, Biff. Him and mommy both changed clothes every three hours.

Mommy Adam's said that she enjoyed my presentation immensely and she bought tickets for all the next three day's seminars where I was presenting. I thanked her but I was even more thankful for the people lining up to purchase my books and to have me sign them. I always try to make the experience meaningful and memorable for each customer. I spent a little extra time with each person than normal to avoid the Adam's Family. The minute the last person in line was takin care of, here they come to play twenty questions. They really didn't seem interested in tending to their tables or selling their products. I thought that strange, as I know they paid $850 per table and I guess another $800 or more for the trees, flowers, carpet and matching colored table covers. I probably went out to smoke three times more than I normally would, just to avoid them. They came to all of my seminars and camped out at or near my table all day long. I couldn't get to my hotel room fast enough that first night. Before I left the convention center that night, I told my assistant not to tell anyone what hotel I was staying at. In the past, I have had fans knock on my hotel room door to visit. The last thing I wanted to do is spend another minute with the 'Adam's Family!'

When I arrived at my table the next morning, I found the 'Adam's Family' sitting at the two white tablecloth tables directly across from me. Rather than buying off on their silliness, I looked at them and nodded towards their 'old tables' and said, "You two kids forgot your shrubbery and carpet." Mommy spat through her teeth as she said, "That mother fucking bitch floor manager said that they rent to the floor location and not the person. We have to rent all new planters, flowers, table covers and carpet and now we have to pay double the price for late requests! I'd like to plunge a knife into her heart! That fat assed self-important bitch!"

I asked, "What gives with your relocation?" Adams said, "Mom and I are actual fans of yours, we really don't have much of a program to sell, we just want to spend some time with you and are hoping to get to know you better and find out what makes you tick. I think I want to become a novel writer and Mom thinks I should model myself after you and your writing style." I said, "That's swell but I'm not a wind up clock and I do not tick."

The Duluth PD Female Homicide Investigator (who I dubbed antsy pants, because she couldn't stop flipping her hair or sit still, but then again Valley Girl had a nice ring too as she talked like a fourteen year old cheerleader) "David, I am totally enjoying your humor, the way you work with words and how you paint a brushless stroke picture but I would just like the hard facts, if you please."

Me: Sweetheart, you just poked the bear. You do not want to piss off the 'golden goose'. Do it again and I walk. I'm not even getting juror's fees and you think you get to give me directions? This is my fuckin story, you don't get to tell me what to say or how I say it. Do you want to explain to your boss how you shit the bed and ruined your only chance to potentially close several murder cold case files? Look around this room at these other faces who are about to beat your ass. Think you can take em? Shut your mouth or you are gone. Do you read me?" She nodded her head.

I got up from my chair, poured a cup of coffee and went outside for a smoke without a further word to anyone.

I came back into the room and there was a collective sigh of relief from everyone. I looked over at the female offender and smiled as I asked, "Still love me babe?"
The room exploded with laughter as she gave me the finger. I sat down and got back to my testimony.

Adam's and Mom dragged their fancy director's chairs from across the aisle at the very edge of the invisible line that separated our tables. Mom said, "My boy has suffered all of his life with ADD and people have been very cruel to him. He is always lonely and depressed. He lives with me, his father left us several years ago because our son was, "damaged goods." I saw you on the TV show, "Good Morning Northland" back in July. Your story was so gripping and so honest that we both fell in love with you. The minute the show was over I ordered your books from amazon and paid for overnight express shipping. My son has an inability to focus long enough to read but a few pages at a time, if that. I read both of your books to him. My boy was so inspired by you and your writings that he has started to read your books by himself for hours at a time. He really does want to become a writer. We came here to ask you to help me and to help us. Would you please help us?

Me: If you want anything from me you better knock all this bullshit off! And I mean all of it! So, you do not own a social media promotions company, you found out my table location, rented a space, and then bought-out the tables directly across from me and you wore clothing like little children playing 'dress-up', all just to get my attention. How much did you pay the people across from me to switch places with you? All that bullshit about you wanting to stab the floor manager in the heart was just to impress me with your theatrical abilities. The way you speak of your "boy" would lead most to believe that they were witnessing a classic case of, "Munchausen Syndrome by Proxy." Oh, you two are slick all right but I'm downwind from what you're spreading. I will give you guy's one chance to come clean, all the way clean. Don't fuck with me, I've been to the circus and I've seen the elephant. Let's

start with this, what the fuck are your real names? And Mom, don't answer for or speak for him. Enough of this bullshit.
Young man, what is your name and age?

Adams: Basil, my name is Basil sir, I am 31 years old and I do not live with my mother and I don't have ADD or any other mental difficulties. I have wanted to be a writer ever since I can remember. I have studied my ass off. I have duel degrees in Journalism and Political Science. I want to write the next great book about the next assassination of a sitting President of The United States of America. Seven years of school and I can't write for shit! Jesus Christ, I applied to be a volunteer for my high school newspaper and they all but laughed at me. Same thing in College, I applied ever year to be a staff writer and submitted several articles. I was turned down every year and they only published two short stories just to get me off their backs. Then a show producer from our TV station that you were on, called my mom and told her about you.

My mom and our family own several local TV stations in Minnesota, Wisconsin and both of the Dakota's. For the fucks sakes, I can't even write fucking copy for reporters who work for my family's TV stations! I got to level with you man, I love you and I hate you. You are so naturally gifted and have the world by the ass and you never so much as took a writing class. Shit, even you admitted that you may have driven buy a few colleges but never stopped in! Nobody should have your level of skills without an Ivy League education! No body writes like you and you sure as hell don't write like anyone else. But yet, people love you and like myself, I am sure that there are many people who want to be you. What is it, what is it that you have, that I and so very many others clamor for, what is that one thing?

I smiled as I off handedly said, "God gifted me an old soul, an old soul like no others. He said I earned it because I suffered well, I learned and now I teach through my public speaking and writing. That's pretty much it.

I don't know if I trust the name Basil, or you, or anything about you or, "Mommy Dearest" over here. I'm calling you Adam's with an apostrophe S. I don't give a fuck if you like it or not you arrogant bastard."

So Mom, you're up, name and age please? And the same rules go for you, don't fuck with me. So let's have it. How about it doll, real name. And GO!

Mother Adams: My name is Charlotte. Please don't call me Char, I hate that!

Me: Well ok Charlotte, that's a cute aristocratic name. I don't like your name either. I think I will call you Pat, or better yet, Patsey. Yup, that's it, Patsey! So how do you like me now? Rhetorical hun, and yes, It's Patsey with a 'Y' just like Adam's with an 'S'. Just me putting your ego's in check. Neither of you cats have nothing on me. Can you dig it? And don't bullshit me with your make believe age. Adam's over here was a late in life baby, probably because you and Hubby (and I don't want to hear anything about that goofy fucker) were most likely living the jet-set life of the rich and famous and couldn't be bothered with dragging around some little snot gobbler. Not to mention that you wanted to protect your smoken hot, movie star body. Sad as it may be, your tucks are starting to slip a bit. Patsey, I'm guessing sixty-four years of living the good life? Still love me babe?

Sweet ole Patsey had obviously never been stripped naked with just words with both of my hands still in my pockets. I think she had goose bumps. All during our exchange my lovely assistant sat quietly with a thin grimacing smile. I looked at her and said, "Kid, help me cover these tables and I'll take you to lunch." She reached into a tote from under the table and pulled out two sheets (much nicer than the ones the convention center supplied). As we were about to leave I turned to the "Adam's Family" and said, "Sorry but you two are not invited, we will continue this lovely conversation when I return. In case you two might have missed it, we have had several eavesdroppers in the last half hour or so. People absolutely love listening to a fellow hard talking to someone, as long as it's not them. I suggest you two go buy tickets for the rest of my appearances. I'm sure they are selling fast. Then again, if they are all sold out, you could make a simple phone call to your, 'On-duty' hitman and you could pull out those tickets from the pockets of a few rapidly cooling body's."

"Well Cops, that's it for me for now. I need a smoke and some lunch. I will be back at 13:00 hours. We will do a brief Q & A and get back into the story. I will leave you with this to chew on along with your lunch. I am well aware that many of you don't see the value in what I've been talking about, up to this point. Well I do and I'll tell you why later. Think of it this way, you don't just throw down a full Thanksgiving Day, turkey dinner for guests and family without first setting the table.

That, and at some point in the next two days you cat's, and I mean each and every one of you, will all be brought to the simple understanding that you're all pissing in the wind. You won't get shit from Adam's. None of you!

That's right boys and girls, this lousy smart ass prick currently speaking, holds the keys to the kingdom. Your job is to figure out a way to bring the information forward that I get from him and to use it to generate several warrants to reopen these cold cases. We all know that judges don't value civilian's testimonies in cold cases. That and of course the civilian to testify is a former police officer who has a past history of a lengthy fall from grace. I am credible today and have been for the last 28 years. Credentials hold credibility, it's your charge to figure out how to get a seventy-one year old sworn into a legit badge toting job. United States Marshals Service, has a nice ring to it. I smell a gold plated badge for dessert!"

Chapter 10   THE SHAMELESS PLEA

"I trust you all had an enjoyable lunch? Who wants the ball?" Carlton County District Attorney Baker: "We currently have a ball in the air. We need to go over to the Saint Louis County Sheriff's Office for a photo and fingerprints." "Bullshit, the county already has my fingerprints from my concealed carry permit. You trying to 'slow roll' me? I have been cleared by the F.B.I., the A.T.F., Interpol and a shit load of other alphabet agencies. You can pull a current photo from the state driver's license bureau. Don't any of you fuckin dare to try to hand me a U.S.D.A. Meat Inspector's badge! I will tell you all as I've told a few others, I've been to the Circus and I saw the Elephant.

Don't try to snow me. You are all out of your league! Tuck in your tiny little pride pieces, zip up your flies and we will get back to work. Anyone dare to venture with a question? No questions? Smart kids! Let's get back to it."

"So, when I returned from lunch with my assistant on the second day, Adam's and Patsey were much calmer than earlier. Patsey smiled as she took a stack of event tickets from her purse. She said, "We learned a lot from you this morning, we will settle down and just enjoy our time with you. And you are right, nobody likes to be talked hard to. Lesson learned, master! No more games. Basil, er-ah Adam's has something to say to you."

"Mr. Brown, I am not trying to stroke you, I will just tell you the truth, the truth about me. I felt your power when I read your books. You are everything that you wrote. I am not like you but I so desperately want to be. I have never established who I am within myself. Then I see you here in person and I felt a huge punch in my belly. It brought back all of my many failures. I am a Geek, I have always been a Geek. I acted that way and everyone saw me that way. I never fit in anywhere with anyone. When I think I am taking a few steps forward, I slip backwards and I'm back to being a nothing and a nobody loser. I have been hospitalized three times, and been treated for depression and taken medications since I was thirteen years old. I so desperately want to be somebody, somebody important!

I feel like you are my only hope. My suicidal ideations are coming more often. I look at you and your life and I look at you now sitting here and I feel hope. Then I shudder when I think of going home alone, just me with me.

I never had the beatings, starvation and neglect that you had to endure. So how can I be such a pussy with living a life of pampered wealth and having a loving family? You made it thru, you became stronger because of it. The loss of love, the loss of family thru death, the loss of friendships and yet here you are like a skyscraper flesh statue. Why are we so different?"

Me: Catch your breath ole son, we are not all that different. We just have and we use different solutions. My mental wellness has everything to do with how well I deal with my mental illness. Most all of my problems have to do with my perceptions, which are not always in line with the reality in front of me. As for you, I can't pretend that I have answers for you or anyone else for that matter. Let me ask you this, but first I have to tell you that I can smell marijuana on you and a faint odor of whiskey. What gives with that shit? Are you just a drunken pothead that would rather surrender his life than fight for your own wellness? If you quit drinking and hitting the pipe would you still have mental health issues?

A bunch of people want to stay sick, that way they get a free pass and don't have to take responsibility for their bullshit. I just watched your mother slightly nod her head and her eyes drop to the floor. My money is on that you are a pothead and have been since you were thirteen years old. I suspect that you are hitting some other shit as well. Get off all that street shit and the boozeand I'm sure everything else will take care of itself. I don't have time to be your sponsor but I will get you an AA meeting list. That's as far as I can go with your living problems. Every question I asked you earlier was rhetorical. You already know all those answers. I'm done with playing patty-cake with you. Now what about you wanting to write. What do you want to write and why?"

    Adam's: David, I want to be famous like you. I want the respect you get. I want people to admire me like they admire you.I have watched every person that you sign a book for. They just about levitate as you shake their hands, sign their books and when you pose with them for a photograph. It would be cool as shit to have people ask me if they could take a picture with me! I know I have never lived like you but when you were on the TV show and you told the story about the newspaper editor from Los Angeles telling you that you were the "Boogie Man" to big people because you trap them into thinking they are safe while reading about some vague person and how it made them cry and at some point they realized that they are crying for themselves. I want that kind of power as a writer. They don't teach those kind of skills in college. How did you develop those skills and will you teach me to write like you do? I want to write gory, snuff books. I want to startle people like you do but in a dark way. I want to scare the shit out of people, I want to give people nightmares that keep them up all night and make them be afraid to go to bed. I want them to turn on every light in their house at night and leave them on even past daylight.

    Me: Jesus Christ Adam's, you are a fucking whack-job bully. You want others to live in your guts and to feel your pain. You're not writing to entertain or to bring any positive messages. You're writing to punish the whole fucking world for you feeling inadequate. That's not just some kind of fucked up, that is ALL kinds of fucked up!

    That is a hard NO on my end. No, I won't be any part of that crap. You got some hate in your head that you need to get right. I don't teach writing, I speak of writing, my own writing. Besides who the fuck wants to read shit that will bankrupt them with electric light bills greater than their house payment?"

Adam's: I knew that you might say no. Correction, I knew that you would say no. Can you give me some book ideas?"

Me: Adam's you told me that you wanted to use me as a side-kick character in your snuff book like Stephen King does cameo appearances in his movies. You wanna pretend you murdered someone or your character murdered someone or better yet, did you already murder someone? I don't know if you just want my attention or if you want to confess a murder to hook my interest so I will write about you.

He had that sly dog grin which tells me that he might do some nasty stuff with his pets or his neighbor's pets. He was just flat out spooky! I made it clear to Adam's that I am not a writing coach, I don't critique anyone's work and my work is my own. Adam's asked me what I would think about my writing a book along with him.

Once again I made it clear to him that I'm a one act show. Then he asked how I felt about my writing a 'as told to the author' book. I said, "Nope I don't do that kind of shit either. Too much conflict, I would have to interview you and then write what you're thinking. There's no accuracy in that and all you'll do is become frustrated and angry and besides, I don't have time for this. I'm a professional writer and I have to work at my craft to make a living." Adam's said "I've got plenty of money, I'll pay you to write a book for me! I just laughed and said, "You couldn't afford me!" Adam's said, "How about $80,000?" I said, "You're going to pay me $80,000 to write a book for you and what's this book about again?" Adam's said, "I want to do a real life snuff book, like being an inside reporter watching a homicide take place as it happens." I said, "Hell you got all those TV cop shows to watch. I'm sure you could find some material and he says, "No, I don't only have the material, I've already got the story!" I looked at him and I said, "Fucker did you kill someone and now this is your way of confessing your crime? I don't want any part of that dance, if you feel you need to confess, go see a cop." Adam says, "Yeah but you used to be a cop and you know how cops think." I said, "Yeah well, I was never a part of a homicide. But I know how convicts think. You ever do any time?" Adam's said, "No, but sometimes I wonder what that would be like." I said, "Sport you keep talking about taking out a seated President of The United States and doing a thrill killing just to see what prison is like and I assure you that you will get your wish, in spades!"

After my last signing for the day I told my assistant quietly, that I was going to go out for a smoke and she was to pack up twenty minutes from now and I would see her in the morning and I went to my hotel room. The next morning (final day) there was one additional person with the Adam's crew, some young lovely lady who had more breasts than she had clothing and I'm assuming that she was a professional brass pole dancer in the late night hours. I asked Adam's what gives with the young table dressing he said, "Well people will stop and pay more attention to us." I said, "You don't have anything to sell. Your whole thing is just one big ruse, you don't have a social media company. I checked you out last night, there is nothing legit about any kind of business or services you're talking about providing. So what is all this bullshit? You and 'Mommy Dearest' buy me a hooker to sweeten the pot?"

"Well we just came here to be next to you so I could learn something and maybe we could entice and encourage you. My mom said I can offer you even more than $80,000. A lot more! I said, "Ole son, you don't have enough money. I don't want any part of wherever you're crazy train is headed or whatever track you're on. I can't help you. There are plenty of other wanna-be authors here that are plenty hungry and would jump at the opportunity." Adam's said, "Yeah but there's nobody as hard pounding as you are. You are a literary bad ass and you don't take any shit from anybody!"

Well Cops that's pretty much it for the Writers convention. Two weeks later I received a package in the mail with a return address sticker that read, 'John Quincy Adam's' with his return address. I almost tossed it in the trash, but then I thought, 'well this should be interesting.' I thought I should at least open it, inside the envelope was a partial manuscript about how a guy was attacked and how he defended himself and it just goes on and on and on. It's written partially like a play would be but then again it's also written like dialog for a movie script, it was just weird. Part of it keyed on the setting, part of it keyed on a main character. His writing was just all over the place. The story line was weak.

I'm a cooperating witness and I will maintain all control of my property. I'll be happy to make you all copies if I can locate it. For right now I need a nap, I'm going home. See you all at 08:00.

The following morning there was one additional male sitting at the table. Carlton County, District Attorney Baker introduced me to the Regional Section Chief of The United States Marshals Office. DA Baker said, "If you have something for us, Deputy Marshal, Clark has something for you."

I pulled out twelve, paper clipped copies of Adam's transcript. I smiled at U.S. Chief Marshal Clark and said, "Give" as I held the copies in my hand. He slid a white box across the table to me. In the box was a silver, round badge that read in blue paint, "United States Marshall" on the outer ring. The center was die-cut with a five pointed star. The center of the star had an eagle with the number 1789. Along with the badge was a Department of Justice ID card with my name and photo.

I smiled as I said, "We are almost there kids. Chief Marshal Clark and I are going to stroll over to the Federal Building to visit a federal judge, so I can be sworn in.
Everyone stay calm, I'm just going to draw my weapon to put it on the table. The Feds don't like civilians to tote firearms into their buildings. Don't anybody touch it, it's in 'condition one'. For you lawyer types, that means the hammer is cocked and there is a live round in the chamber and if you sneeze too loud it could go boom.

This is a 10mm pistol, with a 180 grain hollow point with almost twice the velocity of a 45 caliber and can pass all the way through a city bus engine. Don't fuck with my shit!"

I dropped the copies in the middle of the table as I said, "Read this over while I'm gone, when we get back I will tell you all, how I'm going to get Adam's to confess to your cold cases and how this badge is going to close the deal."

On the short walk to the federal building Chief Marshal Clark was laughing his ass off. He said, "I have never seen a civilian own a room full of lawyers and top cops before. You must be sitting on some kind of case. Please don't tell me. I've got a fishing trip planned with my son's in a few weeks. I don't want to be a witness to any of this malarkey. You do know that you have out maneuvered them, don't you. They don't even know it yet. As you obviously know, they think your badge is just a token. When we get back to city hall I will officially introduce you as a sworn United States Deputy Marshal.

My boss and I laughed our guts out yesterday when we got the panicked call from the Carlton County D.A. that offered us anything we wanted in return.

As I lit a cigarette he said, "I smoke a few cigars when I'm fishing but I haven't smoked a cigarette in thirty years. Can I bum one?"

The judge's clerk was beaming as she led us to the judge's chambers. The judge was beaming much like the clerk was. He said, "I would love to pour you gentlemen a drink, what would you like?" Chief Deputy Marshal Clark apologized for having to decline the judge's offer with, "We are on duty your honor." We all cracked up. The judge said that he had never sworn in a "Gray Hair" to the U.S. Department of Justice before. He said, "I understand that you've been knocking around a bunch of country club lawyers that are scared shitless of you. I don't know what you have that they so desperately want but I think you have been playing your hand brilliantly. Nothing like a good bitch slapping to get them off their pampered asses. Well played, well played indeed, sir!"

I took the oath of office with a smile so wide that it hurt my jaws. On the way out of the federal building my new boss said, "Next time you come in here you can pack heat." We both laughed as he asked for another cigarette. I looked over at him and said, "I won't ask for a corner office but when this case is over with, I'm keeping this fuckin badge!" He smiled and said, "You are the top cop in this area, do whatever you want and when this case is over, I want to take you fishing and hear all about it. I have a feeling that school is still in session and you have a few more lessons to teach back in city hall."

We walked into the meeting room without a word to anyone. I walked to the table, picked up my gun and holstered my weapon as Chief Deputy Marshal, Clark introduced me as: "U.S. Deputy Marshal, David J. Brown."

Chapter 11 Adam's Transcript

It was late spring in Duluth Minnesota with just a touch of snow remaining in the shaded areas. There is still a bit of a chill in the air. You most definitely wanted that jacket when the cool-down came in the midafternoon. I was walking down 1st street with my jacket in my hand, wearing a short sleeve shirt. Suddenly a monstrous size Indian male who had to be every bit of six and a half feet tall and close to three hundred pounds, came out of a stairwell and walked towards me. He had a slit for eyes with a broad forehead and a greatly pronounced high hooked nose that looked like an eagle beak. His menacing stride telegraphed that he was looking for trouble. A fat Indian female and a black, short stocky male fell in line behind him. It was obvious that they were looking to hit a lick. My mind was smiling and saying, "Not with me fuckers, those slabs in the morgue are, "One size fits all."
They all looked dirty and unkempt. It would be obvious to the most casual of observes that they were street slugs. I was smoking a cigarette as they neared me, the monster Indian said, "Nice watch, give me a cigarette." I told him, "Get a fucking job and buy your own god damn cigarettes!" He stepped closer and loomed over me, his breath spoke of rotting teeth and cheap wine. I told him to back off. He said, "Give me your wallet and that watch." He pulled a knife from behind him and held it against his thigh, so no one could see it but me. He repeated, "Give me that watch and your fuckin wallet or I will gut you like a fish." I took three quick steps back as I told him, "Another step and I will pump eight hard rounds of molten lead into your guts, starting in your groin and I will work my way up to putting a double tap into your skull. You

got that, you mother fuckin waste of human flesh, I bet a rabid dog wouldn't even bite you."

He backed up when he saw I was about to draw my weapon. I told him he could either walk away or die where he stood, "I don't give a fuck either way." He looked at his friends as if to check to see what they thought or wanted to do. I sensed there were telegraphing each other to mount a charge. I said, "If I have to draw my gun each of you will get two rounds screaming into your putrid slimy guts. Who would like to be first? Anyone left alive will get to choke to death on their own bile. I will enjoy watching your foreheads explode with the hot brass bouncing off the ground before you drop." All three looked sick to their stomachs like they were going to throw up as they turned and started to walk away. There was a sleazy, scumbag bar twenty feet away. They stopped at the front entrance of the open door of the bar. The black man and woman stepped inside the bar. 'Eagle Beak' stopped and looked back at me and shouted, "I'm going to kill your white fucking ass, nobody pulls a gun on Geronimo, you're fuckin dead. I will find you and chop your fuckin dick off." I calmly said, "I'm right here, let's just do it now, you punk assed bitch!" 'Eagle Beak' charged me. He closed on me so fast from that distance that I barely got my gun out. I think the first two rounds went into him with my barrel pressed up against his belly. He leaned back as I stepped back two steps, he lunged at me again and tried to grab my gun. I kept trying to pull the trigger as I kicked him in the balls and raked his shins with the side of my boot heel. The gun went off a few more times and he let go of the gun as he started to tremble. I thought he was going to go down, he half turned away and spun back and then let out a wild animal roar and I knew he was going to make his last charge. Before he could gather himself to launch his massive body at me I calmly shot him in his Adam's apple. He fell onto the city supplied picnic table (which were placed all over the downtown area for tourists) then slumped under the bench like he was leaning forward with his head up. I was amazed with how calm and satisfied I felt as I said. "I told you fucker and now you're dead." I looked around to see if I would get to kill his two asshole buddies but they were nowhere around. I guess they were slinking out the back door of the bar when the shooting started. I had a spare magazine on my opposite hip, I hit the mag release button and dropped the spent mag into my hand and sent the fresh mag home into my weapon. As I thumbed the upper receiver release it shot forward and chambered a fresh round. The sound of it feeding a round was the sweetest of music. I could feel the heat of the barrel as I flipped the safety on and holstered my weapon. I felt a calmness like I was in a lawn chair at poolside with a cold beer in my hand. It took a few minutes for the shock to finally set in. I became short of breath and everything became real quiet. Suddenly there is no traffic on the street, no people on the sidewalk, it felt like one of those Twilight Zone deals I watched when I was a kid.

    I saw a guy in a white suit at the end of the block. I'm sure he was somebody's pimp. He was using a California style show car dusting wand on his red Cadillac convertible. As I walked toward him I kept trying to dial 911 on my cell phone but I was shaking so badly I couldn't control my fingers to dial. I asked 'old white suit' to call the police because I just had to shoot a guy. He gave me a go away look as he said, "I have to get ready for the parade and I don't have time for your shit!" My right hand started to reach for my holstered gun, my mind told me that I might as well kill this pompous pimp fucker as well, I'm in a killing mood and it feels damn good! He saw me brush back my untucked shirt to draw my gun as he screeched and ran off like a little school girl. I couldn't help but laugh at the funny punk-assed pimp, as I watched the soles of his white shoes pounding down the sidewalk, galloping away like he was riding a stick pony.

    My mind snapped back to what had just happened as I got the chills. I put my jacket on but I started to shiver and my belly got real cold. I looked at my shirt looking for blood. Maybe that fucker did stab me, did I shoot myself as we were fighting for the gun? I couldn't find any blood and I felt inside my shirt I ran my hands over my stomach and chest, there was no blood on my hands or my clothes. I found myself across the street from where I shot him. He was still sitting at the picnic table looking directly at me grinning. My mind is screaming, "What the fuck, I just killed your ass, you sorry son of a bitch!

Now I can see the dust particles passing by my eyes. I watched some particles land on my eyelashes and I did not or could not blink. I was in a physical and mental paralyses. I don't know if I was just in shock or dead. Suddenly the street was full of uniformed white gloved cops marching towards me. All I could hear was the soles of their shoes slapping the pavement and the heavy male voice calling out cadence. The uniforms were from many different departments of police, sheriff and state patrol organizations. I could hear a distant pipe and drum band.

The entire group stopped several feet before me. There were street barricades in front of them that I had not noticed before. Some guy wearing a 'Class A' uniform started telling all of them the course of the parade route. I was dumbfounded that there were all these cops here and nobody saw that huge, dead son of a bitch sitting at the picnic table. I was further amazed that there were no sirens or police cars, fire trucks or an ambulance. Didn't anyone hear the gunshots? No one saw us fighting? The blood and gore are all over the ground! What the fuck is going on here?

Two people were approaching me. I recognize them from many years of the past. There are police detectives and we had worked several cases together. We shook hands and shared compliments on how well the three of us had all aged. Those two detectives had been partners for more than twenty years. They said they were assigned to the, 'strong arm robbery and crimes against persons unit.' Lydia was still a stunningly beautiful Mexican-Asian woman. She still had raven black hair with a very slight wisp of soft silver natural highlights. She had always had a smoldering sensuality about her and she dressed well, she always wore heels and walked as dignified as she looked. She was married and dedicated to her Air Force pilot husband and their four children.

She was a kind and respectful lady. It didn't keep us boys from our dirty thoughts however. We all treated her with the utmost of respect. Of course we all wished we could have met her before 'fly-boy' came along.

Lorenzo is an American born Mexican. He was raised by his grandparents and he had never learned to speak English growing up. He still spoke with a small amount of Mexican accent. He too always dressed well, his suits were tailored and he wore designer shoes. He was always well groomed. Lorenzo was just as much a gentleman as Lydia was a lady. They never talked hard to suspects or used any kind of profanities. It wasn't a strategy they used, they were just both that professional. It was simply that that's who they were. After a few more pleasantries, they asked me if I came to watch the, "National Police Week" parade. I just nodded, as I couldn't remember why I was downtown. They said that there were dispatched to a disturbance here of a possible strong armed robbery.

Lorenzo said I somewhat matched the description of the reported victim. I said, "Yes I am the victim." The street was noisy now with the parade about to start. Lorenzo said, "We have a store front office down the street, let's not say anything until we get there." We crossed the street and approached the picnic table where the, 'totem pole looking' dead asshole was still sitting up. It seemed that he had turned his head to look me in the eye. I was still in shock, in shock that nobody had come to notice that he was dead. The closer I got to him I wanted to slam my spent magazine into his empty eye socket. I started to giggle as I came alongside of him as a thought of slapping him in the forehead and knock him over backwards onto his dead ass. I had to use every bit of self-control as I walked past 'Eagle Beak' to not spit on his cold dead face, as we passed the open door of the bar where 'Eagle Beaks' pals slithered into.

We entered the precinct office that was just really of converted storefront, just a few doors down from the bar we just passed. There were four desks with computers, a small kitchen and a tiny holding cell in the far corner. There was a sloppy looking, grossly overweight woman, wearing a blue faded shapeless tent dress with white buttons the size of Volkswagen hubcaps. She wore a dirty white shirt with stains around her neck line. If she had a red rubber nose you would vote her best circus clown in the parade going on down the block. Olivia poured me a cup of coffee as Lorenzo introduce me to the 'Clown Lady', who is from the city's risk management department. She was there to observe the victim, witness, and suspect interviews. 'Clown Lady' said she was there to do an in-depth audit on the detectives to ensure that all state and federal laws were obeyed and the suspect's rights were being honored

    During her explanation of her duties, I only heard, 'You all better watch out because I'm going to get your asses' which screamed her hatred for cops. I couldn't help myself when I took a sip of my coffee and said to 'Clown Lady,' "So you're carrying a bigger stick than Internal Affairs and you want to lob some heads off because internal affairs are cop sympathetic and always look the other way? Lady, you couldn't be more wrong. Somebody steal your desk stapler or parked in your spot?" That nasty bitch about swallowed her own face. I turned away from her and asked my detective Pals, "You want my gun?" They both looked puzzled and said, "No, you can have your gun." I said, "I just killed the fuck out of a guy down the street! You don't want my gun?" Olivia asked, "What are you talking about, we want to ask you about some street junkies trying to hold you up." I told them about the dead guy at the picnic table. Lorenzo said he thought he was just drunk and passed out. Lorenzo told 'Clown Lady' to get out of the office. She all but flew out of the door. I could faintly hear Lorenzo's radio (they both had ear buds in their ears) he looked a little hesitant as he asked me if he could remove my gun. I kept my hands on the table and nodded my head. Olivia turned her head away, she was crying. After Lorenzo removed my gun and spare magazine he said, "I will be God damned if I will cuff you and put you into that holding cell. The three of us grew up together! We served together! We're still friends! That bullshit will come soon enough!" Olivia said, "I will be God damned if we will read you your rights, none of us are going to say another fucking word about anything. You need to call an Attorney. Don't say another goddam word that would make us have to be forced to testify to anything. Olivia pulled her chair next to me and held my hand, Lorenzo pulled his chair to my other side and put his arm around my shoulder.

With his free hand he radioed that he needed fire rescue and an ambulance at his location for an assault victim experiencing chest pain, with difficulty breathing. The sirens came quick, so did a lot of police uniforms.

    Olivia and Lorenzo introduced me to the two Homicide detectives who sat down. Olivia said, "All he has said was that he is having crushing chest pain, he wants to go the hospital and that he wants a lawyer. He hasn't said anything else, we didn't ask him any questions so we didn't give him any Miranda warnings." Lorenzo and Olivia got up from their chairs, walked to the door and never looked back as they both left the office, heads bowed, hand in hand."

End of Adam's Transcript

Chapter 12   BADGE TOATING

U.S. Marshal Clark, call your federal court judge pal. I want Adam's transferred from Stillwater State Prison to Saint Louis County Jail for an indefinite period of time. If he is here by dinner time I won't be the least bit unhappy. Now for you Mr. Saint Louis County DA, I need you to call the Sheriff. Not his office, but him, him the Sheriff. Tell him that I have a federal shield and want full access to the entire jail, jail staff and all inmates. Back to you U.S. Marshal Clark, call the prison warden, and again not his or her office but them personally. Tell him or her, that I want full access to all of Adam's cellmates, prison pals, his work area staff guards and supervisors. I want copies of all of his records from the day he was welcomed into the open arms of the slammer. Back to you Mr. DA, I want all copies and full access to see Adam's confession, any and all of the interviews that all of you coppers logged from your very first contact with him. I want the entire file, hold nothing back! I don't think any of you really want to be cuffed and thrown into a cell, for interfering with a federal agent doing a federal homicide investigation. I want Adam's placed in a double cell in Saint Louis County Jail with the most anxious inmate that wants to earn an early release. Don't tell him why.

'Valley girl' asked, "So you think you can get him to talk when none of the rest of us could?" I gave her a hard look and leered at her with, "Easy-peasy baby girl."
Valley girl sneered, "Oh you have some kind of magical interview technique that none of us has?" As I got up from my chair I said to her, "On your feet" and walked up to her and said, "Young lady

that's twice now, I have friends in this city. I doubt if you have many if any at all. You are about to meet a whole bunch of new folks that you can get to know personally, from the Street Repairs Department. Are you aware of the repairs going on down on South Lake Avenue? How would you like to be assigned to traffic direction duty for the next few months while they dig up three miles of roadway to replace all the water, sewer and gas lines? You will have to dress like the 'Michelin Tire Man' to survive the 60 below zero wind chills. I hear that JC Penney's has 'cuddle duds' and electric socks on sale. Better clean out your thermos bottle, you're going to need it. By the way, one of those friends I mentioned earlier is your boss, the Chief of Police. I'm sending you home for the rest of the day, get out of my sight and get out now. When you come back tomorrow you had better have a handwritten letter of apology, now get out!"

    Before she could bolt from her chair, tears were running down both of her cheeks. She gathered up her things and quietly tiptoed out the room and silently closed the door behind her. I looked over at her partner to see a satisfied looking smirk on her face as I asked, "You think you are immune from your own ass rippin, you are supposed to be her senior mentor? You and I are going to go to launch, the rest of you can stroll and go make someone's life miserable because your breakfast toast was burnt. See you all tomorrow for: "The rest of the story." We are going to get nasty folks, real nasty! Keep in mind that we are not here to build careers with body recoveries. We are only here to give grieving families a small part of their hearts back and nothing more."

    Well, with that lunch with the other police officer, I was able to pull enough information from her that I made my decision.

    Later that afternoon I got to meet with the Duluth Chief of Police and the Saint Louis County Sheriff in the same office at the same time. Both agreed to my strategy and game plan and gave their full support. In parting from the meeting, the Sheriff winked and with a smile as he said, "You sly son of a bitch! You're going to use all of this in a new book aren't you?" I smiled and said, "You sure as hell didn't get elected because of your good looks now did you!" The Police Chief said, "You are too much of a mouthy basterd for me to want to hire but I wish I had a dozen of you. When you are finished with my rookie homicide detective either bring me back the best of the best or I will bust her down to a meter maid." I smiled as I said, "You don't want her in your department. Perhaps you should learn a bit about your charges. She holds a law degree. She became a cop to understand cops and police work. Your department is a stepping stone, then it is on to the winning team as a prosecutor and finally she will be sitting on the bench in hopes of being known as a ball busting hanging judge. She is the avenging angel to her grandfather who was murdered while wearing your department's uniform and badge, several years ago. I think the three of us would greatly favor a gavel swinging and hard sentencing judge, over a run of the mill homicide detective. The chief smiled with saying, "You are one sneaky bastard, I can't wait to read your new book what are you going to call it, "Dream Makers?" I expect a signed copy!" As I turned to walk out of the office I said over my shoulder, "You boys will both get a signed copy, if you cheap pricks are willing to pay for them!"

It was the final morning of our meetings. I started with, "I trust you have all received emails from your respective bosses. There should be no further questions as to who is directing this marching band, am I correct?

We will be doing this fast, hard and dirty and nothing is to leave this room. Nothing over dinner with your spouses or family, nothing with your office pals, everything spoken here stays here. You are to speak of it to no one. So my charges, it is and will remain hands off of Adam's for all of you. Absolutely no one is to visit him or his mother. None of you are to take or make a call to him or his mother. He or his mother will try to contact your offices inquiring if not demanding to know why he is in Saint Louis County Jail and in seclusion.

I can only tell you this. This case is larger than you think, much larger. Several of the alphabet agencies of the federal government have graciously agreed to give us two weeks to recover and identify our missing and murdered in our cold cases. After that, we are out. Adam's will become the sole property of our Uncle Sam. When I start the interview's we will have four cameras and closed circuit TV's, multiple microphones and everything will be time stamped. Be sure to note the time stamp on the things you have questions about. We will meet each afternoon to work over the questions for the next session."

I looked over to the young lady, (antsy pants) "Did you receive the email from your chief?" Her, "Yes sir, Deputy Marshal Brown."

Good, now this will be your final 'talk down' at least in public. Clean up your act and do it now. You are not the cover model for Lulu Lemon or some CrossFit gym that applauds you every time you lift your CamelbaK to sip some kind of slimy green magic potion juice. You will dress and conduct yourself as a professional police officer. No pigtails with your high school colors in your hair clips. No jewelry, no perfume, no makeup, no lotion of any kind. I want no scent on you or your clothes. I am sending you home early to re-wash the clothes you will need for a five day trip. No detergent, no fabric softener or fabric sheets. You'll have a closed collar without neckwear. You are going to be sitting across the table from the most proficient killers that you will ever dare to dream of. You ever watch silence of the lambs?" She nods her head. "Well Clarice, we go wheels up at 22:00 this date, compliments of the US Department of Justice. A town car will pick you up at your home at precisely 21:00 hours. Be ready, be on time. You buck me any of this and you are gone and your career is over, are we clear?" "Yes sir, you are the boss." I smiled inwardly as I saw and heard the uncertainty in her voice and posture. I stood, walked to the door and opened it and looked back at Clarice and said, "Clarice, nobody will ever take you seriously or will you earn the respect of your peers talking and flouncing around like a little kid. Go home and pack your bags for five days

I dubbed the fresh faced hard-body rookie homicide detective as Val. As in 'Valley girl', every time I call her Val, it is a signal to her that she needs to check herself. I'm sure she will hear me address her as Val, several times in the next few upcoming days.

I arrived at the executive side of the airport thirty minutes early. I checked in with the FBO (fixed base operator for private aircraft) and Val was sitting poking at her laptop. I smiled as I told her to shut it down. Her quizzical look caused me to widen my smile as I said, "We are going dark, give me your cell phones, yes both of them." A second quizzical look was met with a stern glance and chopped words of, "Your career is slipping at break neck speed Val, is this where it ends? Another look like that and you are gone. Don't fuck with me!"

The pilot and co-pilot were already in the cockpit. We walked side-by-side to the staircase. I hooked her arm just short of the staircase and held her back saying, "Do not discuss any part of this case or trip unless we are completely alone. I will key you when I think it is safe to talk. Only I will initiate all conversations. If you have a question or want to say something, first address me as "Uncle Dave." Notice the cute little signs on the door of the FBO office and a second one on the front of the check-in counter that read, "This area may be under surveillance?" You bet your ass it is! Ever since September 11th all transportation facilities are bugged and pick up key words that may cause you a rather uncomfortable visit with a rather large framed gal with knuckles the size of bowling pins. This plane might well, be bugged. Say nothing about nothing, are we clear? Once we get on-board the aircraft we will not talk until we exit the aircraft."

After landing in Stillwater, MN we were met by the Hilton Hotel Van. We rode the van to the hotel in silence. As we entered the lobby I pointed to two chairs and said, "Sit down and put all of your electronics on this table, everything! Anything non electronic remove from your lap top case." I took her cell phones from my brief case and said, these go in your laptop case. I will get you a lap top and phone when we arrive in Los Angeles. Her head almost spun like Linda Blair, the little girl from the Exorcist.

As we checked-in I asked the desk clerk to put her laptop bag in the safe as we were going to be out for a late dinner. I got our room keys and walked Val to her room. I unlocked the door and told her to wait in the hallway. I walked in, turned on the TV to a medium volume, turned on several lights, hung the, "Do not disturb" sign on the door handle. I did the same thing in my room. I said, "Kiddo we are going to work on that cross fit, cardio bullshit. We are on the 18th floor and we're taking the staircase all way to the bottom, I hope you packed lightly!" We went out the back door and hailed a taxi. I had the taxi take us to the nearest car rental agency.

I could see that Val was just beside herself trying to find a way to ask a question. Her head was on a swivel as she was asking in her own mind when it might be safe to ask a question. I climbed behind the wheel of the rental car and pulled off the lot and parked across the street in a bowling alley parking lot.

I looked over at Val as I released my seat belt and lit a cigarette. The look of horror on her face because I was smoking in a rental car was epic. I grinned as I exhaled with, "Uncle Sam will pay for the damages, so fuck em. Our drive to Saint Paul/Minneapolis International Airport is less than thirty miles. We might be parked but you may want to tighten your seatbelt. I am taking you to the big leagues baby girl. If you are ready to turn in your E-ticket to 'Romper Room' I am ready to help you give birth to your first gray hairs.

Here it all is in a very fucking large nut shell. Try to keep up. First off, those several times I left the city council meeting chambers to go out for a smoke was a set up. I had that room bugged for the last three days. I listened to every word that was spoken when I was out of the room. Feel like puking? The short answers to your group are: it is no one's business who the fuck I think I am, who the fuck am I or where the fuck I came from. Yes, I do come from a place where I carried some serious power. I liked your cute little rants most of all with, "Who the fuck is this guy, author my ass! This prick marches around like a commanding general and tries to burn holes in my brain with his maniacal cyborg stares. I'd love to double tap his fuckin skull!"

"Would you like me to continue? I will answer your first question, why did I choose you? You are the only one of the, 'city-hall dirty dozen' without an agenda. Those other fine folks have sugar plumbs dancing in their heads with dreams of great fame, importance and career advancement. I know of your career plans and I fully support them and I'm sorry for your loss of your grandpa. Let's move on. This case is bigger than any of you know, much bigger. First, a word of caution, extreme caution! Listen up and listen hard. If you leak people will die, a lot of people will die, entire families will be wiped out, including children! *CAPICHE*?

Take a big gulp of air, this thrill ride is about to begin. The nucleus of this investigation comes from Adam's supposedly shooting and killing the drunken bully of downtown. Adam's did not shoot him, he orchestrated that killing. It was a hit. It was a drug cartel hit.

That big ugly, foul breathed Indian who was going to stomp Adam's ass, as a deep cover agent for an agency that you have never heard of. He carried an id card (not on his person) that starts with, "From the Oval Office of….." It doesn't matter which one of the alphabets groups he was with, what matters is that he was murdered for a reason. That reason is, that Adam's and 'Mommy Dearest' are suspected of running an importing organization that brings in the weight of a loaded railroad cattle car from Columbia every month. Can you guess what those products might be? The "Adam's Family" runs in the top four families of importing Columbia's finest exported products.

None of that shit is any of our business but we could inadvertently step into it. If we do what I think we can do, you just might get an invite to lunch with the residents of 1600

Val blanched as she said, "I need a drink Several, I'm thinking." "No time for that babydollface, you can drink when we get on the plane. It's a four hour flight to LAX, you can damage yourself then but remember, no talk of any kind about this case in public, drunk or sober."

Val finally snapped out of her horror lock-down and asked, "LAX, what the fuck? Aren't we going to the prison to interview cellmates and staff? And what's this shit about dragging me down 18 hotel floors with my luggage and now we are going to California? Is it you or Adam's who is bat-shit crazy, or both? I need a fucking cigarette, give me one!"

Come to find out that sweet sister Val is a closet smoker but hides it so as not to be judged by her peers. I laughed as I said, "Another twenty minutes and you will be buying a carton of cigarettes. This ride isn't over yet. We are going to a movie studio in Hollywood to meet the principle property master for all three of the John Wick movies. Most, if not all Wick movies were shot in New York and a few locations in Europe. The trilogy titled, "John Wick 3 Parabellum" (as I understand it) was filmed in Morocco. The property master has spent time with Adam's and was paid quite handsomely for that, 'one of a kind gun' and a gold coin that I will tell you about later.

Understand this. We have gone dark because we are in danger. In danger because the bodies you and your pals are trying to recover are not all innocence. They were all part of the Colombian connection on Adam's and Mommy Dearest's payroll. There maybe a few other bodies that are non-mob and were simply considered to be collateral damage.

There is a chauffeur driver, a maid and a mailing store worker, all missing. The chauffer, the maid and the mail store worker (who was dirty) stopped getting pay checks issued from the Adam's clan during the same pay period. I think they overheard or witnessed something that they were deemed to be a threat. All three of the missing had no family to report them missing. You and I sweetheart may fall into that same category. We have to assist the feds for us to keep breathing, it's just that simple. At this point, we can trust no one, until Mommy Dearest and her top dogs are muzzled and kenneled. This trip is a two value ride, it keeps your pals sleeping and away from the case so the feds can do their deal. It also allows them to honor our agreement. Before you ask, here it is. First I do hope you guys can and do recover the bodies of at least the innocent ones. I will do my best to make that happen.

So what's in it for me? You can't possibly think that me having a federal badge makes my dick hard. Remember my saying that a federal badge will lend credibility to 'the witness'? It will and most importantly also lend credibility to a tell-all author. A federal agent, tell-all author. Yea babe, best sellers are not always the best authors but they have the public eye. That badge is my meal ticket to be recognized. The book I have been secretly working on for the last five months, this visit to California and my jail interviews, along with the print, radio and TV appearances arranged by the feds are my payment for being a good citizen. That fuckstick Adam's isn't the only one who's got game!

A couple of weeks ago I visited 'Mommy Dearest' and took her up on her offer to pay me an additional $200,000 to complete my book, six months sooner than the agreed timeline. I told her that I needed to tour the house so I could better get to understand him. She flung open the shutters and showed me everything, including a few mouse traps and some of her undergarments that appeared to have been strategically laid out in several locations throughout the house. As she was giving me the, 'Grand Tour', she was posing like a second rate porn star with several brush-ups against me, followed with giggling apologies.

I of course, paid her no mind with her advancements as I am a devoted, married man. That and I didn't want to muddy the waters with my wearing a button and belt buckle camera streaming a live feed to the alphabets who so graciously supplied me with their finest 'eye spy' gear.

Much akin to her darling boy, she too is a chatty little thing. It is my nature and it has always been, to act only partially interested in a suspect/witness conversation. People tend to give up more than they realize as they try to hold my attention. Making direct eye contact makes people freeze up, especially when you both know they are guilty as fuck.

  Early on, during the 'grand tour' I realized the house staff was either very quiet, or very dead or this visit could be a set-up to whack me. Damn right it creeped me out!
I was looking for three things. His supposed John Wick hand gun collection with receipts, all ammunition that he has stored and a special gold coin that is only specific to the John Wick movies. You want more babe, or are you about to nod off?

  Val: Give it all to me big boy, I probably won't sleep until this time next month, you've got my brain so fuckin twisted up that it's like getting an anchor rope caught in the prop. Continue, you all knowing asshole. Asshole sir, that is!

  I started the car and pulled out into traffic without saying a word. We went a few blocks and I pulled into a convenience store. I looked at Val and said, from this point forward my name is Dave. No other name but Dave. Got it?" Head nod from passenger seat as I said, "You're on the clock and I'm not. Buy your own fuckin cigarettes. I need coffee. I drove back to the bowling alley and parked in the same spot that we had just left.

  Me: Our flight is three hours out, I want to get this shit all out before we walk into the airport. Besides, I would much rather you sleep on the flight with your head on my shoulder and drooling on my favorite sport coat, than you getting silly on booze and blabbering like the cheerleader you like to believe that you still are. Stay with me on this, this is the nuts and bolts of this 'secret' train wreck.

  Here is the why, as to the visit with the property master at the studio. I have a strong suspicion that he built guns for Adam's, full well knowing what that kookfuck's plans were. I'm more concerned about the bullets that he and Adam's have been talking about. I've had several conversations with Adam's about bullet trajectory, weights and velocity's. The list goes on and on. Adam's was obsessed with the "G-2 R.I.P." ammunition. The bullet head is serrated into nine pieces but remains intact until it strikes body tissue. The impact enters human flesh and the bullet now becomes nine separate ragged pieces of flaming hot lead tearing nine individual channels of total destruction. It completely eviscerates the entire body cavity. There is no other bullet out of the one hundred and forty-three known bullet types that comes even close to doing that level of damage that the G-2 R.I.P. is capable of doing. Yup, it guts you from the inside out.

    Adam's repeatedly invited me to go shooting with him. Chris Kyle came to mind instantly. There is no fuckin way that I would put myself in any type of position to being shot by that asshole Adam's. No matter where I am when shooting, I never allow myself to have an empty gun on my person. Too many junkies and whack jobs everywhere you go these days, even at an indoor or outdoor range or just in the woods.

    Adam's as with my many friends, have argued time and time again about gun and bullet selection. Because I'm a former cop they think I should know all about gun laws and they constantly would ask me about when it was ok to shoot someone. They would present several scenarios as to what they would do if in an armed encounter. Most every time they would say, "If someone did this or that, I'd blow their fucking head off!" Each and every time that I had to sit thru that silly bullshit I would just smile and say, "The prosecution would like to call Mr. David J. Brown as our next witness." Don't tell me what you would do in public or even to your dearest friends or even family. If you have to shoot someone, regardless of what they were doing and you were defending yourself, friends or property, you will be arrested, booked and jailed. Every one of your friends and family will be interviewed, neighbors, coworkers and probably your dog will be questioned if you ever made statements as to you speaking of killing or wanting to kill someone. Prosecutors will try to put you away. The rights you think you have still must be defended. Can you afford a half of a million bucks for a defense attorney, a possible appeal and of course the family of the low life you had to shoot or kill now needs to recover damages. If you're not up for all that bullshit I suggest you shut the fuck up!

Of course the same conversations went on with gun and ammo selection. For whatever reasons which I don't understand, people will spend a fortune on the dumbest shit but go cheap on personal protection defense weapons. I even had one asshole say he wouldn't carry an expensive gun for personal protection because if he had to shoot someone in self-defense the cops would take and keep his gun!

There are at least seven or eight court cases that I know of, where a person shot a perpetrator in self-defense and it was a righteous shooting but because they used the 'murder bullet' they were charged with manslaughter. If you use a standard hollow point personal defense load, it's pretty much no harm, no foul but when you intentionally load a firearm with a 'death round' you will pay with your freedom. Prosecutors are all a bunch of pussy's who are elected and if their campaign platform or the majority of their constituents are anti-gun sissy's they will fry your ass. They will make it a point to crucify you to gain re-election.

The same pretty much goes for gun selection. If you shoot someone in a righteous self-defense situation with a low to standard caliber gun, say a 38 or 9mm your probably ok, smoke some asshole with a, "Casull 454 'Raging Bull" or a 44 magnum, you're pretty much fucked, weather they live or die. It's that same old bullshit you hear in the police academy and on TV from the district attorney in court. "Did you shoot to stop your aggressor or did you shoot to kill your aggressor?" It's all about your perceived intentions that will be decided by the jury. As a side note my friends, eye witnesses are completely unreliable and they will destroy you. If you have five witnesses and if you could separate and isolate each one of them you would get five completely different perceptions of what was said and done. You notice I said perceptions rather than factual statements? It's not what you saw or heard, it's what your brain tells you what you saw or heard. Take an anti-gun witness who is a liberal and does not honor the second amendment. They saw a wolfish grin on your face followed by your laughing as you said, "I told you mother fucker, fuck with me or mine and I will kill your ass!" Everyone has their own agenda but will shout out their impartiality to appear to be fair.

With, 'Donkey Dick Adam's,' he felt that the 10 mm was the only gun in the world worth owning. Well, I own a 10 mm and it will stop a city bus, there's no question about it. But due to the extremely high velocity (which is almost twice that of a 45 automatic) there is a significant risk to having your bullet passing thru your intended and striking innocent persons. That's a liability nobody with half a brain or heart wants.

Several of my friends will ask me what gun they should buy for home personal defense or personal carry. My answer is always the same, Buy the very best and most affordable gun you could possibly get. I most often hear, "I found a real good deal on a used gun for real cheap!" I just smile as I say, "So you got a killer deal, do you realize you're betting your fucking life on that gun? You buy a piece of shit from somebody you hardly even know, you don't know how that guns been cared for or what that guns been through. You are the epitome of what a fool is! Buy the top quality or at least the best quality you can possibly afford. Cut out a few restaurant and bar visits, you cheap prick! Buy top quality ammunition and practice your ass off. You know, it's kind of like people falling for that fox in the Carfax commercial, which is just a total bunch of bullshit. The only people that report to Carfax are these straight-up legit car dealers, selling used cars. Good luck with that! Small auto repair shops and shade tree mechanics don't waste their time with reporting their repairs. They will fix something heavily damaged or something major with the engine or running gears and never report to Carfax. The mob run state of New Jersey allows auto dealers to change a "Salvage Title" car from another state to a "Standard Title." There are more car dealers in New Jersey per capita than any other state in the nation! They half ass repair a car and sell it as, "A cream puff." The same thing goes for guns.

So young lady, what we are looking for from this movie property master and what I looked for at Adam's house was the G-2 R.I.P. ammunition. It just so happens that in every autopsy that has been done on the bodies recovered, the Pathologist or Coroner doing the autopsy found very strange looking small pieces of lead that they have never seen before. I of course never had the opportunity to view that data, but looking at the ballistics reports of that particular 10mm round on You Tube, I fully suspect every victim was shot with a G-2 R.I.P. 10mm bullet, fired by a Sig Sauer 10mm pistol. Adam's slipped up one day at lunch when I intentionally let my eyes wonder and fainted my disinterest. He was talking about guns at the time. I offhandedly said, "I wish I could buy a boatload of 10mm Sig Sauer's and a few pallets of ammo." He said, "I have a good friend on the west coast that has a FFL (federal firearm license) and he can get me all the guns and ammo I want and I don't have to do any paper work because they are all unregistered."

I called bullshit and he grinned and said, "I will show you when we leave." We walked out to the parking lot, he opened the trunk of his Lincoln Town Car and it was packed with hand gun cases (50 or more). Adam's said, "Open any one you like, they are all identical to the ones used in all the John Wick movies, check for the serial numbers."

Guess what babe, I opened six random boxes and none of them were stamped. The serial numbers were not ground off, they were never stamped! Totally fucking unheard of!

Our movie prop master is definitely connected. We don't want to spook him so I need to lead and don't ask him any questions that would tip him off that you are a cop or that we are on to him. He would draw a life sentence if it's him who is the supplier to Adam's. Oh, I forgot to mention that Adams and Mommy each had five cases of one thousand count each of 10mm rounds of ammunition. That's ten thousand rounds of ammunition between the two of them, it gave me a severe case of ammo envy!

Mommy is also deep into this shit, much deeper than anyone realizes. I would like to gift her to you. You can burn her all by your little own lonesome as your final act of being a Duluth police officer. Now I bet that you do love me! Right?

So in the John Wick movies, at best count there were seventy-thee different firearms, six knives and swords and even a pencil and few other handy items that killed people. You see hun, what you have to understand is that Adam's very well may not have killed anyone. Yes, he did confess in open court as he being the sole actor in the murders but I don't think he has the guts for it. He orchestrates and directs, it's what he does. Adams wants to have his name as the Author of the $600,000 book I'm writing. I don't give a shit if he wants to have full credit for my work. I have $600,000 in my bank account! I am of the thought that this whole drug importing thing is to fund the movie he wants to write, produce and direct. He wants an Oscar with all the accolades and to go up on stage during the awards ceremony. Don't look at me like that, I know that you and everyone else thinks that he is going to be in prison for the rest of his natural life. You and they, are all wrong!

He has yet to file his colossal and unprecedented appeal. Maybe biblical in proportion would be a better statement. The appeals, yes, appeals with a capital S, will be based on his lead attorney being a cocaine addict. Remember his attorney's office being raided by the DEA? The law practice had all of their bank accounts frozen by the feds. The five partners had their homes raided and all personal assets frozen. All property was seized. They all lost their cars and had to leave their homes without even a bus pass or being allowed to pack so much as a tooth brush.

Adam's could easily afford the top attorneys in the nation. Why did he hire a bunch of country bumpkin locals who never defended a felony case and probably haven't even won a dog bite case? It's all part of his, "Master Plan" my dear.

Remember that on the first day of Adam's trial that they had to move it to the city council meeting room as the scheduled court room was overflowing? I dare say that in part of that crowd, were defense and constitutional law attorneys who the Adam's family had on retainer. He will walk, I shit you not!
Chew on this as a case in point:

When we finally sit down with Adams in the next few days, I will have a form signed by a federal judge that exonerates him from any further prosecution of crimes, if he gives us each and every location of the missing bodies and the number of people killed by his hand or that of his directed executions. That way, there can be no further prosecution and they can't give him the death penalty. He will go to a state mental hospital for the rest of his life. But he will have contact with the outside world and at some point, just like John Hinckley Jr. or better yet, Ethan Couch, he will walk.

Do you remember that charming young child by the name of Ethan Couch? Ethen, the sixteen year old kid who killed four people and injured nine others in a traffic accident while under the influence of alcohol and drugs in June of 2013? His defense was that he suffered from "Affluenza."

In this case, the Couch legal team argued that their "Affluenza defense" had to do with sweet little Ethan needed rehabilitation rather than prison, because he didn't understand boundaries and there were never consequences for his behaviors because his wealthy parents never set any. The whack job judge bought that argument because the Couch money bought her!

At 13 years of age this little dip-shit drove himself to school. He attended a private school of course. The school 'Head Master' confronted him for driving on school property and Daddy Couch threatened to buy the school and fire the 'Head Master.'

Oh babe this gets even better. At age 15, boy wonder was cited by law enforcement for," Minor in consumption of alcohol" and "minor in possession of alcohol," after he was caught parked in a pick-up truck with a naked and drunk, passed out fourteen year old girl. He drew a very short probation, had to attend a brief alcohol awareness program and had to serve eight long arduous hours of community service. It was a different judge but the same buy-off program. Hell the parents had over 20 arrests in a three year period but I guess if you have billions of dollars, rules and laws don't apply. Dear ole Dad was even arrested for impersonating a law enforcement officer with a fake badge. At another time, theft by check, assault and criminal mischief. Of course, all the charges were dropped.

Mom had her own things going on. She thought the car in front of her on the highway was driving to slow, so she rammed them off the road. Mom was fined $500.00 and was placed on, "Self-probation" for one year. Quality folks wouldn't yea say?

The night of the accident, June 15th 2013, the little maggot was seen on surveillance video stealing two cases of beer from a Walmart store. He was driving with seven passengers in his father's pick-up truck.

Ethan was driving seventy miles an hour in a forty mile an hour zone when he caused the accident with a disabled vehicle on the side of the road, struck a parked car that was helping the disabled car which was then pushed into an oncoming car. Three hours after his arrest he blew a 0.24 blood alcohol. That's three times over the legal limit for adult drivers, twenty one years old in Texas. He also tested positive for marijuana and Valium.

The family had several highly respected psychologists hired as experts by the defense that testified that he just didn't understand the consequences of drunk and drugged driving. The psychologists recommended he be sent to a teen mental health and rehabilitation Academy in Newport Beach California which cost up to $450,000 annually. The facility offers a ninety day treatment program that includes horseback riding, mixed martial arts, massage and cookery, interpretive dance therapy, a swimming pool, basketball courts and six acres of land.

Somehow he 'earned' an early release. I think they kicked him out. In December 2015 Couch was videotaped playing beer pong at a party, violating his probation. The probation department asked for his arrest because he could not be reached. He and his mother were reported as missing. Mom took sonny boy and ran off to Mexico.

The U.S. marshals posted a $5,000 reward for information leading to the whereabouts and the arrest of Tonya and Ethan Couch. He and his mother were discovered and arrested and held for deportation.

Tonya (mom) was deported back to the U.S. on December 20, 2015. Ethan fought his deportation based on some kind of presumed paper work snafu and delayed his extradition. Mother was charged in Los Angeles for hindering the apprehension of a fleeing felon. She was initially being held on a million dollar bail, but after her transfer back to Tarrant County (their home county) the judge dropped her bail from a million bucks to $75,000. She was released having posted a cash bond.

I don't know of the outcome of the Couch story and I could give a fuck less. I don't want to ever hear of you being any kind of a judge or lawyer like that. That kind of shit sickens me. Enough of this bullshit! I have a feeling that the case we are working will smell as bad as the Couch deal before all is said and done.

Chapter 13   TWISTED SWITCH

    Here is the 'why' as to the visit with the property master at the studio. I have a strong suspicion that he built those guns with full well knowing what Adam's plans were. I'm more concerned about the bullets that he and Adam's have been talking about. I've had several conversations with Adam's that revolved around bullets, trajectory, weight and configuration.
    The property master might be, or is, every bit as fuckin insane as Adam's is, but I'm not interested in him. We will turn all that all over to someone else, again our goal is to recover bodies, identify murder victims and give the family's some small parts of their hearts back. That's the game for you, the game for me is to become a world famous published author! Yes, that's some selfish shit but I don't work for free. Same as you. As for that gold coin that I mentioned earlier that is a part of the movie structure of how payments are made for killers. The denomination value is immeasurable but at some point I'm sure it cashes in for big money. Adam's claims to have one but I've never seen it. I did however see two of those coins at mommy's house. Ready for this Val? On one of mom's coins, the outer ring of the coin face is stamped, "Movie Prop-Not Legal Currency," which are on all the replica coins that I found on Ebay. Mom's other coin read, "To Basil All My Love, Dad." How is that for a WTF moment?
    Adam's really does think that he is John Wick and he thinks he's committing all these murders (as an avenging angel) that are being done in the movies.
We have a thirty mile drive to get to the airport and hopefully you have nothing to say but please let me hear you snore.

Val: Nope, I'm not ready to go to the airport, I wanna go back to the hotel. This is too much to process right now, besides I'm not sure if I trust you anymore. You have a darkness about you, maybe not dark but at least damn deep. Who the fuck are you, really? You know too much, you are far too connected to be an independent. I have read about people like you, are you one of those secret, secret, society people that are only known by a number and not even a name? I've heard about the secret society of broken and retired law enforcement who still have their hearts in a game. None of those guys carry a shield or have the power of arrest and they don't call the police when they locate a bad guy. The bad guys just seem to disappear and are never heard from again. I know goddam well you're one of those guys. I don't wanna know any more about it, but I unofficially and deniably want to say, "Thank You!"

Me: You are right but only impart. Yeah, I love the game, I love the hunt. I had to give upbow hunting in Colorado several years ago because I can't breathe at such high altitudes any longer. Bow hunting on foot is the ultimate challenge. My biggest thrill is to hunt the very top of the wildlife food chain killers, like Mountain Lions and Bears. There is something that is very intoxicating if not even romantic about knowing that at any moment, man (the master predator) can become prey. So I turned my interests to hunting the most dangerous of all predators to hunt, human beings. Very, very bad human beings, that nobody else seems to be able to find and nobody will ever miss them, if they are gone. My like-minded friends and I do it a bit different than you folks that are controlled by department rules and laws. We set traps offering ourselves up as bait. We allow them to hunt us, we make sure that they know we are coming or them. Get that look off your face little one, and slow your roll. Remember that I am a novelist, a novelist in process of penning a book about a psychotic serial killer. Plausible deniability is the best friend of all novelists. I am a twice copyrighted, registered author. I write what isn't always true and I claim that the truth is oftentimes false. I am a professional mind fuck. My playbook is my business and no, you don't get to even take a slightest of peaks.

I'm trying to grow you up, I'm trying to prime you. You are a bit off course and lost in your career goals. Usually that comes from family or friend pressures. I don't know what your pressures are, nor could I give a shit less. But I am telling you, if you sit on a bench with a black robe and a gavel you will be cheating yourself and your grandpa's memories. It is not what you need, maybe to please those other people but not for you. You've got a position yourself where you can carry the goods. Judges only know of what they're told. DA's only know of what they're told. If you don't know how to properly prepare and bring the case to the court you're never going to get a rightful or righteous prosecution. That's where plea deals were born, because of poor training, not giving a shit cops and inept prosecutors. We're going to clean that shit up, baby girl. I am laying this entire case in your lap. I am your star witness. Go out with a monster win and move on to what your true calling is. You need to be a District Attorney, not an assistant but the District Attorney. You will be the top cop in the entire county. Train the students in the police academies, teach them how to write reports that you can convict with. Give the police officers and deputies of the county refresher courses on report writing and most importantly, how to testify in court. Keep a log in each court room in the entire county. If more than two cases are lost by the same officer because the officer fucked up in the arrest report, he or she becomes a civilian. I will give you five years to do the deal on a local level. From there it's all on you.

You ready for another surprise sweetheart? I reached into my shirt pocket and pulled out a driver's license with her photo but a different name and my home address. I said, "Hold this in your hand until we get to the hotel, we are going to re-register. I'm sure that by now they have had plenty of time to bug our rooms. We are going to get fresh rooms under different names. We will order room service and the only conversation we will have is how you so greatly admire my writing and you may speak of your deep gratitude for my mentoring you in your PhD program. You are a college student and have always been. For the duration of this trip, regardless of where we end up, you are no longer or have ever been a police officer, and I have never been a cop. And again you're a young college student who is working your butt off to get a PhD in some level of law. You think you may even want to write law so you want to study with a master author, someone that knows how to write and has the power that makes sense to a complete stranger. So you are my understudy, you're just a college student who wants to learn how to write and how to put together a story, the right way.

Chapter 14   SANDY BEACHES

    Morning came damn early at 3:00 a.m. Val was trying to act all chipper and ready to go but I easily saw her eyes begging for just a few more hours of sleep. At the hotel check-out desk I had Val remove her laptop case using her actual driver's license from the hotel safe and told her to go to the ladies room and put her badge and gun in the lap top case. I booked two new rooms for another three nights and put her laptop under her new driver's license back into the safe. We headed for the airport. All during the four hour flight, Val drank at least two pots of coffee and kept her head in her rental laptop slapping the keys. We checked in the new hotel in Hollywood and dropped our luggage in my room. Val gave me her, "Oh no you don't" look. I smiled as I said, you aren't that lucky little girl. I have a woman at home. We're going for a ride. I had the taxi driver take us to the Poseidon Paddle and Surf Shop in Santa Monica. Val just stood and looked at the front of the shop and back at me several times without a word. I smiled as I said, "We're going to get you a swimsuit, we are going to lay in the warn sand and sun for a few hours and hopefully you're frozen soul will thaw. Your surf lesson is at 5:00. It's time for some rest, we have the day off. Our meeting is not until 10:00 a.m. tomorrow at the studio SAG member's only restaurant. Val shook her head in surrender as she said, "I suddenly like you again but I do wish I knew who the fuck you are."

    We put our street clothes in a rented locker and walked out the back door of the surf shop and on to the manicured beach. I was shocked to realize that Val had an even better hard body than I first thought. By the looks of several of the beach goers they were tells you they're going to tow your car if you don't use the parking lot. You get anything and everything you want, at any time. Please tell me who you are? Who you really, really are?

Me: Sweetheart I will have to think on that for a bit. It is time you get ready for your surfing lesson. Go splash in the water and feed those hungry eyes that have been locked on you since we got here. Do some of those CrossFit, jumpin-jax thingys that give you your rocking hard body. I pointed to the lifeguard tower and asked, "Have you ever seen five lifeguards in one tower with binoculars so interested in one person whose only 40 yards away? Go play little girl, I'm busy.

Watching Val surf was very interesting and entertaining, she only got up for a few brief periods each time. When she finished her lesson, she did an Oscar winning teasing stroll in the wet sand back to our mats. Beau Derrick has absolutely nothing on Val, that's for damn sure!

I took a lengthy nap when we got back to the hotel before I had to shower and dress for dinner. I knocked on Val's hotel room door. She opened the door. Seeing her in a stunning evening gown that I'm sure is held in reserve for the red carpet Hollywood types, caused me to step back a step or two. I found myself staring at her like I was a nineteen year old again. I wanted to run back to my room, put on my Jami's, call for a burger from room service and call Heather and talk to her for several hours until the need for sleep overtook me. When we got in the elevator, I asked her about her outfit and the jewelry that would cost a Duluth cop five years of pre-tax wages. She smiled sweetly as she said, "This is Hollywood darling. You can rent anything you want in Hollywood, especially when you give them a credit card number that can buy any six houses on most any beach in Southern California. Remember my dear man, I am your understudy. I am here to learn from the great master and world renowned author, Mr. David J. Brown!" This time I did slap her ass, but just once.

I took Val to the Stinking Rose restaurant in Beverly Hills. It has everything garlic, heavy garlic, right down to the deserts! It has an Italian motif with linen overhead tents at each high backed booth. You do get a great deal of privacy. I had made those reservations early in the morning for a private room. When you make a reservation at this particular restaurant you pre-pay the price of the table that will easily rival the weekly pay of any Union master journeyman. When we were seated the maître d' left the room and closed the doors. A waiter came in and latch locked those doors as he said, "You will not be bothered during your dining experience with us tonight, Mr. Brown." As he was latching the door, Val grabbed my arm in questioning panic. I smiled and patted her hand saying, "This room is reserved for only the top Hollywood celebrities. It's how they protect their privacy and keep out the paparazzi, we're fine. Nothing to worry about. It's a bitch not to be armed, isn't it baby?" The maître d' approached and asked if I preferred a male or female wait staff for our meal. I asked for his best bottle of red wine and told him we will need a few minutes to decide on our wait staff. Val was all eyes as I told her that the electric candle at the center of our table will softly flash for a full ten seconds before a wait person will approach our table. If we are still in conversation, they will turn around and go back to their station and wait for two minutes before the candle flashes again. I went on to say that the entire wait staff are aspiring actors hoping for a break into the movie industry. If we asked for male servers you will see some of the most handsome and charming men on this entire planet. It will be the very same for the women. You call it babe, wanna meet your competition or go the other way and you'll never look at your boyfriend quite the same way again.

    Val chose a female wait staff and they did not disappoint either of us. Val shook her head after her wine was poured and the 'Cleopatra' of modern times left the table.

    Val: How the fuck do you know about all this stuff? You've been here before, everywhere we have gone people have known you. I saw the room clerk and even the guy at the surf shop grin when we walked in, like you've been there before. I'm betting that even the airline pilots know you too! And you say you live in Duluth Minnesota, right. You are so full of shit!"

I don't know what I enjoyed more, the meal or Val sitting in stunned wonderment. Her only comment was, "I have never had a seven course meal, let alone had a different server for each course." I smiled as I said, "Federal cops live much better than city cops, consider that when you decide on your long term career choice."

I told our taxi driver to take us to the 'CUT Lounge' on Wilshire Boulevard. Val gave me the 'oh face' as she said, "Oh one of your favorite haunts, you lying bastard? I will kick you square in the balls, if anyone in that place acts in any way that they might even possibly know you!" I could only laugh as I said, "We are going celeb watching but for only one drink. We have a big day tomorrow. The CUT Lounge is an invitation only, number one nightclub for the top actors and recording artists in all the land. Doubt if we will get to press any flesh but I just thought I'd give you something to tell your Duluth pals about."

The door man was happy to accept my reservation number and the all but required fifty dollar, handshake tip. The host was just as appreciative with the standard cash handshake as he seated us.

I told Val that she could only order table pour wine. She gave me her patented (what is this shit?) look that I have seen way too many times from her in the last seventy-two hours. I smiled as I asked, "You coppers ever hear of date rape drugs? The hatchery for that kind of shit usually starts in a bar. Remember the, Jell-O Pudding guy?
No mixed drinks when I'm with you, do what you want on your time but keep in mind that you are on my time and I still call the ball."

I don't know if Val saw any celebs but she was ready to go before she finished her single glass of wine.

Our appointment the next day was at 10:00 a.m. with the Property Master. I was told by him to mention his name at the main entrance and we would be escorted to the SAG member's only, restaurant. The taxi driver let out a low whistle as he said, "I very rarely get a fair that gets to go to the SAG and I'm here several times a day!"

A surrey covered golf cart pulled up and asked if I was Mr. Brown with a guest. I said yes and we hopped on board. Val's eyes were wide with her head on a full swivel once we passed by the studio tour groups and entered the hallowed grounds of the 'no admittance'. We saw hundreds of people in costumes everywhere we drove. As we stopped at the SAG restaurant the driver said that he must escort us into the restaurant to introduce us to the Host. As we followed the surrey driver into the restaurant, I noticed his, in-the-pants holstered gun under his shirt. He introduced us as guests of Mr. Henry Bronson. I handed him a twenty dollar bill as I said, "Thanks for the lift, Officer." He grinned as he said, "Sergeant, Hollywood P.D. seventeen years." We shook hands and he left. We were seated by the Host with him saying, "Mr. Bronson will be with you shortly. Val shook her head as she said, "You spotted him for a cop, how in the hell did you know that? I responded with a simple smile, "I don't stand down, ever! No matter where I am, you shouldn't either, ever!" I saw the impact on her face as I said, "I saw the imprint on his shirt from the butt of his gun. He carries a full size Commander 1911, guessing either a Colt or a Kimber. We ordered coffee and Orange juice while waiting for our breakfast host.

I looked up to see a very common looking man of medium height and build, clean shaven and just a few years younger than me, approach or table. I stood and offered my hand in welcome. I introduced him to Val. He warmly smiled as he said, "We finally get to meet in person, Miss Bergquist. You are just as pretty as your voice is!"

I felt a gut punch as Val sheepishly said, "I've spoken with Henry of few times, but that was a few months ago. Val looked like she wanted to throw-up after I gave her my patented, thousand mile death stare.

Chapter 15 A KILLER UNMASKED

    Henry Bronson was a charismatic and engaging gentleman with soft but alert eyes.
    Henry: I would like to save our conversation as to the why of your visit until we can sit in my private, sound proof office, if you don't mind. My building is a very noisy machine and fabrication shop. I own the only privately held building on the entire studio lot. Hell, I should, I've been here for forty years! I hold a hundred year contract with the studio to produce any and all movie props that they desire. I have thirty four employees. They are my employees and not studio employees, I pay them much better than studio wages. Nobody has ever left me, other than retiring or dying. Then the applicant's in line for the job goes around the block. I have to interview job applicant's off-property because studio security goes nuts with having to do all the escorts. I am also the studio Prop Master. I am nothing more than a glorified librarian that catalogs inventory and locations for props that the studio has used from the very day one. Absolutely nothing is ever thrown away,"
    We had a very pleasant breakfast, except for Val of course. I could see that she was quietly begging for a quick beating. She knew that I was going to tear into her for her withholding the information of her having prior conversations with Henry. So the whole understudy story with the great author, David J. Brown was out the window. Henry knew that she was a cop. That meant that he would be guarded and measure every word before he spoke it. Fuck, fuck and fuck!
    As we walked out of the restaurant Henry said, "It's a nice warm morning, we could walk the three blocks to the shop or catch

a surrey." We walked, I think that Henry knew I needed to lower my blood pressure. Henry's three story, city block long and half as wide building exterior look like an entrance to an amusement park. Except for the concertina wire on top of the ten foot high fence. There were two truck size private property signs that read, "This building is not part of any studio tour. Trespassers will be arrested and jailed." I laughed at the sign as Henry said, "Movie crazed fans want to come in and touch the movie props and pocket or carry off any thing they could get. We have to turn them away to protect the props and of course, the huge liability of potential injuries. People will take anything that isn't nailed down, not to mention the autograph seekers.

It's also the reason we have the SAG restaurant, so everyone can eat in peace. That is why we have tall fences all around. The studio does three tours a day and averages six thousand visitors a day. The studio has several levels of security and there is a police precinct on the property. My nephew was just one of the thousands of memorabilia and autograph seekers. As a matter of fact, Basil has a life-time restraining order from this studio and all of it's personal. He has been thrown off of every location set as well. He has repeatedly snuck on to this property and locations in disguise. He held a SAG card as an 'extra'. He was a terrible distraction as he was always trying to talk to the actors, directors and writers. He was a complete pain in the ass, even for me. Every time he was detained he used my name. I received several phone calls from studio security."

Henry used a key access card and open the front door. The first office I saw was an all glass enclosure with a gilded silver sign that read, "Safety and Security Services."

The very large, flat stomach gentleman who greeted us could probably carry a cow under each arm all the way out to the pasture. I'm guessing that he is the runt of the litter and all of his brothers and cousins all work here. I guess old Mr. Bronson isn't fuckin around when it comes to his security. The entire back wall of the security office was one oversized fire and alarm panel. Yes this is a serious business all right, for sure! As we entered Henry's glass office another shapely 'Cleopatra' type beauty, welcomed us. She was wearing a very smart and expensive business suit. Henry introduced us and asked her to bring a craft of coffee and to order a large platter of Crow for Miss Reba Bergquist. As we entered the private office I couldn't help but notice how stark the walls were. There was none of that wall to wall, floor to ceiling celebrity handshake autographed photos stuff. Henry read my mind as he said, "I have come to learn that less is more, my home is full of photos and gifted memorabilia from the last 40 years. Yes, I have met and spoken to most all of the greats, however this is a business and not a museum.

Feel free to interrupt me at any time. I am of the thought that you would rather hear answers as I speak. Please let me know if I miss anything or if I'm boring you. First, Mr. Brown, I have read both your books which in my opinion, deserves at least a first reading if not a full movie script. I became aware of you and your writings from my nephew Basil. Basil is my sister's adopted son, we of course are not blood related.

My sister Charlotte was married to Basil's father, Clark. Basil came from Clark's first marriage. Clark designed and built experimental aircraft and manufactured do-it-yourself small, single passenger airplane kits. Clark was testing a new plane that he designed and built. His plane disappeared off radar over Lake Superior near Silver Bay, Minnesota. Neither he nor any part of his aircraft were ever found. He went down in the heavy thunderstorm, there was no oil slick or any floating debris. Basil was only four years old when Clark died, so he had no recollection of his father. I'm the only male image he has ever had. He calls me dad and I welcome that. Let me tell you of what I know to be true in reference to Basil or as he likes to be known today as "Adam's." I understand that I have you to thank for that and yes I agree, Basil is not a very masculine name for a man in today's world. Basil or Adam's, is a bit of a contrary fellow but I assure you he is not mentally ill. What he is, is obsessed. Obsessed to the very edge of his sanity, but he has never gone over the edge. He refuses to grasp reality, he is much like a twenty-eight year old gamer living in his mom's basement. Adam's so desperately wants and needs to be recognized. He needs, perhaps clambers (is a better word) to be seen and known as a person of fame and stature. But he is so afraid of rejection that he never ever tries. He just sits and dreams, he dreams and he cries, with knowing that he will never realize his dream as anything other than just a silly boys dream. You my good Sir, have been the only one to ever reach him, to inspire him and to give him hope.

Me: Henry let's not leave out that tiny little matter that his renewed hopes to achieve great fame is to very publicly murder me. Val let out a gasp with a look of horror on her face. Henry dropped his head as he said, "Yes that was his goal."

Me: Henry I know that he did not shoot that man in Duluth, he just happened to be crossing the street when it happened. He confessed to it because he thought he would get his fifteen minutes of fame. He thought because the victim was a homeless drunk and the local bully, that the penalties would be minimal.

Henry: Yes he did confess to several other killings that he is using to keep what he calls his "Fame Train" alive. I personally think he needs to stay behind bars to keep him from killing you. You do know that he will kill you anyway he can, at any time and in any place. He doesn't hate you, he actually deeply loves you. It's much like when John Chapman, who was a die-hard Beatles fan, shot and killed John Lennon in December of 1980.

Val started to vomit as she ran from the room. When she returned to the office she asked if we could just leave. She was visibly shaken with a weak voice. I stood up and held her for a moment and said, "Yes honey just a few more questions and we will be on our way. She moved her chair next to mine and grasped my hand, she had no intention of letting go, that's for sure!

Me: Henry tell me about the whole John Wick deal and the handguns in Adam's car trunk. Where did they come from?

Adam's said that you gave them to him. I know Henry that you are a convicted felon. Convicted of murder I believe, you only did three weeks in jail with no prison time. You are on lifetime probation, you do know where I'm coming from with that don't you? It is that whole thing about you being a felon in possession of a firearm right?

    Henry: You my good man, sure do your research. Yes I was convicted of manslaughter fourteen years ago, on your birthday as a matter of fact, June 3rd. Yes I do my homework too! I was standing at the bar of a working man's bar. Some biker pukes came in looking for trouble. Two guys came up on each side of me and started to squeeze into me. I told them to stop it and to go play somewhere else. The guy on my left shoulder shoved me. I shoved him back and he fell back on to a table and the table flipped over. He came up swinging, I ducked his punch and drove my right fist under his chin. He was out cold as he fell back, he struck his head on the foot of the leg of the upended table. He died right there on the floor. I had an FFL (Federal Firearm License) manufacturer's license and of course a concealed carry permit. I was carrying a gun at the time. Because I had drank three stiff drinks, I was intoxicated and in possession of a firearm. If I would not had the gun on my side I would have been found innocent, but because I was armed I couldn't plead self-defense.

    So on to the guns in the trunk of his car. Yes they came from this shop. Did you work the actions? I answered, "Yes they were so smooth that it was like farting through silk."

    Henry: If you looked a bit closer you would have found that there was no hole machined for the firing pin and the barrels were all plugged. None of those guns are in any way operable, hence the serial numbers or the lack thereof. They are nothing more than inert display pieces, Knick Knacks if you will. Anything else?

    Me: Yes Henry, you've been a very gracious host. I like you and I appreciate your candor. There is something you should know about Adam's. I had him removed from Stillwater State

Penitentiary and he is currently being housed in the Saint Louis County Jail under the guise that I wanted to interview him about the missing people in our area. The truth is, that I too know that Adam's didn't kill anyone. The deal is this, I know a guy, who knows a guy, who knows a guy that said there is a green light, a hit if you will, out on Adam's. If you want to visit him for one last time you better fly back with us in the morning. It seems that the drug cartels and the street gangs don't much like people who claim to be one of them when they are not. Tomorrow afternoon I will honor my contract and deliver my completed 325 page, 123,017 word novel to Adams. The author of record is Basil Adam's. I will hand him his completed novel as the two deputy U.S. Marshall's fit him into his belly band and his leg shackles for his trip back to Stillwater State Penitentiary before the dinner hour. There's a great chance that he will not rise for breakfast in the morning.

    Henry nodded his head as he weekly said, "I understand, thank you for telling me the truth. So, is there anything else?"

    Me: Yes, I take it that you're shop made those John Wick coins? (Henry nodded his head) Could we each have one? Not as a souvenir but more of a remembrance. It was the first time Henry smiled since we sat down. He said, "If you would like to stretch your legs, I'll take you two for a brief tour. We had to go to the 'safety-security' glass office to sign a waiver and to be issued a hard hat along with hearing and eye protection. Henry wrote a few things down on a notepad and gave it to the security guard and said, "I trust you will take care of this immediately" as the security guard nods his head and said, "Right away sir."

    We had a very interesting twenty minute tour. I had to do a double take as we went into the caged 'money room'. I had to shake my head as I said, "That mother fucker, he has killed himself with his own bullshit!" Val and Henry had puzzled looks on their faces as I said, "A friend of a friend of a friend, showed me a picture of Adam's kneeling with these identical foot lockers, overflowing with cash the very same as these are. Even the back drop is the same. That little prick posted pictures of himself with these foot lockers on the internet. He wanted people to think he was a drug kingpin. Well fuck me!

That is why the feds are after him! They think that he is moving tons of cocaine every month and that he is laundering the drug money thru the TV station business. The Secret Service thinks that he is counterfeiting. I have seen the Interpol alerts on him.

That silly bastard set all this shit up! I've got to get some pictures of this shit. Val, go kneel behind those foot lockers, I'm going to make you famous! I cannot wait to show these to the poor bastards from the 'alphabets' who are chasing a whack-job's fantasy."

We returned from our tour, signed out and returned our issued hard hats, eye and hearing protection. The security guard nodded at Henry and said, "Those items you requested Sir are with Sally." We walked back into the executive suite. Sally stood and handed Henry two shiny vinyl blue gift boxes stamped in bright gold letters, "John Wick." Henry fully smiled as he said, "As requested, for my honored parting guests from Minnesota." Val opened her Box first. It was a glistening gold, John Wick coin. Instead of the coin edges stamped 'movie prop-not legal tender' hers read, "To my friend Reba, truly a cop's cop." Mine read, "To my friend, David J. Brown, my all-time favorite author."

Sally asked if she could call for a Surrey for us. I said, "No thank you, we could use the exercise." Handshakes all around and we left the building. Val and I walked over to a bench and sat down. She was visibly shaking. Obviously she didn't know that Adam's only goal in the last year and a half was to kill me, anyway he possibly could. She said, "Please take me back to the beach. I need to walk in the wet sand, I have to get my head right and put my heart back into my body."

I sat in the sand and watched her walk down the beach and out of view. She was gone for almost a full hour. A Lifeguard Jeep pulled up with a smiling Val. She patted the lifeguards arm and kissed his cheek and said, "Thank you for the ride handsome."

She hopped out of the Jeep as the blushing lifeguard drove

off. Val started to giggle as she said, "The lifeguard asked me for a date for this afternoon but I told him that my grandpa was waiting for me on the beach." I started to bring my hand back to swat her ass but then I thought better of it.

We had an early dinner. I was relieved to see Val wearing street clothes. She asked, "Do you really think that he will be murdered in prison?" I smiled as I said, "I sure do hope so!" Val gulped a bit of air as she said, "I feel absolutely terrible about this, but I hope so too." The rest of dinner was just common chatter. I walked Val to her room, she stopped at her door, turned to me and said, "If you didn't have Heather in your life, I would bed you tonight and marry you in the morning. I think a beach wedding would be nice!" We shook hands goodnight.

After a quick breakfast we headed to the airport. Val said, "I think that you will like our seat selections." I gave her my best WTF face as she smiled sweetly and said "I have learned much from being under the tutelage of the great author Mr. David J. Brown. The greatest of all lessons that I've learned on this trip is how to use a federal credit card. I upgraded our seats to first class! I want to be close to you during our trip home. I smiled as I said, "You better knock that shit off. This card and my credentials expire at midnight tonight. But I am keeping this fucking badge!"

Val cuddled up to me during the flight and fell fast asleep. I put my arm round her and thought to myself, "This is what it must feel like to be a father, maybe even a grandfather. I found more than just one tear.

Chapter 16 LIKE-MINDED

Holy shit, what in the hell was that? More of those smaller airplane windows. First on the left than on the right and then dead center. It's the same as before with the way the window faded away from me. And as before I was suddenly slammed into total darkness, black darkness! I do know that my thinking earlier that they were taking out my eyes was nonsense. The only thing that makes any sense is that they must be opening my eyelids to give me eye drops. I'm guessing that people in comas don't have any tear duct functions, fucked if I know. All I do know is that, I've got to keep my mind actively working. What the hell can I think about? People, places, and things, shit I don't know. Well hell, there is no place I care to visit or revisit. I've been everywhere I wanna go. I'm not a sightseer, don't care for festivals or historic tours. Things don't hold much value to me as far as possessions, other than my guns and trout fishing gear. So all that leaves me with is people. I am outgoing if not a bit gregarious and I do enjoy people. But then again there are times that I could and have gone a week or even two without speaking to another soul.

We all have different levels of friends. Work friends that we rarely socialize with outside of work, organizational, service and church friends, who we don't associate with outside of scheduled events.

I have a fairly large group of 'reading friends'. I guess I always refer to them as 'reading friends' rather than fans, because it just feels so phony to call them, 'my fans'. I think it is arrogant and dismissive to refer to my readers as fans. In my mind, they carry more value than many of my daily friends where we just speak of day to day common shit. My readers have a depth and a shared interest with me and other readers. I am quite active with reading groups and do my best to answer their email questions and attend their annual events.

I started to recruit like-minded Facebook friends about six years ago. Since my writings are about First Responder and abuse survivor wellness, I friend requested Police, Fire, EMS, Nurses, School Teachers, Mental Health and Social Workers.

I built 5,000 Facebook friends as a marketing strategy to bring my books to them. I secured friendships with people that I thought I could help directly. I never had any visions that my writing would appeal to the masses or national book store chains or the big box retailers. As time went on, I found that people who fought with depression and loss, benefited the very most. Professionals seem to have a higher level of denial to protect their jobs and to avoid criticism from their peers. Of course, the super stoic professionals have the highest number of suicides. Appearances obviously holds more value than wellness.

Some, maybe even many, say that Facebook friends are not real friends. I strongly disagree. I have had many deep heartfelt conversations with Facebook friends and readers that I have never met. Sadly my actual friends fall far short when it comes to gut honesty. Yeah I guess I could start there.

It's been said that if you want to limit disappointment and frustration in your life, tighten your circle of friends. My experience tells me, that if I have to practice tolerance and acceptance of my friends, then they never were friends in the first place. They were just people that needed to use me. I have further found that money is not the root of all evil. Envy and jealousy are the roots of all evil.

There is a group of people (10 to 12) that I see twice a week. We have lunch every Friday or at least we did up until just recently. When my first book came out, I gifted each of those fellows a signed copy. Not one of them have read it, but each of them wanted me to gift them a signed copy of my second book when it came out. God has blessed me and gifted me with a unique smile that simply says, "Go fuck yourself," without me muttering a word. As this whole impeachment bullshit from the democrats has gone on they have gotten more boisterous and more aggressive with their disdain for President Trump. Of course, these guys are all retired union members and tradesmen. In their small world, the union is their God. If the union says it they believe it, if CNN or the rest of those liberal pukes says it, they believe it. The last time we lunched, (and the last time for me forever) most all of the group wanted to argue with me about President Trump as I'm the only Republican in the group. I smiled as I got up from my chair, looked at each one of them and said, "Gentlemen, I have suddenly lost my appetite. I don't debate with one dimensional people." A few aggressively looked at me and someone asked, "What is that supposed to mean?" I smiled as I answered, "You all have the mental process of a tree stump, see you around fellows."

It's all about knowing the difference between an acquaintance and a friend.
I have sponsored dozens and dozens of young fellows in AA. Once they got their job back, their wife back and their court/probation activities taken care of, I very rarely ever see them again.

Chapter 17   THE COP AND THE CONVICT

Probably the most notable of all of my experiences with a friend in AA had to be with my friend, Jim Abby. I met Jim after an AA meeting where a group of us always went out for coffee after the meeting. Jim was an interesting looking fellow. He was about five foot, four inches tall, probably two hundred and sixty pounds. He was just as heavy in his shoulders and in chest mass as he was in his stomach and a very powerful looking guy. Jim was full-on with his dedication to his sobriety, there's no question about that.

One of the meetings we both went to, was in a very large room in the basement of a church. We had to set up sixteen banquet sized tables (4x8) and chairs for approximately eighty people at the tables and sixty additional chairs along the walls for late comers. I was part of the set-up crew along with Jim and six others. Jim was a blur and out worked everyone else, every time. He would just be covered in sweat like an old hound but he wouldn't stop until everything was laid out properly for the meeting. He would go home to quickly shower and be back before the meeting started. It was the same thing after the meeting with breaking everything down and putting everything away. Jim and I became friends and spent quite a bit of time together. As with all the people I have met, (Jim was certainly no exception) I told them and him that if there was any crime that they had committed or witnessed that they had not been adjudicated for, that I didn't want to hear about it. I don't want to be the one to turn them in or to have to testify against them, so again keep that shit to yourself!

Jim had the physique of a felon who had thrown around a lot of free weights as most prison inmates do. Jim and I did quite a few things together. We went to the weekly stock car races, went to the mountains looking for gold, did some trout fishing and swilled coffee frequently during the week nights and after meetings.

As time went on, Jim confided in me that he had been to prison. Seems that him and four of his buddies, (who were all drunks and drug addicts) often times found their highs were not high enough, so they would go and rob banks. They robbed seven banks, one of those banks they robbed twice in northern California. Jim said they would be drunk and do a mess of meth before each bank job. He would rob a jewelry store on the way to the bank job, just to get his juices flowing. Jim got caught and served eleven years in prison. He never gave up any of his bank robbing buddies. The prison parole board tried to give him an early parole at the start of his seventh year. Jim told them no dice, he told them to take him back to his cell. He wanted to walk out of prison a free man without the strict conditions of parole. He said that he knew he would violate the conditions of parole and would end up doing a life stretch. Jim had some other stories that I highly questioned but never confronted him with. Like a lot of other guys, Jim wanted to be known or stand out as a crazy bad-assed fellow. Jim presented himself as a sensitive, tough guy and he certainly was all of that. He helped out a lot of people, he was actually a very kind and sensitive man.

One of Jim's claims was that he was a 'patched enforcer' for an international motorcycle gang who wears leather vests with a skull on the back who didn't like to be called a gang. They would much rather be referred to as a, "Motorcycle Club!" I didn't quite buy that story, nor was I interested in pursuing it as to its authenticity.

I just chalked it up as a story of a man with a weak self-image. Jim and another fellow made their living doing freelance demolition work on small buildings. All they really had was a couple of power saws, crow bars and a small flatbed truck. They only would do cash paying jobs.

One day, Jim had a great deal of chest pain and was hospitalized for six days. The doctors told him that he had a very serious heart problem and that he needed surgery. Jim didn't have any health insurance so I dragged him (screaming and kicking through the social service agencies and got him registered and he received Medicare and Medicaid and he had the surgery. Jim was a proud man and didn't want welfare but at the same time he couldn't work and had no savings. By the time we got him set up for help with housing and food, the finance company repossessed his car and he was evicted from his apartment. A friend of ours let Jim stay in his dilapidated two person camping trailer that was parked in his back yard. After two months of heated debates (his ego) I convinced Jim to sign up for social security disability due to his health restrictions that wouldn't allow him to work. As most people know, most every person that applies gets denied the first and even the second time when applying for SSI. For some strange reason Jim was approved in less than five weeks!

Jim told me that he was still married to the same woman for the last eighteen years. He said he hadn't seen her or his daughter (who he only saw once in her first month of life) that live somewhere in Arizona. I found that more than a bit odd to still be married to someone you haven't seen for seventeen years but then again, that's none of my business. One day, Jim said his wife was coming to Colorado to visit him for two weeks and he wanted me to meet her. She was a very nice woman and they got along very well. We had dinner several times and went to the races twice. She went back to her home state and Jim fell into a depression that caused me to fear for his life.

It wasn't but a few weeks later when Jim said, "I think I'm going to go back home and be with my wife and my daughter. My daughter is pregnant and I want to meet my granddaughter when she's born. I couldn't be there for my own daughter and I have always felt that I let her down and I've always felt ashamed."

I thought that would be wonderful, Jim left with my full heart-felt blessings. We would talk on a phone (him and her both) at least once a week for several months. Then late one night Jim's wife called me and she was crying. The first thing out of her mouth was, "They got Jim! They got Jim!" My response was, "Who got him, holy Christ who got him?" She said, "The feds, The U.S. Marshals!" I said "The feds, what the hell is this all about?" She said, "Well I have some things to tell you and I am very sorry for having to lie to you. You are the best friend Jim has ever had. Jim is not who we claims to be. His name is not Jim or James Abby. His real name is 'Monte Von Ripper the 3rd'. He is not an American citizen, he is a Canadian citizen. Jim escaped from the 'Remand Centre' prison in Medicine Hat, Ontario, seventeen years ago. They were transporting him to, Millhaven Federal Maximum Prison in Bath, Ontario. He was doing a life sentence for arson, kidnapping and murder. Jim was an enforcer for a motorcycle club and was ordered to kill a rival club, chapter president in Medicine Hat, Canada." I asked her what jail they took him to, she said, "I don't know for sure, they were talking about the Immigration Center or the Maricopa County Jail. After the S.W.A.T. Team arrested Jim, the Marshal let me kiss him goodbye and told me that I would never be able to see him again. He told me that Jim's case was his very first, "High risk, International Fugitive Case," that has been haunting him for sixteen years. He said that he drove by my house every day for the last sixteen years on his way home from work. He saw Jim watering the flowers yesterday and had several agents hidden in the area waiting for me and our daughter to leave the house for our safety.

    Jim was walking down the driveway to walk the dog and they pounced on him. It scared the shit out of me! S.W.A.T. guys, flash bang and smoke grenades. Cops were everywhere. Jim didn't resist."

    From that day to this day, I have had no further contact with Jim. I did however talk to an Assistant Warden at the prison in Bath, Canada. I asked if I could put some money in Jim's commissary. The assistant warden said that prisoners with Jim's status (solitary confinement) don't have commissary privileges. They are not allowed visitors, are not allowed to send or receive mail as well as phone calls. When I asked what I could do to make Jim's time go better, he said, "Absolutely nothing!" I said, "Well does he have or is he allowed to have a radio or television?" The assistant warden said that they're allowed to have clear case radios and televisions that can only be bought from the prison commissary. I made arrangements with the assistant warden and sent the money to his account. Six weeks later I received a blank letterhead from the prison and a receipt for Jim's TV. I guess that if I'm going to be conned, I'd prefer it be Jim more than anyone else. I was very grateful for my opening statement when I first met him, "Don't tell me anything that you have not been adjudicated for." In this case, that was a pure God thing.

    I did get a call from the U.S. Deputy Marshall that had Jim's case. After I listened to him introducing himself, I started laughing as he said, "I am just doing some follow-up to close your friend's case. Is there anything more I should put into the file before I close it out?" I laughed much harder this time as I said, "Sport, you going for the trifecta? You charge Jim's wife for, "Harboring a fugitive" and now you think that you can take me too? Go fuck yourself!"

    The agent quickly started to back pedal as he said he did not and will not charge Jim's wife or daughter. He said, "I have put in the papers for my retirement, I think I want to write a book on Jim's case and a few others. I have read your first book, I am asking you if you might give me a few pointers?" I laughed even harder than the first two times.

    I gathered myself as I said, "Listen hard, I will say this only once. No two people, know the very same person in the very same way. Each and every relationship is unique onto itself. You know Jim as a wanted and recovered fugitive. I knew that very same man as a kind and loving soul. I love the man and I pray for him every night. I make no apologies for calling Jim, my friend and my brother."

Chapter 18   GENERATIONAL ENTITLEMENT

    Without question the most difficult relationship I have ever had to maintain and endure was with my stepdad. I loved the guy, he was a good friend of my dad's before my dad died and pops took care of my mom afterwards, as he had promised my dad. Mom was living in a house that she couldn't afford to keep without my dad's income. My parents always thought that my dad's union would take good care of the family if dad died. Mom found out the blind faith myth behind that when dad passed.

    At some point mom and pops decided that they were in love and they got married. Pops and I were good buddies that is, right up until I moved out West. Pops was a die-hard union member, he hated the fact that I moved to a, "Right to Work State." He further hated the fact that I became a Police Officer. My pops hated anyone with authority that he couldn't get around. My pops had worked for the same company for forty-two years. He worked for a large grain elevator company that had locations all over the country. At this elevator they took in grains from semi-trucks and railroad cars from all over the country. They loaded into ocean going ships in bulk and bagged loads. Of course it was a Union operation. My pops worked afternoon shifts and actually bragged about only working two or three hours in a ten hour shift, the rest the time he spent sleeping. He joked with his friends and anyone else who would listen to his bragging about how he screwed his employer and they would all laugh. My mother would comment on how rested he looked after working ten hours and they would both laugh. It sickened me. For reasons I don't understand, he felt that the company owed him.

But yet, the company were the ones that gave him the job, paid him his wages, and give him his benefits with full medical along with generous sick time and vacation pay. He however didn't see it that way, he thought the union did all this for him. It is a very common attitude amongst many northern Minnesota union workers. In turn he followed the unions overpowering mandate that all members must vote a straight democratic ticket. And of course, pops blindly followed union mandates and always voted democrat. I remember him showing me with great pride, his collection of hand tools all stamped with his company's name on them. I think he must have had every screwdriver, wrench, plyers, saws and hammers by every manufacturer ever made, every size and every model. His basement looked like a trophy room with displays of all the tools that he stole from his employer. When his company put in fuel tanks for diesel fuel, he immediately went and bought a diesel pick-up truck and of course filled his tank along with a number of his other work buddies every Friday afternoon. He bragged about not having to buy diesel fuel for his pick-up truck for more than twelve years.

I'm of the thought that just because your dad has a union job you should not automatically be hired because your dad or uncle work there. You should have to apply for it and actually compete with other applicants. It's not that way with the unions however, at least that's the way it used to be. When I would come back to visit my family my pops immediately wanted to talk all about the asshole cops in this town, his horseshit employer and all the terrible things that people were doing to him. Probably my best time with him was when GM went on strike and all the dealerships went out along with the factory workers. My pops had a GM pick-up truck. His truck broke down and needed some parts.

So he drove up to the local dealership and there were picketers with signs everywhere and they were blocking the driveway of the dealership. He said, "Hey I'm going to go down the street and drop you off and you can go walk in, right past those guys and get me the parts I need." I laughed my ass off as I asked him, "Whatever happened to your loyalty to the union brotherhood? You know, when any trade union goes out on strike the whole world goes out on strike. You know how everyone honors picket lines, right? But now because you need something the union membership can all go fuck themselves?" With a smirk I told him, "You know that your truck in going nowhere until your union brotherhood decides to go to the bargaining table and the meantime you could always take a bus or rent a car!" The look on his face was priceless!

There was one period of time where pops union was out on strike for nine weeks. He of course was bragging about his strike fund payments, unemployment and food stamps and he didn't have to go to work and he still got paid. I couldn't resist asking him if he knew who was still drawing a full paycheck. The look on his face when I said, "The guy who promoted that you all vote to strike, your union business agent!" I followed up with, "I have to ask you, why does the taxpayer, have to carry a union worker because they're not getting their way? If you don't like your job and the benefits, go get a different job. Your employer owes you nothing!"

There was never any reasoning with my pops when it came to union matters. I found it sad that someone can allow their union to dictate who they should like or not like and who they should vote for. Of course I told him that as a police officer we did have a union but we did not hold out, we did not slow down, we did not reduce services and we sure as hell never went on strike, because we had a responsibility to our community! He didn't care for that much.

But the best of the best, of the very best, came the day when my wife and I came to visit (we were living in Colorado) for Christmas. My mom and pops had never met my new wife and neither of them knew that she was a corporate executive and oversaw the human resources division of a Fortune 500 company that bought raw products from his company. My pops is old school and doesn't value women in the work place. He thinks women who work are all secretaries or typists. Pops loved to talk and was holding court as to the value of his great service to our country, to his employer and more importantly his steadfast loyalty to his union. Of course he lamented over the good old days of being allowed to drink on his lunch break. My wife sat quietly as he told us about his 'chicken shit' employer that just installed time clocks throughout the plant (up to that time the employees wrote down their own work hours). He was quite proud to announce that after the five technicians left, after three days of installing the time clocks, he poured a full can of soda down each time clock saying, (as my mom giggled) "I showed those assholes."

My wife smiled as she stood up, reached into her purse and pulled out two business cards and gave one each to my mom and pops. She stood and watched the color drain from their faces. She then said, "My Company is your company's largest customer. I personally know the executives of your company. I will pretend that I have never meet you, for David's sake. I have to think that you will put in a 'work order' to fix those time clocks, the moment that you get to work tomorrow?"

We left their house and returned to Colorado. The few times I went back to Minnesota to visit, I had to go alone.

I remember when my dad was the union "Shop Stewart' for his company. If an employee felt he was being mistreated he reported it to my dad and dad would speek to management on the employee's behalf. If the matter could not be resolved the employee would file a grievance with the union business agent. My dad would come home all kinds of pissed off because the employee would secretly meet with management and withdraw their grievance and it made my dad look like an asshole. In most every case (I even heard workers bragging about it) management would offer the 'offended' a months of Saturdays of overtime where the worker only had to show up to clock-in, go back home and return ten hours later to clock-out.

In the mid 70's I took a job in an open pit iron ore mine, where you have to join the union as a condition of employment, so the employees couldn't go out on a "Wild-Cat" strike. I remember my first day on the job when a boss came up to me and didn't even ask my name before he started chewing my ass for working to fast. He said, "Son, we have only one speed here and we set that speed. Slow down and follow our pace. There are a lot of nails and spikes all over the parking lot. It would be a shame if all of your tires became flat!"

The company had the right to search your person and vehicle at any time. There were paved, four-lane roads on the property. If security was checking cars leaving the property everyone used the established and well-practiced hand signals to alert the car behind them.

That really wasn't necessary however because you could see the cars in front of you throwing tools and parts out their windows. You couldn't drive in the other lane because it was littered with company property. In the one year I worked there, no one to my knowledge got fired for any reason. The union held the power.

Chapter 19   FEAR DRIVEN RAGE

Now what the hell is this? Is this actually light, am I really seeing real light? It's kind of like a moon dog light, defused for sure but where is it coming from? Is this the light that people see in their final moments? Now I'm starting to feel something. It's like I'm drifting but I'm not feeling or hearing any water. Then again it feels like I'm floating in the air but I can't feel or hear any wind. Is my body waking up or am I just rebooting my brain. Is this the final spike just before I crash and become dust? I don't feel frightened or worried, I would just like to know what's next and when. Guess I'm ready for all of this to come to an end, either way.

I have no concept of time. Some people think that water boarding of terrorists is a cruel treatment. They ought to try this shit on them. I feel like I'm in a torrent flooding river being dragged under water. I stroke my arms and kick my legs to struggle to the surface, I break the water surface gasping for air, I franticly look for an overhead branch to grab onto, but I get sucked under the surface again.

Well shit, listen to me. Hell I would give anything to have the chance to fight a fast flowing flooding river and risk death over having to lay here with a dead body and a dying mind. At least give me a fucking chance to fight!

Guess that little rant isn't going to take me anywhere. Where was I with the friend's thing? I fully know that many if not most people don't like the truth. Especially when that truth is about them. There are tons of Facebook posts that define friendships.

Stuff like, "When you start seeing your worth, it's harder to stay around those that don't." Or, "The truth is the truth even if nobody believes it. A lie is a lie even if everyone believes it."
Or, "People don't abandon people they love. People abandon people they were using."
Or, "Some people only hate you because of the way other people love you."
Or, "Don't feel sad over someone who gave up on you, feel sorry for them because they gave up on someone who would have never given up on them." Or, my personal favorite, "Money isn't the root of all evil...Jealousy is..."

Guess the 'root of all evil' statement is a good place to land on.

I have always been warm and engaging, respectful and courteous with most all people I meet. But my life has taken a rather sharp turn, perhaps a hair-pin turn and I'm not the one who changed! Ever since my first book was published people started to treat me differently. I think my hard pounding, gut twisting search for my truths may have embarrassed them. There is a part of me that wants to call them mentally lazy but I know the real truths about that. I was no different for many years. I used people, places, and things to avoid having to look at my own truths. My truth was that I was a drunk without purpose. The only thing that mattered to me at that time, was that I owned enough stuff to distract me from looking at me. I looked at my stuff as my identity. Everything had to do with what I had and what I did. It was never about who I was, other than my physique and my looks. I knew, as I believe that most everyone else knows, that comfort and image is far more important than self-discovery.

So back to that jealousy thing. There are a great many people that like and respect me as an author and a contributing human being.

Then again there are people that I resent as well. I have no stomach for the proud peacocks that strut around wearing their college degrees like combat ribbons, hiding behind what they think they know. I want to look at them and ask, "Tell me true, how many assignment papers did you buy or plagiarize? How many times did you pay to have another student take your exams for you? Tell me about the ingenious cheat sheets you developed and carried into test sessions. Or did you just throw down a stack of cash and buy your grades from your drug addicted professor? You know, kinda like those pieces of shit celebrities that bought their kid's way into collage. Someone take your SATs for you?"

I have never been impressed or swayed by peoples status, be it social or professional. I smile inwardly as I silently say, "Fucker, don't tell me what you've learned, tell me what you've discovered! Not what you were taught but what you yourself have discovered. What is your contribution to society and to all of mankind? What have you brought forward, what have you or are you leaving behind other than some overblown obituary that nobody gives a shit about and is forgotten the very moment the mourners close the freshly printed pamphlets produced by the mortuary? Have you ever written any books that sit and will continue to be on the shelves of the United States Library of Congress for all of time? Go fuck your entire self!"

Holy shit that's some crazy rage! If I come out of this shit I will definitely have to work on that!

Yes, I too suffer from envy at times.

Chapter 20 SEARCHING

Names, where are all these names coming from? This screen crawler is in warp speed, all of a sudden. It's just a blur of letters, how can I slow this down? Am I waking up to a new and beautiful world or is this a runaway train careening down a hill at break neck speed, just before it derails and fucks everything up? Does derailment and smoldering wreckage have a message?

Am I about to die and be sent into the flaming bowels of hell? Well that sure as fuck is a comforting scenario of the end of a person's life. Wait a damn minute, this is not just about some random person's life. Jesus Christ, this is about my life!

How many other rosy thoughts can I come up with that will energize me to want to keep fighting?

I must be panicking, that is the reason why I can't read that damn crawler screen. I've got to slow down. I can't tell what my heart rate is, so I don't know how to gauge how fast I'm going. I just I have to sit with a clear mind and not think of anything. I need to give myself a timeout or take a nap, whenever the hell that must feel like. I've got a slow this thing down so I can figure this all out.

Now there's a different light, it's a cast of light which I can only describe as a kind of sand color or maybe it's more like a muted tan or something. But at least it's nowhere near as black as it has been. Maybe I am coming out of this deal. I just have to control myself. What is the most important thing right now is that I can't allow myself to do any further damage. I have to keep fighting but balance myself. At the same time I have to be able to read the screen crawler to stay on track.

What did I see in the screen crawler that turned me around? Up until just now the screen crawler was black and white. Now everything is in color! I haven't been this hopeful since all this shit happened!

Now the crawler is at normal speed and still in full color. I'm seeing the word, stub, stub what? Check stub, ticket stub, what is the stub's stuff all about? Now there's the word lance. Lance, as in a spear kind of thing? I think a lance is for throwing and a spear is for thrusting but I'm not sure, just my guess. I don't think it's a person's name. I have only known one person named Lance from forty or more years ago. That can't be it. Now, it's the name, Marty that keeps coming to me. Who is Marty? And now there is a Mike, an Adele and a Steve. It's going to take some time to work thru all of this. Well it seems that time is all I have, until I run out of it…that is.

Adele was my mother's name. My mom has been dead for ten years now. If I'm seeing my mom, that must mean I am on my way to her. I guess I'm ok with that but this Adele person on the crawler, is spelled differently.

Something, something about the internet, something about a popular local (and one of my favorite) websites. What is it, what is it? Am I having delusions or am I hallucinating? Shit, if I'm hallucinating, I have either been doped-up or I've become schizophrenic!

Zenith, what about zenith? I think the word 'zenith,' has to do with the highest point of something or some kind of double-talk of a celestial sphere directly overhead foolishness. I've never been much of a fan of that star and planet silliness.

Damn it! I hate being stuck in my memories. I know it's there, come on, where the hell is it? Websites, why websites, why zenith? I don't do charades or care to play all those silly assed, kid games. Zenith website? It can't be that tough to figure out. Has my brain become like a cell phone or IPad where when the batteries start to run low and it automatically slows down to save stored data of whatever the fuck it's supposed to do?

This pisses me off, where the fuck is my memory? I'm a writer for the Christs sake! I have written and published two lengthy novels and damn good novels! I have never had that bullshit, "Writer's block." That's just a bunch of made up excuses people use when they are in fear of not being understood or they come to the realization that their writing is just so much dog shit. Well that sure as hell is not me!

    I'm suddenly feeling calmer, did I go too far with my rage and my mind rebooted to cool itself down? I wonder if these monitors are picking up on my silent outbursts. I've got to be showing some kind of electrical, if not muscular activity of some sort?

    Back to that Zenith stuff, I'm not going to let this beat me. Waite a minute, is it this simple, am I trying to out think myself? Why the fuck do I think I need to suddenly go all cerebral? I don't live like that, leave that bullshit to the enlightened with their scholarly vocabularies. I don't go in for all those fancy words when an everyday common word suits me and my pal's just fine.

    That was a rather boring ride, where the hell am I going with all of this nonsense?

Zenith is part of a title of a Facebook group. Well hell, that was simple, "Duluthians of Zenith!" So why is that dancing in my head?

    Yes I'm a member of that group and I do enjoy the fantastic photography of the area of Duluth and the North Shore of western Lake Superior. Wait a minute, North Shore, North Shore and 'Duluthians of Zenith' what is the tie-in with those two? There it is, it's called 'North Shore Tribe'. It's another local Facebook group for the surrounding communities. But both sites reach far beyond the local area. People who were raised here and left the area and visitors who live all over the world are very active on both sites. There are stunning wildlife and nature photos and videos. Of course there are the ships that travel the great lakes and the sea going ships as well. There are several, live feed cameras that show the ships coming and leaving the port and the frightening and treacherous lake storms. Both of those sites are quite enjoyable.

Now it's coming, I wrote something about something about or for the police department. What did I write for the police department? I love the police department, I love cops, I was once one myself. But what was I doing writing for the police department? Oh I know, I wrote to publicly thank them for saving my life when I was nine years old!

I wrote a public letter of appreciation to the officers currently serving the Duluth, MN Police Department. I also slanted the letter as a supportive statement or maybe even a plea to those who suffer from depression and suicidal ideations during the Christmas season.

Christmas season? Are you shitting me? My first dated memory since I've been this way is October 10th with my cousin Lori and the Ladies of Floodwood. Now it's Christmas? Hell, I wrote and published that letter on December 23rd! Damn it, I wish I had paid more (hell any is more accurate) attention in school.

I am seventy-one years old and I still don't know how many days are in each month. I vaguely remember some kind of silly little rhyme to memorize the days in each month but I never locked that down. Ironic how I hated school as a youth and now I have to live with that regret every day. OK back to how many days in October, November and December. I can only do best guess practice like those pricks at the IRS do when you don't file for the year and they send you a bullshit bill for the price of a new car.

I'm guessing October has 31 days. Subtract ten days from the thirty-one and I was "out" for twenty-one days. November might be thirty days, and I think I posted that message on December twenty-third. If I did the math right that would mean that I have been, "out" for seventy-four days. Far, far beyond the point of no return! I have never in my life wanted to be so wrong! But how do you explain my being so mentally active when I am supposed to be all but brain dead? Are there multiple levels or layers of brain like there are multiple layers of skin? Guess it doesn't really matter at this point, I'm about as fucked as fucked can be.

Well I guess I should do something with my time until I run out of it. Back to my open letter to the police officers. It somehow seems that I just wrote this yesterday.

Chapter 21 WHY I WRITE

"To the currently active officers of the Duluth Police Department. Your predecessor's have left a legacy that few of you know of. In 1957 a nine year old boy was going to take his life on Christmas Eve. The kindness and generosity of your entire department turned that little boy away from his darkness.
I am that little boy. David J. Brown
Work safe and Goodspeed
Merry Christmas"

I wrote those eight short sentences in just a few minutes. I posted the letter on my Facebook page (approx. 4,980 friends) and on "Duluthians of Zenith" and "North Shore Tribe" and many of my favorite first responder groups on Facebook.

I received several thousands (yes, thousands with an 'S') of emails of appreciation from civilians and police officers and their families. I received an email from a Duluth police officer who said he was going to forward my post to the people within the department. He also volunteered to research who those officers may be. I gave him all the pertinent information that I had. I have put out the plea to identify these officers for the last several years so I could hopefully locate their children and grandchildren so I could tell them that these men made a difference in a suicidal child's life.

Next came an email from Mr. Mike Tusken, the Chief of Police for the City of Duluth. He wrote and sent it on Christmas Day! The Chief said he read my post and said it was a powerful message and went on to say officers don't often know the full impact of their efforts. He finished with saying, "I will share this with my staff to reinforce the importance of kind and compassionate policing."

Admittedly, I often times rough up law enforcement administration in my novels due to my personal experiences as a police officer. In this case however this chief is the exception. For him to acknowledge and respond on Christmas Day from his home, tells me that Chief Tusken is truly, "A cops, cop."

Never in my life did I expect to impact so many people with so few words. I can't even try to acknowledge the many kind words and heartfelt messages of gratitude. And then it started, it started and it has yet to stop. People from my past reached out to congratulate me and several said they would like to reunite with me.

Now all these names make perfect sense. First was Lance Sundquist. I worked with him and his dad at a small clothing store chain. His dad worked in the Duluth main store and Lance managed a store in Hibbing, Minnesota. I saw Lance at least once each week. He was a good guy and a good manager. I haven't seen him for more than forty years. It was my honor to send him a copy of each of my books. Lance's message was tagged by Marty Mehling. Marty and I worked together at Wilcol Ambulance Service and we were Pals. We spent a fair amount of time cruising in his GTX 440, his Jeep Wrangler and we sampled most all of the nightlife in Duluth and Superior, WI.

One cold late fall night, Marty pulled me from my car and did CPR on me. I remember coming-to with Marty doing chest compressions on me. I remember the shame I felt and have never found the courage to look him in the eyes and to thank him for saving my life.

I blacked out from drinking on a regular basis. Obviously I drove to Marty's house and parked in his driveway. Him and his girlfriend came home and found me unconscious in my car with the windows rolled up and the motor running.
Was I just drunk and innocently passed out or was this a suicide attempt?

Marty went on to become a firefighter for the Duluth Fire Department. We hung out a few times every week for several years. I was also honored to send Marty copies of my books.

Now there is Adelle Whitefoot. Adelle is a reporter for the "Duluth News Tribune" which is a daily newspaper that has a large countywide following. I sat with Adelle for two hours along with her photographer Steve Kuchera. As Adelle was interviewing me in a spacious conference room, Steve was contorting himself to get the perfect shot. What surprised me was that Steve showed a keen interest in the interview itself. After the interview Steve and I drove to the Duluth Police Headquarters for photos next to the two Police Officer bronze statues, titled, "Cooperation, Safety, Honor." It was then, that after I asked Steve a few questions, I fully understood Steve's interest in my story.

The following day the article was on the front page of the Duluth News Tribune. My buddy, Eric Bomey bitched that he had to spend $1.25 to buy a paper with my picture on the front page when he usually sees me every week. All I could respond with was, "Money well spent, you cheap prick."

The newspaper article caused several emails and a few phone calls from people in my distant past. More than just a few of the hundreds of the newspaper readers shared with me some very personal and sad stories of their own lives that they have never spoken of, to anyone. All I could do is lower my head as I thanked God for giving me purpose.

I received an email from Mona Mar who is a TV producer from KBJR Channel 6 News, that brodcasts to most all of Minnesota. She asked if I would do an "ON-AIR" interview with her reporters. I of course said yes but I don't remember if that actually happened.

Wait a minute, Stubbs name was on that crawler too. That is Jim Stauber!

Jim sent me a message and reintroduced himself. I remember him well. Jim was a dispatcher for Wilcol Ambulance Service, became a paramedic and then went to work as the manager for Gold Cross Ambulance. Jim went on to be a city councilman. I always enjoyed talking with Jim. Jim was best buddies with Gary Wilson, the Duluth Police Detective Sargent who was killed (murdered) in the line of duty. I also greatly liked Gary. I happened to be in town for a one week visit when Gary went down. I attended Gary's funeral and ran into Jim at the funeral service. Jim took it hard. I could easily see his brokenness. Jim and I have exchanged phone numbers and plan to meet for lunch soon.

Yes, now I remember that thing with Mona Mar. Mona set up a joint television interview on January 6th 2020 with me and Duluth Police Chief Mike Tusken. Reporter John Cardinale of CBS 6 Duluth did the interview.

I always make it a point to arrive fifteen minutes early for all appointments including casual coffee with friends. I think it to be a great injustice to be late for meeting someone who shows a genuine interest in me and freely gives me their time.

As I entered the Police Administration building I saw John Cardinale sitting in the lobby with his oversized camera bag and tri-pod. I introduced myself and we lightly chatted. I asked John about his home town, his education and training as is my standard question when I meet someone new.

John is from California and fresh out of the prestigious, "Edward R. Murrow School of Broadcast Journalism." I got an instant memory flash of my past. I remember watching Edward R. Murrow on TV as a kid. I remember him smoking cigarettes, I thought he had a great official sounding voice. I did a paper on him when I was in the fifth grade. Of course I had to use the, "Kardex" system in the library and then locate his books using the, "Dewey Decimal" system.

Mr. Murrow actually reported live during the, 'Battle of Britain' from rooftops while bombs were dropping all around him and London. He set the standard for broadcasting the news on location. If memory serves, I think he was nominated for seven and even won five Emmy awards for news broadcast excellence. Once the United States entered into World War 2 he visited the airfields and hitched rides in American bombers so he could actually report as they were flying and dropping bombs. During the 'Blitz' Mr. Murrow opened each broadcast with, "This is London." He ended each broadcast with, "Goodnight and good luck." That phrase was used by Londoner's when parting company as they could not be sure they would ever see each other again.

Mr. Morrow was one of the first journalist to enter the Nazi, Buchenwald Concentration Camp. As he described to his shocked radio audience the piles of bodies that he witnessed, he was crying. He called the prisoner camp, "A factory of death."

As I watched reports of the Gulf War in 1990 all of America watched Scud Missiles screaming down the streets of Bagdad with CNN reporters filming and hanging out of the 9th floor windows of the 'Al Rasheed Hotel', was all but laughable as they tried to copy-cat and one-up Mr. Morrow with his rooftop reports of fifty years past.

Mr. Morrow also busted Joseph McCarthy that was a republican senator from Wisconsin. McCarthy came up with this whole bullshit story about, The United States Army was being operated by communists in the top command positions. McCarthy was the chairman of the, "House Un-American Activities Committee." He developed and promoted, "The Second Scare" that ran for ten years. McCarthy was loose with his baseless accusations and evidence but his, "Black List" of suspicion of the people he labeled as communists harmed many people. McCarthy went heavily after the Hollywood entertainers and reporters who didn't agree with him. He destroyed many, many carriers.

I remember when I was a kid that we had air-raid sirens mounted on the roofs of every school and governmental building throughout the city (not the storm warning sirens of today) and when in school we had to sit under our wooden stationary desks, (with ink wells) tuck our heads down between our legs with our hands behind our necks. That went on for several years. That's some laughable shit to think we were safe under our desks when the class room outer walls had several windows in every classroom.

Where the hell did this all come from? I can't believe that I can remember all this stuff! How much crazier can this get? Damn, I need a cigarette!

OK, I was about to meet the Chief of Police. I guess John Cardinale triggered me with his telling about his attending the Edward R. Murrow reporting school.

Back to the Chief. I found him to be very personable and engaging. He is a nice man and he was very welcoming. We were just like any two other fellows who would chat over a cup of coffee. We talked for about an hour and forty-five minutes. At no point did he act rushed or check his watch or make any kind of gesture as to that we were taking too much of his time. I think he's just a real classy fella. We talked about his officers and a need for his officers to be recognized from their many efforts, which rarely happens. At the end of the taping he asked the reporter if he could have a copy of the raw tape to use for his in-service training with his officers. I thought that was classy as well. The chief gifted me a shoulder patch, several pins of both the shoulder patch lapel pins as well as a badge pins which I thought were really cool. The chief said with a grin, "Please do not sew this to the shoulder of your shirt."

The response from the TV interview was again overwhelming. If this goes no further, the chief assured me that he would do his utmost to locate those officers who took care of me when I was a child. He has sent out letters to all the retirees and requesting them to bring forward any information they may have. And again, if this goes no further I believe it's served its purpose.

From my initial post on Facebook to a newspaper reporter picking it up and interviewing me, publishing the following day on a weekend with a large front page layout and then on to a television news show that humanizes police officers. I believe I've served my purpose because without purpose there is nothing else.

Chapter 22 COMING HOME

Holy shit, what is this? There is light, I can see actual light. Not like that muted tan or gray light like I've been seeing, this is actually real light! It's real thin like I'm looking thru window blinds but they are more like door blinds, I think they are called vanes and they are vertical. I think I'm using both eyes but I can't quite tell but it's a real thin light of different widths. I must have both eyes open but there are these tiny thin little black bars that are hard to see through. The little black bars seem to be flickering or bouncing around. What the hell am I looking at, this is some wild shit! Now the little slits are getting wider and taller. I think I'm blinking, I think my eyes are blinking. Damn, those aren't little bars, they are my eyelashes! I'm sure of it, that's what they are and now they are fluttering. I can't seem to control them, they just keep fluttering. Now the light is getting bigger and it's too bright, it feels like my eyes are burning like I have been staring into a welders arch light. It's too bright but I can't close my eyes and I can't make my eyes focus either. I know I'm seeing something, I can see dust particles floating in the air, I can see them landing on my eyes! They look massive, about the size of pancakes! They are landing right on my eyes but I can't feel them but I can see them landing right on my eyes! I can see them floating down from far above me. They just keep coming down and coming down. It's almost like laying on the ground and watching snowflakes come right in into my eyes. I can't blink or close my eyes. This is some weird shit.

I can still hear Laine Hardy's music, it's getting louder it seems that the lights are getting brighter. Hell I must be waking up! Jesus Christ, I'm waking up!

Now I can't see the floating dust particles anymore butI am looking at something. I think I'm looking straight up. I'm looking at an off white, maybe a kind of a beige color with different size small dots. Those are not dots, those are holes. Those are ceiling tiles, that's what I'm looking at, I'm looking at ceiling tiles and those holes are the perforations that are for sound proofing and now I can see the metal support strips for the ceiling tiles. Jesus Christ, I'm coming around, I'm coming out of this shit! I can't tell if I can move my eyes or not and I don't know how far open they are. I'm trying to move my eyes but I don't think anything's happening. I'm just going to try to stay quiet with my mind and just listen and look and see just what the hell's going on here. Now I just heard Laine Hardy's song change to another of his songs. Why am I hearing this song? It has to be Heather, she must have put this music on for me. I have heard that people are told to speak and read to people in a coma or when they are unconscious in the hopes that they may hear what you're saying and it might help bring them back. Well if that's the case, it sure as hell is working! Now I can just barley hear a voice, not a singing voice but a speaking voice.

    I would give anything to hear a live speaking voice. Please let me hear Heather's voice. I love her so much, I would give everything I own just to hear her voice and to see her beautiful face. I hope she is ok, I hope she is here with me now.   That's a strange sound, I'm guessing I hear feet but they're not really walking they're kind of like sliding, like someone's walking with those hospital paper slippers on a hard floor surface. What am I hearing? Jesus Christ, there's a face I can see a face it's far away and it's a little blurry but I know it's a face. Where did that face come from? I think it might be a woman, I can't tell they're wearing a surgical mask and a hair net. Now their faces look bigger but I can't tell who it is. It's coming closer, coming closer, Jesus Christ it is her, its Heather! I can tell by her long hair and I can just barely smell her perfume. My God I can smell, I can see and I can hear! Jesus Christ I'm through, I broke through to the other side! Oh my God, Jesus Christ if I haven't had a heart attack I'm about to! I'm just sure that it is her. I see her hand reaching out to me, she must be touching me but I can't feel her touching me. She must be touching my arms or hands. If I have any arms or hands. I can't feel anything. Maybe it's going to be a little bit longer but this shits making me crazy. Man if I could just jump up and hold her that would be the happiest moment of my entire life! I have got to think, I've got to find a way to talk how do I talk? I've got a let her know that I'm OK. I haven't talked to her forever. I have to stay calm. Now there are faces coming real close to me. They seem so big but she's tiny, her face can't be this big but I know it's her face. I guess my eyes have to adjust just as my brain must from this sleep thing. I just felt something. I felt something, it's Heather she just kissed me! I know she kissed me and now there is something wet. I feel something on my face. I can see she has tears, her tears just hit my face. She pulled her mask backup and stepped away. I sure hope she isn't saying good bye. Good bye like I'm dying right now. I hope that isn't it. I've got to find a way to talk to her.

    Now there's a lot of noise, there's people everywhere. Jesus Christ there is such a big crowd it is like people going through turnstiles like at a NASCAR race. Holy balls what the hell is all this? Everyone's wearing masks and hair nets and they're laughing they are all laughing! My eyes are starting to move. I can see things now and my eyes are starting to adjust. I can make out faces a little better, well just eyes because their faces are covered with masks but I'm seeing a lot of different eyes. I don't think I know any of them, they must be nurses or doctors or somebody but I do know that it was Heather that kissed me. I could not miss her eyes, she still has her beautiful tender little fawn like eyes. I have been in love with her for sixty years.

    I'm feeling something, holy shit I think I just swallowed. There was a big blur that blocked my view below my eye line. I don't know what happened but I think I just swallowed again. Was

I intubated? Did they just pull the tube? I can't feel myself breathing or my chest rising but I must be breathing.

OK I have to try to talk, I've got to find a way to talk. Did I just say something? I think I just said something and I heard Heather say, "Thank you baby, I love you too! I'm so glad you came back to me, you're going to be OK, I promise. We've all been praying for you, I'm so glad to have you back. It will take some time sweetheart, but I will stay with you. I'm not going to leave your side and you're going to be just fine."

Now these people talking to me must be doctors? What is he saying? He's talking too fast! Slow down damn it, I can't understand you!

He just patted my arm and he took off his mask. It's not a doctor it's Sean Carrigan, my best friend! What is he doing here, he lives in Colorado. Oh my God, here I am with my sweetheart and my best buddy! Now there's a bunch of other people coming up close to me, now they are taking off their masks. It's Kirk, it's Kirk my brother-in-law. He is more like a brother to me. It is so good to see his face and next to him, that's Mary it's clearly his wife Mary! Holy shit there are a whole bunch of other people that are kind of standing in line. Jesus Christ, now it's Paul Roberts from Chicago, I can see his $300.00 neck tie like the one's he gave me.

Why are all of these people here? I'm almost wondering if maybe there looking at me in a coffin. Maybe this is my funeral and Heather has an open coffin! Holy Christ which one is it? Am I coming to life or am I losing my life or worse yet, am I losing my mind? I have to be coming to life. People do not go to funerals wearing surgical masks and hair nets! What the fucks wrong with me? I have to snap out of this shit. Stop thinking and just observe. Watch and listen. Don't try to figure this shit out, just go along with it.

I'm alive and things are starting to come back. OK now, who's this guy? He has a stethoscope, he must be the doctor. Just a minute, yes he just said his name was doctor something, I couldn't understand him. He said I'm going to be just fine, everything is going to be just fine and if things keep progressing I'll be home by the end of the month! Holy Christ I'm going home! Jesus Christ this is a fucking miracle!

Laine Hardy, I can faintly hear Laine Hardy's music. I love his voice but even more than that, I love his soul. That kid absolutely amazes me. I remember his first audition on 'American Idol'. Just a shy and awkward seventeen year old kid from the Louisiana bayou that has a hair style of a nine year old.

He sang "Hurricane" by 'The Band of Heathens.' He has this innocent, gritty but soulful voice that moms and daughters would probably fight each other to date him. After some research I was even further amazed to find out that he started to play a 'Walmart' kids guitar when he was six years old. He did most of his guitar playing and singing alone in the swamps. He idolized Elvis Presley and even wore an Elvis type jumpsuit when he was eight years old. What I like most about Laine is his sprit. He failed on his first attempt on American Idol mainly because of his shyness and self-doubt. He came back the next year and won the title of, "American Idol 2019," at the age of eighteen. I think he won because he wanted to more than anyone else. He just did not sing but he performed! He found the courage to completely change everything about himself and he challenged his comfort levels to win but he hung onto his Louisiana roots. He changed his hair style, his clothes style and his singing style. No one pushed him harder than he did himself. He proved that dreams are worth dreaming, if you're willing to do the work.

Hell, it took me sixty-one years before I found the courage to even dare to dream.
That and a giant shove from God. Ever see videos of railroad trains blasting thru a wall of snow in some mountain pass? Well, that's what God's giant shove felt like.

I guess it's now safe to admit that I had a second spiritual awakening as I started to write my first book, "Daddy Had to Say Goodbye" in 2009.

I couldn't get started, my lack of education and self-doubt had me frozen in place. It was never my desire to write a book of any kind, especially a book about me! God was trying to bully me into it and it pissed me off that he wouldn't let me go. After three days of finger spinning my ink pen while staring at a blank legal pad with coffee gut so bad that I wanted to throw up, I took myself for a ride in the mountains. I went to Estes Park and across Hwy #7 to Camp St. Milo which is a Catholic retreat and conference center. I didn't try to enter the property, I just parked on the roadside, got out of my truck and went for a walk. Nothing came to me during the drive or the walk.

I drove to St. Mary's Lake and saw that the trout were rising. I always carry my fly rod and spinning rod along with my fishing vest in my truck.

For the first time in my entire life, I tried not to catch a fish. I cut the hook off of the imitation fly just to enjoy seeing the fish rise to the fly. After a bit of time, I put my fly rod down and sat on a rock with my feet in the water. For the dozenth time or more I asked, "God, why me, why not someone else who has the talent and skills necessary to do this? I am without skills or desire. Why have you chosen me? Then it happened. I clearly heard God say;

"David, I gave your Grandfather an extreme challenge when he entered into Father Flanagan's "Boys Town" in 1917. Your Grandfather was taught well and he learned well but in his young adult life he squandered his teachings and he lost his life at the age of 40, through the very same violence that he had himself brought to others.

Your father was a violent, stubborn and bitter man. I gave him a chance to redeem himself and he did. He found success thru his sobriety for himself, your family and many other alcoholics that he sponsored. You should be proud of your father and his accomplishments. You ask me why you, I ask you, why not you?

David my son, it is no secret that I have gifted you an old soul. I have given you both your Grandfather's and your Father's souls. You have a challenge of three generations to bring forward the message. David your challenge is to bring hope to the masses and future generations thru your writings. Church attendance and bible reading has gone much to the wayside. Speak of your truths and others will seek their truths. Teach them well my son.

Now to answer your question as to why you. I have chosen you because you have suffered well. You have learned and all but mastered the power of understanding and forgiveness. Your writings and future books will serve as my voice.
You will first reach the most damaged of souls, you will teach of emotional neutrality and freedom through forgiveness, hope and prayer. You will show the human condition and fears as normal emotions. Your task is to deliver validation to all. David you must never allow any man to walk alone."

Chapter 23   ROLLING THE DICE

Laine Hardy, only one person knows of my respect and admiration for him and that is Heather. Is Heather playing his music to help me come out of it? She is that thoughtful and loving. I hope she finds the strength to walk away and start a new life, if my brain is nothing more than a handful of wild onions. My heart hurts for her.

Am I hallucinating again or am I coming out of it, am I actually hearing Laine Hardy or is it that I just want to hear his music. Have I floated down the swollen flooded stream far enough to escape the rushing waters? Do I just need to try to stand up and walk to shore? Can it be that simple? Is my waking up just a matter of willpower? Have I been hiding out to avoid one of lives cruel or uncomfortable truths? What is my most uncomfortable truth? That simple truth is my accepting my deepest of all fears. The truth is that I fear that people won't trust me or believe me. Am I like the rest of the cowards who don't want to hear the truth because I and they don't want their well-guarded allusions destroyed? Is it because I and they know that if we were to face our own truths, that we have lived a life of lies? We most all deny our heartaches and failures for the appearance of normalcy.

Writers often hear that to write a great story you must first have, an even greater back story. Take JK Rowling for instance of Harry Potter fame. Today of course she is a highly successful British author, film producer, television producer and screenwriter. She has sold well over 500 million copies of her books and her wealth stands far beyond one billion dollars. She has written some of her books in long hand.

She has donated half of her wealth to a number of charities. Her back story (if it can be believed that it wasn't produced by some literary agent) goes something like this. Joanne Rowling, aka JK Rowling was a book worm at a very young age. At the age of six she wrote her first book. The story goes on with her graduating college and working as an interpreter and teaching English in Portugal. She was married, had a child and divorced. Some say she and her daughter lived in an abandoned car and was living on welfare when she wrote her first novel. Others say she lived in a tiny apartment with her sister. It is further rumored that she sold that first novel to a publisher for a paltry $4,000.

    Next is Ernest Hemingway. In his case it's not his back story but just in the way that he lived. He was a reckless and drunken bully. He was an insanely avid hunter and thrill killed many, many, exotic animals in his many world travels. After several car and motorcycle wrecks (all of which he caused) he had several concussions which resulted in multiple electric shock therapies which rendered him unable to put together a simple sentence. It is reported that his final words were to his wife on July 2nd 1961. He said to her, "Goodnight my kitten." He then went to his study and killed himself with a shotgun blast to his head. I never liked anything about that arrogant son of a bitch, especially after I read about his "Baby Shoes" story. The story goes that Hemingway was lunching with a group of this writer friends in his favorite restaurant located in the East village of Manhattan which is known to be the preferred restaurant of the who's who of the rich and famous. Supposedly the gentleman at the table had a bet as to who could write the best short story. Hemingway wrote only six words, "For sale, baby shoes, never worn." His lunch buddies applauded his genius and paid for his lunch. As myself, being a grieving parent who lost his child at birth, I so much wish I could have been in that restaurant with them motherfuckers! They all thought that it was so cute. I would have loved to have plunged his steak knife into his fucking neck and told his uppity asshole buddies that, "Warm fresh neck blood was what was for dessert!"

Then of course we have that lovely former First Lady of the White House (that is of course if she actually is in fact a lady) there is much debate about her sex as well as her name being Michelle or Michael. It was Clint Eastwood who said, "One day we will realize that the Barack Obama presidency was the biggest fraud ever perpetrated on the American people." I've got no arguments there. Obama was the most divisive racist of all time and singly handed unraveled every bit of the work that Dr. Martin Luther King Jr. did. We have never experienced such disrespect for police along with the staggering assault and murder rates in this nation's history!

It has been recently discovered that Michelle Obama, who claimed to graduate from both Harvard and Princeton with a PhD from both schools and was a professor teaching at each of those schools is not true. The Obamas were said to have raised in excess of seven million dollars for each school. There are many in the know who believe that they got a fifty percent kickback from those large donations. It's common practice for colleges to give out honorarium degrees to their top financial supporters. In Michelle Obama's case she was given those PhD diplomas, she never earned either one of them. Currently, her law degree is under scrutiny for its validity. There is just no end to the lies and corruption of the wealthy and powerful.

So as of late, Michelle Obama has received a Grammy award for narrating one of her books as an audiobook. A Grammy is a music award for the fucks sake! Michelle Obama also claims to have written seven books. Well in a pig's ass she has! There is one very wealthy ghost writer who just grins with a full mouth of teeth as he or she slithers away with their pockets bulging. It took me eight years to write my two books and I worked my ass off! Don't fucking tell me that she wrote seven books in two years!

Now, it is my turn. I have the 'greatest of all times' backstory to promote my third novel.

I was contacted by a top twenty University staff member that booked guest speakers and managed, "The students of disability's" program. She seemed quite impressed with herself and her title, whatever the fuck that was. She made the grave mistake of telling me that the top benefactor of their school was approached by his nephew who had heard me speak at some event in the past. She asked if she could book me for an entire student body engagement. I was asked to speak twice a-day for three days. Knowing that she was told by their top money man to book me, made my speaking rates skyrocket from three thousand dollars a day to eight thousand dollars a day in a matter of seconds. Normally a nationally known author with only one book authored is offered between $5,000 and $10,000 dollars for an eighty minute presentation. I of course know who I am. I am unknown as both a speaker and novelist in the big leagues. I've got 2 and 3/4 books and I'm shooting for the moon. Since I knew I had her by the pony-tails, I thought I would have some fun with her. I told her I expected the full payment of $24,000, two weeks prior to the event.

    She balked of course, as she said they only pay 30 days after the event from the Box office receipts. I about lost my shit with her as I asked her if the airlines collect from their passengers their fees upon arrival at the destination? "You pay me in advance or there's no deal. I also now require a $700 daily stipend for incidentals to be paid upon my arrival." She begrudgingly agreed as she told me that I could sign my books at the University bookstore and nowhere else while I was there and the split was 60/40 in their favor. The bookstore would of course take care of the sales and they would pay me 90 days after my visit. I declined as I thought, 'fuck you.' I have to pay more than 70% of the retail cost to buy my own God Damn books and I have to pay to have them shipped and then I have to pay to have the unsold books return shipped to my house. Now I'm stuck with thousands of books that I have all of my money tied-up with! Jesus Christ those money grubbing pricks at Amazon pay better than that! I went on to tell her that if there was a lecture fee charged to the students that

I am staying home. "You don't get to make money off of me by screwing your own students!"

I arrived two days early to acclimate to the altitude. I live at 1,000' above sea level, this college campus is at 4,600' my voice would not hold out if I didn't allow myself time to acclimate prior to my speaking. I received my check for the full amount of $24,000, ten days before the scheduled date. Along with that check was a letter from the college asking me for, "The customary donation" of a speaker of $10,000 to go back to the University. As I read that letter I gave it my very best country wide smile of, "Go fuck yourself!" The second day I was there, I met with the 'booking' lady who I had been speaking with involving the event. I was there to collect my stipend of $2,100.

She said she would have it for me the next day, after I complete the morning and evening speaking engagements. I told her, "No dice, you will give me that check before I take the stage in the morning or I don't go on." She had a beyond bitch look on her face. She had very tight small ringlets of poorly dyed black hair. It looked like she was twisting her hair to lift the wrinkles off of her forehead.

The next morning she was wearing a pair of stomping shoes like the "River Dancers" would wear. I guess she had the need to announce her presence for at least a full city block prior to her arrival. I had to bite the inside of my cheeks to suppress my giggles as she all but 'goose stepped' to the auditorium. I held short behind the curtains of the stage and put my hand out and said, "Check Please?" She dug into her purse with a huff ass he said, "I will be damn happy when you are off of my campus!" I smiled as I bowed to her with, "Thanks Babe!"

There might have been a bit more than 2,000 students seated with several still coming in. It was ten minutes before my scheduled appearance. Little miss, 'Stomper' escorted me over to a seated group of obvious faculty members. I guess those robed and plasterboard head wearing with tassels fucker's don't have to show the common courtesy of rising to their feet when being introduced and shaking hands with a visiting guest. Maybe this was their protest of having a 'nobody speaker,' shoved up their asses by their #1 financial supporter. I could only smile as I knew that I had made the right decision on my plane ride. That decision was even further reinforced when the 'stomper' showed her disdain by having me demanding my stipend check. What really locked down the deal was those phony professor pricks that thought they were better than me. I might have upset those sissy ass hats.

As I understand it, it is customary when being introduced to a robed professor that you state the name of the college you graduated from, the degree you hold and your course of study, followed with your GPA. I thought a few of them were gonna puke when I said, "Central High school, lifted each year and graduated with a .04 GPA!"

The Dean of students (who was not seated with the robed crowd) was wearing a simple dress and gave me a very nice introduction with a brief account of my lifetime's achievements. When I took the podium and looked out at the almost now, 3,000 fresh looking faces (except for the stoners and still drunk from the night before group) I did the necessary thanks and appreciation for the invitation that I've done for dozens and dozens of times before.

I then said, "Students, please close your laptop's, put your writing instruments down and close your notebooks. We are just going to talk rather than you trying to figure out a way to find an angle to write a paper on or to ask me a question. I'm simply asking you to just listen to my very short presentation. I'm about to ask you a rhetorical question, I needn't an answer of course. Here is the most important question of all time. Are you getting your money's worth? I would like to emphasize, "Your moneys" worth, from these people sitting behind me?" I could see a lot of puzzled faces. "It is your money, it's either from your family or from your student loans but you're paying for this ride contrary to radical and liberal beliefs that you will not have to repay your college loans. That is false information. You will in fact, have to pay it all back." I took the microphone from the podium and stepped to the very front edge of the stage. I looked down at a very plain looking young lady, probably in her very early twenties. I asked her to step forward to the edge of the stage and I asked her name. She said her name was, "Mary Margaret."

I reached into my coat pocket and took out a check for her to look at, as I asked her what it was. She said, "It looks like a check." I said, "Yes, It is a check, what is the name of the payer on the upper left hand corner of this check?" She answered, "It's from this University sir." I asked Mary Margaret, "What is the name on the payee line on this check?" "It is your name sir, David J. Brown." I than asked, "What is the amount of this check?" She answered, "It is made out for the amount of $24,000." I smiled at Mary Margaret as I said, "Thank you, you may return to your seat."

"Ladies and gentlemen, I am a total nobody author from nowhere important. I was lifted every year in high school without ever earning a passing grade. I never attended college or took any writing classes, yet I have published two very well received novels and I'm about to complete my third and final novel, which I believe will surpass both of my other novels in sales and popularity, in a very short period of time. I can tell you this, I am successful because of God's loving grace and his unwavering guidance. My only true skills have to do with my finding the courage to believe. I found the strength to dare to dream to become a successful novelist. I dared to dream and I dared to dream big! Beyond that I had the will to succeed. I trusted that God would not allow me to fail.

You people are taught how to study and how to pass tests and you think that that is success. Are you taught how to succeed in life or just to pass tests? I dare say that many of you have a very large, hairy-assed student loan or loans to repay. Much like the rest of your fellow college students throughout the country, many of you have pissed away your student loan money.

The booze parties, the bar crawls and of course all of the seemly mandatory, exotic Christmas and Spring Break trips aren't cheap. I believe that it is safe to say that most, if not all of you carry a nagging question within your darling little skulls. That question is, "How in the fuck am I going to pay all this shit back? How am I going to find a job where I can earn enough money that I can live on and pay my student loans?"

You kids want to get you your own apartment, drive a decent car, by your own house, and someday start a family with this boat anchor the size of the cruise ships that you were party on hanging from around your neck? Take charge of your lives and take charge of your education. You need to call the ball. You must demand that these people sitting on the stage today, teach and prepare you for success outside of this campus.

Now, 'Miss Mary Margaret', please return to the front of the stage, as a matter of fact, please come to the end of the stage, up the stairs and join me please." I handed her the same check that she held earlier as I asked, "Mary Margaret, is this the very same check I had you look at a bit earlier." She said, "Yes sir it is." I said, "Good, I just want everyone to know that this is not a stunt. Mary Margaret, please take the check in both hands and hold it as high as you can reach, for all to see. Make sure everyone gets a little look at it. Ok thank you for doing that, now Mary Margaret, please tear that check in half." She of course blanched and looked at me like I had lost my fucking mind. I again said, "Mary Margaret, please tear that check in half." She reluctantly did so but very slowly waiting for me to stop her. I did not stop her. When she finished tearing the check I told her to put the two pieces together and to tear them again. When she finished that, I said, "Again Mary Margaret, please stack those pieces altogether and tear then again." She struggled to tear the, eight pieces of the check. I said "Now Mary Margaret please throw these into the air like you would throw a bouquet of flowers at your wedding." She did throw the pieces of the check in the air and had a slight chuckle. She threw her arms around my neck for a brief hug. I escorted her off the stage.

I then said, "Ladies and gentlemen I am under direct and I do mean, "Direct Orders" from God. He told me to, "Teach them well." I turned my back to the audience and took a few steps forward to the clowns sitting in their silly little bathrobes and said, "Don't teach them (as I gestured to the audience) what you know. Teach them what they need to learn! I turned back to the students and said, "Manage your disappointments as well as you do you successes. Embrace your blessings and speak of them often. God-bless you all."

The lengthy clapping and thunderous shouts escorted me as I turned and walked off the stage and out of the building to my rental car without saying another word to anyone. I drove back to my hotel, put on my swim trunks and went out to the pool to sit and enjoy the warm sun and to finish the final chapters of my new book. Several times I broke out into laughter. Some of the people around me give me the strangest of looks. After ordering my 4th cup of coffee in the first half-hour, the pool area waiter asked if I would prefer a carafe of coffee. I said that would be swell. I also ordered ice cream cones for everyone at the poolside area, children and parents alike. I broke out in laughter several times as he was serving the two dozen or more ice cream cones. When he came over to me to have me sign the bill he stood with a big smile as he watched me add a $50 tip. He said, "Sir you must be writing some really funny stuff." I nodded and said, "I'm a novelist and I do believe that this is the funniest stuff that I have ever written!"

After he walked away I looked down at the seven words that I wrote, one word on two lines with two lines of spacing and I laughed again as I read those seven words.

I
Sure
As
Shit
Hope
This
Works

I thought, well if not, I just pissed away $24,000! I probably will never be invited to any college campus ever again. But I sure am enjoying this all-expenses-paid vacation and the $2,100. Yeah, I sure as shit hope this works!

The next two days I made it a point to not check my emails or messages. I just sat at the pool and wrote. I Left for the airport four hours early, turned in my rental car and just thought I would people watch for a bit. A half hour before they started boarding, I finally looked at my phone which I have been ignoring for three days. I opened my messages and it was two pages of nothing but 911 calls from the same person at the same number. I smiled to myself, took a deep breath and quietly repeated to myself, "I sure as shit hope this works," for the hundredth time in the last three days! The name and numbers were from my publisher's customer service rep named Jason. Jason has been my agent for over three years. We've never met but we talk often, at least once a week. I called his cell phone. Jason almost sounded like he was out of his mind as he said, "We've been hacked dude! We've been hacked hard, real hard! Orders for your books are coming in like a fuckin Tsunami, we are at almost 85,000 book orders, what the fucks happened?" I said, old friend, "Those orders are legit, grease-up the printing presses. You want to know what has happened Jason? ………..I happened!"

I hung up the phone. I sat and smiled all during the flight home. The lady next to me asked me if I worked. I said with a grin as I answered, "I guess I work for a print shop" and went back to my smiling.

Chapter 24   HOMECOMING

Wow this feels weird. What is this, it's not physical or even mental and not even emotional? I feel calm but excited. What the fuck is wrong with me? Calm and excited don't even belong in the same five word sentence! What the hell is this? I feel warm, not an overall warm but an isolated kind of warm. Kind of like the warmth in your belly when you do something good for someone in dire need who have absolutely no way to pay you back. They often times don't even know your name, it's that kind of warm but it's not coming from my belly either! Holy shit, have I just truly connected with my soul and where in the hell does my soul live? Is a human soul actually located in our bodies, is there actually such a thing as a soul? I have been to some very gruesome murder scenes where I just knew that it could only be the work of some soulless psychopathic son of a bitch who could have done it. Is the soul simply a barometer of good and evil?

As I understand it, years back and near the turn of the century, a doctor in Massachusetts named Dr. Duncan MacDougall performed a series of experiments trying to actually weigh the human soul. He was intrigued with the theory that the human soul actually has measurable mass. Through his questionable research he came to the conclusion that upon immediate death, the body loses approximately 21grams of weight (3/4 of an ounce) at the very instant of death. His claim was the weight loss at the time of death came from the soul leaving the body. Dr. MacDougall was thrust to the top of the fame pole and was the talk of the medical world.

As happens most often times, some descending asshole physician named Dr. Augustus P. Clark not only disputed Dr. MacDougall's theory but made cruel sport of him with belittling his findings and his charictor. The jealous prick did however, have an interesting take on the weight loss at time of death phenomenon. Dr. Clark surmised that at the time of death the lungs stop cooling the blood, causing the body's temperature to rise slightly, which makes the skin sweat, accounting for Dr. MacDougall's, missing 21 grams of body weight. Those two went back and forth with claims and counter claims as to who was in the right for a number of years. Arguing theory is like shooting pool with a rope.

Regardless of those theories the soul leaving the body is some freaky shit. Is everyone born with a soul? Is a soul given or earned? Do people lose their souls? I knew one soulless bastard that I don't believe ever had a soul from birth.

This clown was known as, 'Roofer John' from Estes Park, Colorado. Roofer John owned two residential roofing companies that only worked in the mountain towns. One of his companies was an 'all girl' operation. There were two crews of five each. Pink hard hats, pink tool belts Pink hammer handles and two pink pickup trucks. That, and each crew also had a pink dump truck. The 'Pink Ladies' were always busy and made Roofer John a lot of money.

Roofer John was a strange fellow who rarely bathed. His breath would knock a train off the tracks. He was 5' 4" tall and weighed under 145 lbs. He was a shouter and had a lot more character defects than most. He thought he was the King of AA. He didn't care who was chairing the meeting or what the topic was. John held court and would loudly and publicly belittle anyone who would take exception to his bullshit. He bullied and controlled everyone. Everyone but me that is! I never acknowledge that phony piece of shit.

It is common that after most all AA meetings that small groups would visit outside, after the meeting for fellowship and brief chats. John acted as though he was on patrol and stopped at every small group to interject and correct anyone speaking. If anyone voiced an objection, John would brush back his untucked shirt to show his roofing hatchet tucked into his belt.

He tried that shit with me shortly after we met. I brushed back my jacket to expose my Kimber 1911 45 semi-automatic full size pistol. I smiled as I asked, "Wanna play fucker? Go ahead dick breath, pull your tomahawk and I will make you famous! Don't ever try to play that shit with me again. I will smoke you in a New York second, get and stay the fuck away from me!"

Roofer John never exposed his hatchet around me again. Roofer John was just another coward who so desperately wanted to be somebody. Well, that ass face did become somebody. He became a murderous madman!

Winter comes early up in the high country. After the first big snow, Roofer John would go to Florida for the winter and stay with his sister. Well, ole Roofer John became famous overnight. John for whatever reason, lost his shit and murdered his sister and pregnant teenage niece. It is rumored that he raped his niece on his last visit and she was about to deliver the baby he fathered. It is suspected that he again attempted to rape his niece but her mother (his sister) caught him and was about to call the police so he killed them both. Roofer John was the chief suspect in the double murders and there was an arrest warrant and B.O.L.O. issued for him. A state trooper spotted him and attempted a felony traffic stop. John jumped out of his car and shot and killed the trooper and drove off. A short time later, two county deputies spotted him and pursued him in a high speed chase. John ran out of gas and engaged the deputies in a gun battle. John wounded one deputy and killed the other. John was wounded with a non-life threating injury. The last I heard, was that he was found guilty of all charges and sits on Florida's death row.

I wish I could have goaded him into a fight and killed him the first time he brushed back his shirt. It would have saved several innocent lives.

I guess what it comes down to is: either you've got a soul or you don't.

Chapter 25 A TRAGIC LOSS

Holy Christ, I've got to break away from all these horror stories but how do I do that? It's the life I have lived, it's just what's happened. We can't change our history. There's a lot of good in this world, I've had a lot of experience with good people. I'm thinking about Sean Conohan as one of those good people. Sean is the producer and host of, "UP Talk" podcast radio, which is for first responders who are or have suffered from PTSD. His blog talk radio station is based out of Nova Scotia, Canada and broadcasts worldwide under the banner of, "Mental Health News Radio Global Network."

I listened to two of his broadcasts and thought, "Finally, someone who knows and admits his truths." I thought that I would like to be a guest on his show. I sent Sean an email and introduced myself with an attachment of my website. We corresponded back-and-forth for a few weeks and he scheduled me for an upcoming show. Sean asked me if I would like to dedicate my interview to anyone in particular. It didn't take me much time at all to say, "Yes an old friend of mine, Firestone, Colorado Deputy Marshall Richard (Rick) Hart who lost his life in the line of duty." I sent Sean the story on Rick along with a photo of Rick in uniform.

That evening I sat up all night reminiscing about Rick and the days and years that followed his murder.

Rick Hart worked part time for the "Firestone, Colorado Marshals Office." There was a Town Marshal and three part-time deputies. Rick worked a few nights and weekend shifts. Rick also had a full time job driving an oil field tanker truck and made damn good money. Rick was an easy fellow to hang around with. I was with the adjoining police department so our jurisdictions bordered each other. We would meet for dinner or coffee every night we were on shift.

Most oftentimes Rick just had coffee and would not allow me to buy him dinner. Every now and then he would allow me to bully him into ordering pie with his coffee. Rick was damn tight with his money and he had good reason to be. Rick was a Vietnam Vet and was hit heavy with Agent Orange. His son was born without ears or hearing and the US military denied benefits for his child saying, it was not due to Rick's exposure to Agent Orange. So Rick was saving every dime he made to pay for his son's surgery. Rick's only interest in life was taking care of his family and giving his son the gift of hearing. What's not to love about a man like Rick?

We met late one Wednesday afternoon and had coffee. We decided that it would be nice if our wives could meet each other and we could do a few things together as couples, every now and then. We decide that we would have our wives join us the upcoming Saturday night at this restaurant at 8:00 p.m. before the area bars got revved up for the, 'Saturday Night Fights'. About 5 o'clock that Saturday afternoon I received a call from dispatch to phone home. I called my home and my sister-in-law answered and said my wife wouldn't be able to come to the dinner tonight because she had an extremely severe migraine headache. I radioed Rick on 'private channel' and told him of the deal and we would have to cancel but I suggested we still meet briefly for a cup of coffee. For the last several weeks I had been trying to twist his arm (not much hope as he was two heads taller and carried fifty pounds of nothing but solid muscle on me) to attend an upcoming three day seminar in Denver sponsored by Paladin Press (a law enforcement tactical book and magazine publishing company). The seminar was for law enforcement only, the subject was on, "Officer Street Survival."

Rick could certainly handle himself but greatly lacked situational awareness.

Rick's town was small and the marshal's office was of course, greatly underfunded. They did not have a training budget. Rick would not even consider to dip into his child's surgery fund. I offered to pay for his registration but Rick had his pride and I respected his right to it.

That Saturday night we had coffee and pie. I of course pushed for him to attend the street survival course and to prove my point, I raked my fork down his forearm and left a three inch long red welt with four perfect tine marks. I didn't mean to use that much force to leave welts. Rick just calmly grinned as if to say, "If we weren't friends, I would fuckin tear your fucking face off!"

We went 10:8 (clear of call, available for service.)There were two driveways in the strip mall where the restaurant was located. I went north to return to my city, Rick went south to pick up his partner for a night of patrol. I was dispatched to a bar fight to assist three on-scene squads that needed additional back-up 10:33, (emergency) with twenty or more participants. When I arrived I found a hell of a lot more than thirty combatants. It was not my goal or concern to break up the fight. I was solely there to protect my fellow officers. I wadded into the battle and made contact with several bad actors with my PR24 (police baton) and a few times it sounded like a stand-up double in most any baseball stadium. I'm sure there will be at least a few heavily bruised and bleeding if not broken shins and elbows.

During the bar tussle I picked up some broken radio chatter about fire rescue calling for air-medical. When the fight was over I was walking to my squad car and I heard the Firestone's Marshal's voice screaming into the radio, "Where the hell is that Helicopter, my deputy is dying!" I jumped behind the wheel, radioed my dispatch that I was out of service and enroute to assist the Firestone Marshals Office.

I knew in my heart that is was Rick and I also knew that I would never see him alive again. I buried the speedometer as the front end of the squad was lifting off of the wet pavement. By the time I arrived the helicopter was airborne with the patient. I had to run more than a full city block as the street was jammed with police vehicles. I went to the closest officer (a county deputy) who pointed to an ambulance and said, "The Marshal is in there, he might be having a heart attack." On the way to the ambulance I saw another Firestone Deputy Marshal. He told me the story.

Rick picked up his partner and they went on patrol. He stopped for a stop sign. They heard and saw a vehicle sideswiping parked cars. Rick pulled over the El Camino. The deputy marshal I was talking to said he came in as a cover car and saw the driver was drunk and argumentative. The driver was gunning the engine as Rick was repeatedly telling the driver to shut off the vehicle and get out of the car. The driver reached for the shifter to put the car in gear as Rick reached into the car to pull the keys out of the ignition. The driver put his car in gear and rapidly accelerated with Ricks arm inside the vehicle. Rick fell back and struck his head on the asphalt. Rick was unconscious and bleeding from his ear. He never regained consciousness. Rick was pronounced brain dead two days later.

His wife thought he should have an open casket and be buried in his uniform that he was so proud to wear.

The day of the funeral, myself and several hundred other police officers from Colorado and several surrounding states attended his funereal. There was a private, early viewing for friends and family. As I looked at Rick in his casket my eyes locked onto those four raised welts from my fork tines on his forearm and it absolutely broke my heart. Nobody knew where those welts came from or our conversations about Rick attending the, "Officer Street Survival Seminar." Nobody knew that I was the last person that Rick ever talked to except for his partner and the EL Camino driver. Rick's radio log only showed the time that we went 10:6 (busy but available) at the restaurant and when he went 10:8. (Assignment complete, available for service). The only other radio communication was when he made the traffic stop. His final radio broadcast was that he had an uncooperative 10:55

(drunk driver) suspect. I never told anyone that we were together just before he died, other than my wife.

I was in the front of the receiving line with my wife at my left side. She knew to never stand on my right side (gun hand). As the pallbearers were removing Rick's coffin from the hearse the color guard took up their position and we were called to, 'Attention'. The command of 'Salute' was given and several hundred white gloved right hands were raised to hat brims.

I can be as stoic as a rock most any time that I wish to be. This day however the tears flowed down my face as I held my body statue still. I could feel my tears dripping from my chin and landing on my uniform shirt as I continued to hold my white gloved salute, until his coffin was placed onto the lowering device over the open grave.

My poor wife had never attended a Police Officers funeral before and didn't understand the proper decorum. She started to reach over to try to wipe my tears away. I didn't flinch but I guess the set of my facial muscles, the flex of my cheek bones and my blazing eyes, telegraphed that she shouldn't be touching me at that moment. She later told me that she had never in her life, seen such deep sorrow and loosely bridled rage at the same time.

Cops don't drink in the bars of the districts they patrol. It's not wise to be in a bar when some asshole whose lip you had to bust a few nights before and he now has retaliation on his mind. But the night of Rick's funeral fifty or more of us made an exception. We took over a, 'Beer and a Shot Bar.'

It was a rough, bad ass biker joint. We cleared the joint out of the, "rocker vest" folks. Something about pistol wiping a few loudmouths with a couple of four dozen drawn and pointed guns with eyes of murder behind the business end of their pistols, sent them on their way. The few shit-heads that tried to reenter the bar (some with reinforcements) must have missed the fact that many of us initially came in the bar with shotguns. We gently reminded them that this was a private party with our hardware that makes real big, loud booms.

There were probably eight or nine guys in law enforcement that knew Rick well.
One of those fellows pulled me aside and asked if I knew what had to be done? I grinned as I responded with, "Damn right I do, I just don't know if I can trust you!"
Between us, we picked four more officers that we knew we could trust. This wasn't about trusting another cop to have your back. This was about trusting another cop to keep his mouth shut about an execution of a bad guy. When we had fresh Intel to share we would announce, 'Pizza at Pete's.' We only met in the far corners of parking lots and kept it brief. Several law enforcement agencies in the state and the adjoining states were looking for Jacobs, but we were hunting him. Not for arrest or justice, he was to be exterminated.

Chapter 26   THE ENDLESS HUNT

The violators name was Bernie Wayne Jacobs, 39 years old of Evanston, Colorado. It took us three hours to find him. He was found hiding in the reeds down by an irrigation ditch, eight officers were coming up the hill with him in handcuffs when I arrived. I had my weapon drawn and was ready to drop my safety off. I just wanted to get a clear shot at him but with all the officers around him I couldn't get a clear shot. Every bit of my fiber wanted to kill that mother fucker! Jacobs was taken to the Weld County Jail in Rick's patrol car. He was booked on suspicion of, Drunk Driving and Vehicular Assault. His bond was set at a bullshit, $2,000 by a cop hating Judge and District Attorney. Jacobs bonded out (without travel or behavior restrictions) and paid a $200 bond to a bondsman before the ink was dry on the arrest reports. No police agency was notified of his release. I think they figured out that Jacobs wouldn't live long enough to enjoy an early morning breakfast. I'm sure that that piece of shit was, "In the wind" ten minutes after his release. There were police vehicles stationed around Jacobs house 24 hours a day. There was no movement inside the residence during that period.

Rick was actually pronounced dead two days later. The Weld County District Attorney issued an arrest warrant for Jacobs with the amended charge of Vehicular Homicide. Once again he set a bullshit bond of $50,000. The D.A. of course held a news conference (it was an election year) and spoke of his deep love and respect for all law enforcement. You would have thought he had a movie script writer, prepare his flowery twenty minute speech.

    The DA stated that because of Jacob's three drunk driving convictions and that he had just had his driver's license suspended for five years and along with the results of his blood alcohol which was above .20 (twice the legal limit)when he murdered Rick, that he wanted to have Jacobs back in custody. None of the guys bought his grandstanding bullshit.

    There were several different police agency cars parked all around Jacob's house. When the DA announced the arrest warrant, we crashed thru his doors and broke every window out of his house with everyone hoping to put a bullet into him. Jacobs was gone.

    We hunted for that son of a bitch every waking moment. One of the guys got to dispatch and the six man, "Hunting Party" was left alone during our shifts. We were only dispatched to hot calls. The other squads took the common routine calls for us and never complained. Our days off, were full hunting days that went well into the night. We never let up, we went for weeks and months shaking every bush, many times over. We made deals with bad guys and looked the other way if we thought we could get useful information from the local pukes. The thief's and drug dealers were fully enjoying the hands-off honeymoon. Every cop wrote pending arrest reports on these assholes to be executed at a later date. Every time I cut loose a bad guy without charges, I would inwardly grin with the oath of, "Fucker, this ain't over, I will come for you and I'm gonna be coming hard!"

    As the weeks, the months and even the years passed the original six of, "The Hunting Party" never stood down. We of course lost the insane intensity that burned within us but we never lost the desire or hope to someday kill him.

    The mystery of what happened to Bernie Jacobs was solved four and a half years later, when his body was found on April 29th 1987 on a riverbank near Weaver Reservoir in Lyons County, Nevada.

    The official report released by the Sherriff of Lyons County, Nevada was that Jacobs had committed suicide with a 38 caliber revolver with a gunshot wound to his chest. When they found his body it was thought that he had been dead for up to four days.

What I found interesting was that the 38 caliber handgun was never found! The Sherriff surmised that a wild animal must have run off with it. CASE CLOSED.

There was a nationwide teletype issued by the F.B.I. as to the "Capture" of suspect Bernie Jacobs. There was a state wide broadcast on the "State emergency band radio system" followed by a Weld County Colorado dispatch, "Attention all cars and stations, standby for 10:33 information. Fugitive suspect, Bernie Wayne Jacobs has been located and is dead."

The next morning the six member, "Hunting Party" met at the Hillside Cemetery in Fort Lupton, Colorado, ten minutes before sunup. We all noticed the dark blue Chevrolet Biscayne that pulled up twenty yards behind our vehicles. Two suited men got out and leaned against the front fender of their car.

We six stood in silence at Rick's grave. After about ten minutes, we came to attention and saluted in unison without a command or word spoken. We turned and walked as a group towards the suits leaning against the blue Chevy. I stopped in front of them and said, "Go ahead and ask." The two suits, with their F.B.I. badges hanging from the breast pockets said, "Can you gentleman tell us where you all were on or about April 25th and 26th?" I smiled and said, "I was either working, sleeping, fighting or fucking. Pick one."

The rest of the guys all said, "Me too!" The senior Fed smiled and said, "Thank you gentlemen, there will be no further questions, ever! If you gentlemen don't mind we would like to pay our respects to your friend."

We went to our cars and drove away as the Feds were walking to Rick's grave.

Chapter 27 MY DAD'S LEGACY

My dad's legacy was that he taught me as a young child how to take a beating, on a daily basis. He taught me not to cry with the threat of a greater beating. He taught me how to take verbal abuse, using cruel and harsh words with glaring looks of constant hatred. He taught me to feel unwanted, unloved and trapped. One day he joined AA and sobered up. He taught me kindness, he taught me understanding, tolerance and acceptance. Those are not words, those were his actions. He showed me that a man can change, he become a good man with love in his heart and with his actions. My dad died at the age of fifty from lung cancer. Dad died with 14 years of rocking sobriety. Because and due to his powerful examples, I am sober today. I am no longer harming others or myself. Thanks dad I miss you. I think you would be proud of me as I am of you.

Then there's my old pal, Brian Cook. Brian was my divorce attorney for my fourth marriage. Brian was a true study of what strange people are and do. I didn't think Brian owned a wrinkleless or a newer T-shirt. His law office was in an old house, semi- restored, he shared the bottom level with another attorney which was a real arrogant prick that I couldn't stomach. Brian was a piece of work. Brian paid his way through law school by playing piano in a bar at the world famous Breakers Hotel in Palm Beach, Florida. Brian could play any musical instrument (I believe) that's ever been made. Each time I went to meet with him he would start singing the same song, each time.

The song was titled, "Little Boy" that he wrote himself and he was kind of making fun of us weepy little pricks who we're going through a divorce and having our hearts broken, full well knowing we are going to be broke for all of our lives with mountains of child support and fighting to see our kids on a regular basics. Brian could play the fiddle, the guitar, ukulele, banjo and piano. You name it, he could play it. I would be sitting in conversation with him and he would suddenly grab one of his instruments and start singing and playing that damn song! He had one of those, old grade school back room coat racks with his instruments hanging from the pot metal hooks behind him. When the day came that we were supposed to go to court I wondered if the judge would kick us out with Brian wearing one of his finest t-shirts. I was pretty sure that he didn't own a suit. I was in disbelief when I walked into his office that morning and found him not only clean shaven (a true rarity) but wearing a rather smart looking professional suit.

I had been in arrears in my child support for about five months according to court records but that wasn't the whole truth. I was working in a large retail pharmacy. I was the manager there but I didn't make a lot of money. My boss let me buy diapers, formula, baby vitamins and prescriptions all at cost. My wife was sickly and had a severe cold. I brought her over the counter remedies and her doctor's prescriptions. I paid for all that and gave her money orders to make up the difference of the court order. She never reported either the goods or money orders to the court. I was pretty sure that I was going to go to jail that day.

Brian drove a beater (matched his wardrobe) car that almost never started if you didn't push it. We left his office and sure enough I'm pushing his car down the street.

When the court clerk called the case the judge looked at me and looked at Brian and asked, "Why isn't your client in jail?" Brian answered, "Your honor, the complainant has been giving false information to this court for the last four months. My client has receipts for the purchase of goods for the child and the complainant. I have the purchase receipts and the money order receipts that my client actually paid more than the court ordered. My client does not earn enough money to comply with the generous and unreasonable demands of the complainant. She is demanding support for four children when there is only one child." The judge looked at the receipts, took off his glasses and looked at me and said, "Sir these receipts are keeping you out of jail today, in the future you will follow the court orders as they are stated, you seem to be an honorable man but a bit foolish as well. In the future you will do exactly as ordered by this court." He turned his head to my wife and said, "Young lady, if there wasn't a small child involved I would jail you today. The man that you are divorcing is paying for your prescriptions out of his own pocket, you and I both work for this county. We get free medical and prescription coverage. It is obvious to this court that you are trying to punish him for him not making your life perfect. You, young lady have much to learn in life, and I'm giving you your first lesson. You will report to the county probation department on next Monday to avoid felony fraud charges. I am vacating your request for divorce and granting the defendant the divorce. If you, Mr. Brown and your attorney agree sir." I nodded, Brian nodded. The judge told me that I didn't have to reappear and the attorneys would work out reasonable child support and visitation now. "This court is in recess for one hour. You attorneys are not to leave this room, I want a fair and reasonable agreement in one hour."

    I bolted out of the courtroom for a smoke. I waited for Brian on a park bench in front of the court house. He came out in just a little bit over an hour with a big smile. He said, "This is the best deal you could ever hope for. Read it and sign it but only if you fully agree." I read it and signed it. Brian went back inside the courthouse and submitted it to the clerk of court.

    Ten minutes later and I was pushing Brian's piece of shit car from the courthouse into downtown Greeley. We stopped at every bar on highway #287 from Greeley all the way down to Longmont.

    We avoided one brush up just outside of Loveland, Colorado. It was an old farm house that was converted into a bar.

Strange as it might be, the bar was named, 'The Old Farmhouse Bar!' Brian didn't drink but I had two fast beers.

Brian put a quarter in the jukebox. As soon as the record started, two obvious local country boy's in bib overhauls were making loud comments about Brian's song choice and our "sissy citified suits." Brian being the sport that he is, went over to the jukebox and unplugged it. He smiled broadly as he took a few steps towards the pool table, picked up a cue stick and twirled it like Bruce Lee. He asked in a mimicking country drawl, (while still twirling the pool cue) "How much trouble would you gentlemen like on this fine day?" Everyone in that bar was real busy studying their drinks. We left the bar and hoped that piece of shit car would start because we knew those shit head clowns would be coming out shortly behind us. Brian parked on a bit of an incline so I had to only push for a few feet when he popped the clutch and it fired up. More than a few of those local boys came out of the bar to wave goodbye. We laughed as I said, "Good thing I didn't have to shoot those fuck sticks. Brian looked at me and asked, "You carried a gun into the court house? Me too!"

Chapter 28   WELCOME BACK

    Holy Christ what's going on here? I can see light, I can see people, I can see people moving, I can hear people, what the fuck is this? Just another one of the many hallucinations that probably could be stacked up like cord wood at this point? Now I can feel myself. I'm looking now, I can see, I can really see! I can see my hand! It's swollen and looks dark like a big bruise with an IV line with a lot of tape marks. I can wiggle my fingers but just a little bit and I count all five of them. Holy shit, I can lift my arm but just a little bit, I'm trying to lift and turn my head but it won't go very far, it's like everything is trying to work but just a little bit.

    This has got to be real! Is this fuckin nightmare finally over? In front of me, at the foot of the bed, on the wall is a big white grease board. It has my name in big letters at the top left than a bunch of doctor's names on the same line. The next line below it says, "Today is Wednesday" in big block letters the whole length of the board. There are a bunch of names in small letters below that that take up the rest of the whole board but it's just too small to read. I know they use those boards to keep patients oriented.

    I can clearly see Heather standing next to me. She is crying and smiling at the same time. She is not wearing a mask or a hair net or a hospital gown like when I saw her in my other dreams. Now I see a bunch of people standing like a church choir, they all have books in their hands like they are singing but their mouths are not moving.

I can't see what those books are, but they don't look like any hymnals that I have ever seen. I feel real sleepy now.

I must have fallen asleep because those choir people were gone now. It was just Heather and a bunch of people that looked like doctors and nurses. I knew it still had to be the same day because Heather still has the same clothes on. Heather is a clean freak and she would never wear the same clothes two days in a row. I looked at Heather to ask her what happened but nothing came out of my mouth but I know my lips were moving. A woman in a white lab coat with a stethoscope patted my arm and said, "It might be too soon to speak yet, we will give you some ice chips to sooth your throat and maybe in an hour or two you will find your voice. For now I need to ask you some questions. Just nod you head for yes or shake it for no. Are you in pain?" I had to think for a few minutes as I was trying to mentally identify everything and to check my body out, limb by limb. I couldn't really tell but some parts felt different than before whenever the fuck "before" was. I shook my head no. She asked, "Do you know your name?" I leaned a bit forward and nodded my head toward the grease board on the wall at the foot of the bed. She looked and smiled as she said, "That is very smart, the way you showed me your name. I'm going to enjoy working with you." She went on to say that she is my primary Physican in this matter and she would direct my care and recovery. The lady pulled two chairs next to me and motioned to Heather to sit down, the doctor sat next to her. She said, "I am going to ask you some basic multiple choice questions. There are only three answers for each question, nod your head when you hear the right answer. Who is this lady sitting next to me? Is she a friend, is she your sister, is she your wife?" I nodded at wife.

Two nurses came into the room. One had a big gulp cup of shaved ice and the doctor reached out for it. The doctor told her to, "Stay here." The other nurse had a tray with two IV bags (one was a piggyback) the doctor nodded at her and the nurse took down the hanging IV bag. The doctor said, "Use the other hand, we have violated this hand long enough for a while. The nurse removed the port from my left hand and bandaged it. She went over to the other side of the bed and hung the new IV's. She said, "Just a little stick and you might feel a little cold." If I could have laughed I would have. I can't feel a fucking thing!

The doctor smiled as she lightly patted my left hand and said, "You are quite a fighter, and you have torn your IV's out several times. There is a bit of chaffing on your wrists and forearms and you might have some sore neck and chest muscles. I am sorry but we had to restrain you a few times, because we were fearful that you may harm yourself further." She handed Heather the cup of ice chips and told her, "Just a few at a time," as she went on to play the standard twenty questions to see if I had my wits about me. I was waiting for her to ask the, "Golden Buzzer" question but it was taking her for fuckin ever! I was loving the ice chips however, I could feel them all the way down to my toes. That is if I still have toes!

I know the game and how it's played. She will (hopefully soon) ask me if I know what happened, I will say, "No fucking clue" and the nice doctor lady will tell me what she thinks has happened. "Get to it damn it, what the fuck happened to me?" The doctor let out a deep breath and here it came, "Do you remember what has happened to you?"

Suddenly I had tears in my eyes and I shook my head no. Heather tried to dry my tears and kissed my cheek. The doctor took a deep breath and said, "All things considered, you are in relatively good shape. You should fully recover and go on to live the life you had before the accident." So now I'm thinking, a car accident? I looked over at Heather and studied her face and body of what I can see of it, to see if she had any injuries. She looked normal.

The doctor said, "You were struck by lightning while you were mowing your lawn. It was not a direct hit but is what is known as a, 'Side Flash', which still can be deadly. Lucky for you, Heather was standing on the deck and saw you go down. Her being there at that very moment is what saved your life. You were unconscious when the paramedics arrived. You went into cardiac arrest as they were loading you into the ambulance. They couldn't defibrillate you and risk further damaging your heart. You have more than a few broken ribs from the CPR, but they brought you back before they arrived at the hospital. You are luckier than most, I would say, damn lucky!

You have been here for eight days now and you have had two surgeries. It will take you a few days to regain your motor skills and speech patterns. I will do my best to manage your pain through your upcoming surgeries and therapy."

I must have had an involuntary eye movement that told her, "What the fuck are you talking about surgeries, as in plural, what the fuck is this?" She reached over and picked up a syringe that was on the IV tray that the nurse brought in earlier. She didn't add the contents to the IV bags, she slammed it fast into the port next to my hand. She sat back a bit, patted Heathers arm and smiled at her as she rubbed my forearm and smiled. I knew she was waiting for the drugs to kick in.

The doctor went on to say, "You have third degree burns on your right hip and all down your entire right leg. You have a nasty little entry wound high on your right hip and a larger exit wound on the inside of your right leg, at mid-calf. It looks much like a large caliber bullet wound. I understand that you have plenty of experience with those kinds of things, probably more than I do. You will need skin grafts for several days, you will spend full days in the 'burn unit.' I will do my absolute best to manage your pain without turning you into an opioid addict. The pain will be intense and will be all but unbearable at times. You must keep in the forefront of your mind that the pain you will be experiencing is all part of your healing process. I also want you to know that you are safe with us.

Heather has been here every moment from the time you first arrived. Your family has brought her toiletries and clothing. She has showered in this room and slept in a rollaway bed next to you every night. I don't believe she has left this room. I will give you something to sleep in a few minutes, I am going to take

Heather to a nice restaurant for dinner and then I'm going to send her home to sleep in her own bed. Now that you are awake I can finally see those gorgeous eyes that Heather and your friends were talking about. Before I discharge you in a few weeks I hope you will sign your books for me if you don't hate me by then. I snuck your first book and finished it with my breakfast this morning. You sir have some incredible talent. Believe me when I tell you that your time writing, has been well spent. Well spent indeed!

Heather, kiss this Adonis goodnight, we are going to dinner!" I think the lights went out for me before they left the room.

Chapter 29 MAKING NEW FRIENDS

I woke up to my bed being raised to a sitting position. There was Heather and the lady doctor from the night before, the lights went out. Heather rarely wore any kind of makeup or lipstick. This morning she had on eye shadow, a soft pink barely noticeable rouge, with bright almost wet looking red lipstick. She is wearing a thin Hawaiian style silk dress with big yellow and Red Lehua flowers (I think it means fire goddess and represents volcano fire). Heather looked beyond stunning, she was absolutely delicious. She had a tall cup of coffee with a straw in it. She smiled as she said, "I would like to give you a lot more than this," as she slowly turned a full circle with her patented, 'come take me baby' smile. "This will have to do for now sweetheart." I looked at the straw bobbing in the steaming coffee cup like a fishing bobber and I laughed.

It made me think of a friend of mine who spent an absolute fortune with her dentist to have perfect gleaming white teeth. She still goes to her dentist every six weeks for a polishing and buffing. She drank her coffee through a straw to keep her teeth from staining.

Well for now it's coffee through a straw. I took my first sip and it felt like heaven. The lady doctor said we have an hour to get to know each other. "No doctor no medical talk, we will just sit and visit until your first test this morning. We will sit and visit with a team of doctors this afternoon to design your treatment program, for now let's talk." I said, "OK doctor, what's your first name?"

She answered, "Katherine, Katherine with a K not Kathy, its Katherine. Dr. Katherine Phillips.

I smiled as I said, "Cath there is something you need to learn about me, if we're gonna get along. The few people that I actually like all get nicknames from me. You will learn that when you swipe my second book, "Flesh of a Fraud." I like you Cath, I think I'll call you Gwen!" (I'm guessing sweet ole Katherine to be mid-thirties or something close. She has a clean fresh face and athletic build with a rather generous upper body).She gave me a disappointed look as I smiled and said, "Gwen pull up a chair and I will tell you about your namesake, my sweet old friend Gwen." She and Heather both took a seat.

"Gwen was the graveyard shift switchboard operator at the hotel that I was a stowaway in for three years." Cath now Gwen, nodded her head and said, "Yes I read about the hotel life of yours." I smiled as I said, "Gwen, I don't like being interrupted, you will want to learn that about me too. You and Gwen could be twin sisters. I hope you find that flattering. Well, Gwen and I were buddies and we both loved beer. At 2:00 a.m. every morning, when everyone was quiet in the hotel and the dust had cleared. I brought a six pack of iced beer for Gwen and me. She drank four beers to my two in the same period of time. I brought the front desk clerk who was studying for his college classes two, iced wine coolers and the night auditor/acting manager on duty (he only drank coffee) a carafe of steaming fresh coffee to keep them quiet about Gwen and I (I was only 15 years old) drinking beer. I also brought the night manager the latest hustler magazine when it came out each month. He seemed to spend an awful lot of time in the bathroom.

Gwen was very pretty, well-groomed and very busty. She wore very tight blouses. She put a great deal of trust into those buttons of her blouse. As we were visiting I was always of the hopes that those buttons would burst and go flying across the room. That never happened however.

Gwen was a world traveler. She worked for Pan-American Airline's. She was an internal auditor and spent six days in France, six days in Italy and four days in Spain every month. Gwen spoke the language of each country fluently. She quit her job to marry an Air Force Lieutenant Colonel. They have been married for fifteen years. Gwen was my buddy, she cared about me. Sometimes she almost cared too much about me. She bought me two sets of bed linens, a nice pillow and two warm blankets. She said, "I know that you sleep in the elevator shaft control room, on the roof. I don't want you sleeping with that hotel crap for bed clothes." She knew when it was my birthday and always gave me birthday and Christmas cards along with expensive gifts of clothing that always were a perfect fit. We talked about everything. She taught me more than most anyone. I trusted her and she believed in me.

When my girlfriend got pregnant I had to quit the job at the hotel and move back home with my parents. I never got to see Gwen again. Not until my newborn baby girl died. Gwen came to my baby's funeral, she was crying. She introduced me to her husband and handed me a thick, #10 envelop as she said it was from all the hotel employees to help pay for the funeral and a headstone for my baby, Saundra. She told me that they were being transferred to an air base in Michigan. Gwen gave me the most loving hug I've ever had at that time in my young life. After the funeral I never saw her again. Gwen was the first woman that ever truly cared about me. I still think back about the times that she made those lonely times bearable. I think I enjoyed the close contact with her spirit warmth, even more than staring at her breasts. Gwen had an understanding kindness that made you feel safe.

Well Dr. Gwen, the tenderness in your eyes tell me that I am safe with you, just like I was with Gwen. I trust you like I did Gwen. So Gwen, let's have it. I want all of it, I know that doctors don't give newly awaken patients the full story all at once. I want it all Gwen and I want it now. Bring it Gwen, bring it hard, bring it fast and bring it dirty!

Gwen cleared her throat, looked at the remaining nurse and said, "Hand me my briefcase." She wrote something down on a notepad and said, "Call these doctors, change these appointments for today and reschedule them for the same time tomorrow. Please put the, 'Do not enter sign' on the door when you leave, thank you." The nurse smiled and said, "Yes Doctor." Then Gwen said, "Nurse, the name 'Gwen' is not to be spoken again by anyone outside of this room. I don't want to hear a snicker or see a grin, it seems that Mr. Brown here has blessed me with a pet name. It is not anyone else's pet name to use, I want that to be clear. Am I clear with your nurse?" The nurse smiled and said, "Yes doctor we are perfectly clear," as she left the room.

Gwen pulled out a folder of sheets of paper from her briefcase. She said, "I'm going to read this to you, so you fully understand and that I don't miss anything. First it is very rare to have somebody who is struck by lightning to die. Ninety percent of all the people who are struck by lightning survive. The injuries very greatly from person to person. Most all patients suffer mental and emotional injuries as well. People who have experienced a lightning strike may also experience symptoms that are delayed. These symptoms may include depression, chronic pain, headaches, personality changes, self-isolation, and difficulties with carrying on a conversation. The person may feel irritable or embarrassment because they are unable to remember others, their job responsibilities, or key information. Family members, friends, and co-workers who see the same person they knew before, might not understand why the person they know who has experienced a lightning strike is so different. Friends might stop coming by or asking them to participate in activities, or survivors may self-isolate due to irritability or embarrassment. It is important for family members, friends, and others to continue to participate with people who experienced a lightning strike.

So please know David that people are trying to help you. Try not to become frustrated with continuous short visits, with little conversation. They just want you to know that they're pulling for you. When a bolt of lightning strikes the human frame, very bad things happen. In addition to the 30,000 volts of energy coursing through you, the power of the strike heats the surrounding air to 50,000 degrees, causing 3rd degree burns at the bolts entry and exit points. I took care of those wounds three days ago. A lightning strike can also cause lightning bolt or tree branch shaped burn marks called "Lichtenberg Figures," which are caused by bursting blood vessels. There look much like the henna tattoos that tourist's get in the South Sea Islands. For the most part those will disappear in time.

Now about you immediate post-strike symptoms, they can include, cardiac arrhythmia, myocardial damage and pulmonary edema in the circulatory system. You could suffer brain damage (because in the cellular structure of your brain literally cooks from the current) resulting in short term memory loss and amnesia. Longer neurological maladies include personality changes, learning disabilities, sleep disorders, seizures along with Parkinson twitching like symptoms. Last, victims commonly report numbness and weakness of limbs, temporary or permanent paralysis, concussions, blown ear drums, cataracts and a whole lot of pain. All of that is quite difficult to measure.

The actual brain damage appears to come from the one time flooding of the brain with neurotransmitters that are released from the dying neurons. This causes a rewiring of neurons, providing access to areas of the brain that were previously inaccessible which in many cases means you will have a complete change of not only personalities but abilities. There are people that could never play the piano that became concert pianist and just a matter of months. I don't know if that's going to make you a, better writer or a better public speaker, we will just have to wait and see." I grinned as I said, "Well Gwen, I have always wanted to learn to play a, "Hammered Dulcimer" what do you think my chances are?" She smiled as she said, "I don't like to be interrupted either, let me finish. Beyond that, I don't have anything more to offer you at this point. We are going to run a battery of tests to establish a base line and treatment plan and to measure the level of damage you received. Heather has assured me that you're a fierce fighter and that you'll do whatever it takes to recover, I trust in her words. You have done an awful lot of talking while we had you under. As your physician I have to ask your permission to allow certain people to visit with you. Under the federal 'HIPAA' patients' rights act, we bent some rules to allow your close friends, Mr. and Ms. Quinn to record your ramblings while you were sleeping. They have spent five days recording your musings, this is something that you will have to agree with. I have those tapes they recorded you with and if you say no I will turn them over to you. If you would like, I will be happy to destroy them. There has been a lot of media attention because people just don't get struck by lightning very often and because of the following you carry as a local celebrity novelist.

There are two boxes over there from the US Postal Service that are full of nothing but get well cards and letters from all over the country. Our hospital switchboard has been overwhelmed with phone calls enquiring on your condition and asking for the mailing address. Well as you can see, they have been using that mailing address. Alright, now tell me about those four cases of books over there. Even when you were under, you clearly and firmly directed Heather to bring those books here, on several occasions. Could you tell me why?"

I smiled as I said, "Well Gwen, here's what those cases of books are about. I was having eye surgery a year and a half ago. I was afraid that I would lose my eyesight so I had approximately two hundred books of each novel in my home. I signed all of them before I went for my surgery, in case I was blind or worse yet, in case I died. I wanted Heather to have those signed copies so she could sell them for full price to help pay for the cost of my burial. Heather and I have a running joke about my dying and that I will have one of the largest attended funerals of all times. People will be in line all the way around the block wanting to come into the mortuary just to make sure that I'm dead. She says she's going to charge a $20 cover charge for entry and then another $20 for a

"Split the Pot" like they do in Bingo parlors. For an additional $15, you can buy an old lady type hat pin, for the non-believers who want to stick me just to be sure that I'm dead."

Gwen leaned back and smiled with, "You two are really fucked up. It's gotta be a lot of fun to live in your house. I'm going to leave you kids just to hang out for the rest of the day.

 Today is my day off and because of you, 'Mr. Smart ass' I'm taking the other copy of your book that I was about to pilfer. You owe me for having to put up with your twisted mind that I believe is pre-electrocution. I'm a power reader and I'll give you my report tomorrow morning. That is if, you give any part of a fuck."

Chapter 30   CAN'T YOU EVER BEHAVE?

The doctor left the room and in just a few minutes, in came a parade of nurses. They came in several waves. Some to change my bandages from my earlier surgeries, some to change the bed linens. I pulled the one nurse up-short when I asked, "Since when does a, "Unit charge nurse," fluff up a patients pillow?"

She blushed heavily with a meek smile as she said, "You are the only patient that I've ever meet who has donated one million dollars to our, "Burn Unit" I just wanted to say thank you, but we are all under strict orders not to bother you." I thought, "That fuckin Paul Roberts."

I called a halt to the nurse 'Cake walk' of the five or more nurses like you might see at your local community center during Harvest Season. Ladies, stand still. I know you are pretending to provide care for me, but I have watched each of you allow your eyes to drift at the books on the table over there. I am not a famous writer like you may think, I'm just a regular, local guy who just happened to write a couple of novels. As for that million buck's donation, that came from a friend of mine whose heart is as big as his bank account. Ladies it would greatly please me if you all were to take a copy of each book. Let's call it a gift of gratitude for all that you do. These books are gifts from the patients of past, present and future." There were several sheepish smiles and softly spoken, 'Thank yous' as they scuttled out of the room.

I took a deep breath to summon the courage of opening the door before it got kicked in. I knew I had to hear of my "Sleep

talking." I talk in my sleep at home all the time. Heather will always tell me that most of my talking is gibberish but at times Heather will say that I speak clearly when I'm talking to the dogs and that I love her with all my heart. Well, I saw her wince when the doctor was talking about my recorded 'sleep talk.'
Well, I guess it's time for my scolding. I reached out to take her hand as I asked, "Did I embarrass you enough to make you plan for my future demise?"

Heather smiled as she patted my arm as she said, "Of course you did! It was actually music to my ears. It told me that your brain was not affected by the strike. It actually made me cry with joy. All I could do was smile as I thought, yup that's my asshole sweetheart!" I smiled and asked, "Am I grounded?" Heather smiled as she said, "You asked me to show you my 'boobies' several hundred times and of course there was always some nurse here and I could hear them giggling as they left the room. Strange as it might sound, you made perfectly good sense. You said you had to call Paul to get Chicago to redistrict the grocery stores, something about classrooms in the grocery stores, you told me to tell 'Satins' little sister to stop busting thru walls and kicking down doors. I lost track of all your orders that you were giving but I think you had either a comment or a task for everyone in both of your books. But mostly it was, "Lift your shirt baby, just for a minute, it will be ok, just for a minute."

"Now the entire hospital and many of your friends know what a pig you really are. Congratulations!"

All I could say was, "Sorry Babe it's just my way to say, I'm still crazy about you. Did I see a bunch of people in the room, like a church choir? It felt like I saw a bunch of people a couple of times at different times." Heather started to laugh as she said, "You've had friends and acquaintances and even a large number of people who you've never met before, who've come to the hospital to volunteer to read to you.

The hospital claims that due to so many inquiries about your condition from the public and the media, with the media requesting a press conference on lighting strike victims the hospital held a press conference.

Dr. Phillips was interviewed during the press conference. She mentioned your condition and how physician's use the patient's favorite music and have voices familiar to the patient read to them, to sooth and hopefully wake patients who are unconscious or are in a coma.

That started a firestorm of people who wanted to come to read to a famous author, to read his own books to him and hopefully aid in his recovery. I probably shouldn't be telling you all this, but a lot has been going on for the last several days. I think you would want to know. I'm sorry to tell you this baby, but the dedication and Grand Opening for the 'Boys and Girls Town' library and study hall was last Monday, three days ago. I'm so sorry that you had to miss that. During the ceremony Father Martin mentioned you and your accident and offered up a prayer for you. Of course there was every national and International news agency standing in the crowd. They went nuts after the dedication. media surrounded Jane, Amanda, and sweet little Missy. The reporters obviously sniffed out a back story. They wanted to know who you were and why you were mentioned in Father's special prayers. Jane told them that you are the man who took on the entire City of Chicago to reduce street crime, and about the two grocery stores being currently built with an additional 14 stores being planned all over the City of Chicago. Cities throughout the nation are currently inquiring about the program to add to their own cities. Amanda told them about what you did for her entire family. When they got to Missy, all those tough reporters were in tears when she told them about what you did for her (with you not even knowing) that she was convinced that there was no place on this earth for her until she met you). Those very same reporters and national news satellite trucks have now taken over the parking lots all around this hospital. Babe, we always joked about you being famous, I guess the joke is on us! You made it baby, you are now famous! What is so funny is that you are not famous because of your writing and your books but because of who you are and what you are and what you've done. Honey, I've always been proud of you and remember that I fell in love with you when I was just a small child and you were just my dad's friend Dave, Dave the nice man.

Heather started to cry and I followed suit. When our 'tear fest' was over we both started to laugh. I couldn't help but giggle when I said, "Babe remember when that newspaper editor from back east told me that the best way to get well known as a novelist was to either be killed or kill someone else in a very public way with several witnesses? Well I beat that by country mile! I was laying here in a coma and became famous in my sleep! Now that I am famous and a big deal, I don't feel a tick different. Shit I don't feel much of anything. I'm getting sleepy would it be OK if I took a short nap?

I didn't know if I had another crazy dream or if Heather and I actually talked about all that media stuff. Heather took off her headphones as she said with a smile, "I see his Royal Highness has awaken. You have only been sleeping for about forty-two minutes. How do you feel?" "I don't know but my feet are itching." She said, "I'm going to get the doctor, they told me that your feet are of great concern and you may never have feeling in them again." I said, "Could you brush my teeth for me first so I can kiss the prettiest girl in the entire world?" She used a funny looking foam stick with some kind of putrid sweet stuff on it. As she was wiping my mouth there was a tap on the door, just before it opened. In walked Doctor Phillips. She was laughing when she held the door all the way open to point at the 3' by 4' professionally lettered sign on a white poster board. We all started laughing. The sign had my name in block letters. Doctor Phillips name was below mine and in huge cursive letters it said, "Wild Thang!" She closed the door still laughing as she went to the white grease board and erased my name that was in big block letters and wrote my name in much smaller letters and added in large cursive letters, "Wild Thang." At the end of her name she wrote in parentheses, (NOT GWEN!)When I told her about my itchy feet she pulled back the covers and smiled as she said, "Your feet are sweating! This is a wonderful sign, I will be right back!"

Chapter 31   THE RX FOR HEALERS

    Doctor Phillips came back with another doctor who she introduced as Dr. Fisk, my neurologist. After the introductions a nurse came in with a cart with a bunch of stuff on it that I couldn't see. Dr. Fisk said, "I understand that you told Doctor Phillips that your feet itched. Did you then or now feel anything else different, anything else anywhere?" I said, "I don't know, I've only been able to reach out my left arm a little bit and wiggle my fingers. The doctor came over to my left side and said "Reach out your arm and wiggle your fingers." I did what he told me to do. He put out his arm towards me and put out two fingers. He told me to grip his fingers and squeeze, he said grip harder, he again said harder. I was gripping with all my might but it wasn't much. He said, "Put your arm to your side. Now grip my fingers, as he stepped back." I reached out but I couldn't touch his fingers, it was all the further my arm would go. He said, "Your brain controls your muscles and joints. I want you to tell your brain to tell your arm to reach out further." I had to think for a minute before I reached my arm out again, as I was reaching out he took another step back. Now he was twice as far away from where I couldn't touch him.
Then he said, "I interviewed your wife a few day's back, she told me that you are a pretty tough guy. Your friend, Paul Robert's claims you are a total bad ass, but I'm just not seeing it!" I took a deep breath like I was about to lift something heavy and pushed my arm out and easily grasped his fingers. He smiled and said, "Your body is starting to wake up, it has been in a very deep sleep. You just did what you did, using sure will power. I just called you out and you even surprised me. It also tells me of your charictor and maybe just a bit that I don't want to piss you off.

Before we exercise we always have to warm up our muscles. Your muscles and joints are cold from lack of use. I'm going to test your muscles with a few simple procedures and none of this will hurt you." He went over to the nurse's tray and picked up a big thick towel that almost looked like an oversized bathmat. He said I'm going to place this over your face and eyes like a blindfold. I want to see if I can trick your muscles." I could hear him walking all around both sides of me, all the time asking, "Can you feel this, can you feel this, can you feel this, can you feel this? Then he stopped for a minute and before he could ask, "Can you feel this," I jumped and said, "Jesus Christ that's cold!" He asked where it was cold. I said, "My lower stomach and my groin, get that shit away from me!" The doctor I laughed as he said, "I'm taking your blindfold off." He was grinning and was holding up an ice bag to show it to me. He sat down shaking his head as he started to talk. I looked at the hospital gown and said, "Would you mind covering my junk please?" He smiled and said, "Sorry" as he covered me up and put the blankets back on me. He again smiled as he said, "I examined the paramedics EKG strip from nine days ago. You were as dead as dead could be. I have examined all of your body and brain scans. I can find nothing that would point to any permanent damage.

You came to, late yesterday afternoon and now you are talking as normal as anyone. The test I just did, shows that you should have a complete recovery. The reason I covered your eyes was so you couldn't see when I did, and when I didn't touch you. Remember when you were a kid and you tried to fib your mom? Just because you told her a really good fib and thought you got away with it, doesn't mean that she believed you. She just let it pass because it was a harmless little fib and you are her sweet little boy. Well your nerves and muscles are much like that little fibbing boy. Your brain is like the mom and it is all-knowing, you can't trick the brain!

With Doctor Phillips approval, I will have the physical therapy people come in and start working with you within the next hour." Doctor Philip's smiled and said, "The powers that sit high above the both of us, have directed me that it's hands off with Mr. Brown's treatment until tomorrow. It seems that Mr. Brown has become a celebrity. Doctor Fisk, have you by chance noticed the encampment of satellite media trucks all around the hospital property? These news network trucks are here to interview our dashing celebrity patient here. Compliments of hospital administration, Mr. Brown, you, me and hospital admin, along with a contingent of some VIP's from Chicago thrown in with the mix, will be doing countless interviews for the rest of this day and well into the evening, I would have to think. Any questions Doctor Fisk?"

Doctor Fisk smiled and said, "Yes just a few. Doctor Phillips how does a man in a coma present a one million dollar check for the Burn Unit three days before he wakes up and how does this very same patient take a solarium with the best view of Lake Superior, on the outer wall, outside of the Burn Unit and turn it into a, Patient Critical Care Room and in less than 24 hours, while still unconscious?"

I smiled as I said, "Let me take this one Gwen. Doctor Fisk, I am a nobody, but I know someone, who is a 'somebody' and that's pretty much it. And Doctor Fisk, there is something you need to understand about me as others have already learned. I like to give nicknames to the few people that I actually do like.

Doctor Fisk your nickname from now on is, 'Ice Man' for obvious reasons! It was laughs all around. Doctor Fisk, now 'Ice Man' said, "I've enjoyed this day more than many days in the past. Thanks for the entertainment, I will check it on you tomorrow morning."

The 'Ice Man' left the Room. Gwen went over to the white grease board and after Doctor Fisk's name she wrote, 'Ice man'.

I looked at her and said, "Gwen it's supposed to be your day off. You were going home to read my second book, what gives?" Gwen answered with, "I no sooner picked up your book, when Hospital Admin called me into work. They want me to plan for all this media stuff!" I smiled as I said, "Bullshit Gwen, you do understand as I'm sure you do, that the eyes are the windows to the soul. Let's have it."

"Damn it David, I am a professional, I am a Physican, I am a Scientist. We only deal with facts, hard cold facts. We don't play around with theory, you are a patient and you are under my charge. Yes, you are a human being, but to all Physician's, you as all other patients are seen as a project. We cannot allow ourselves to get emotionally involved with our patients. We can only look at you as a challenge.

I was waiting for you in the Emergency Department when they brought you in by ambulance. The paramedics called in a, 'Trauma Alert' while in route to the hospital. There was an entire trauma team along with all of the pertinent equipment ready for full action. I have watched paramedics arriving with, 'Trauma Alert' patients hundreds and hundreds of times. I personally know these paramedics, we have worked together quite often and we've even had coffee and lunch together on several occasions. But on that day, they both looked different, they even acted different. These are both heavily experienced paramedics but I could clearly see that they were personally affected by this patient. I don't think it was that you 'Coded' and they brought you back, they do that stuff all the time. They saw or felt something about you that was different. Something about you changed them! As I started to examine you I got the chills. I don't get the chills but I certainly had them that day. I stood back and looked at your entire body and I felt something from you. I quickly realized that you were special, there was something very special within you, not about or around you, but you yourself. It startled me that I had allowed myself to go so deep about an unconscious patient. It took me some time to shake it off. I just told myself that I was just tired and overworked.

When I got home this morning, I immediately took your second book out of my briefcase, kicked off my shoes and sat down to read. I read the "Readers Praise and Reviews of Flesh of a Fraud" and found them to be extremely complementary and quite accurate. Suddenly I felt a foreign stirring in my belly. I only got through the first two paragraphs of the, "Introduction" before I locked up. My chest was heaving, my heart was pounding and I couldn't catch my breath! I was overwhelmed with emotions. The emotions that I thought I couldn't allow myself to have as a Physican.

David, you and your writing has brought me back to who I really am. Not who I and every other Physican think who we have to be, as a professional. You gave me back my own humanism. Yes David, I cried for you. And then, I cried for me, I actually cried for myself. I have never felt so fresh, so clean. I set your book down, slipped on my shoes, grabbed my handbag and got in my car to come back here to ask you to forgive me."

I could only smile as I asked her to lean over as I kissed her cheek. I said, "Gwen, I need not to forgive you, God already has. He allowed you to cry, he showed you who you truly are.

It's all about balance sweetheart, allow yourself to breath just like every other person on this planet. You are a treater and a healer who just so happens to be a human being. I notice your neckless has a cross, are you a Christian?" Gwen, "Yes I am, I'm Catholic."

Chapter 32   THE LOVING NUDGE

Me: So then I did hear Laine Hardy?

Heather: Yes my love, 24/7 and it about drove me out of my flippin mind!

Me: So there were people in a line that looked like a church choir with books?

Heather: Yes my love, they were reading your books like you guys do at your AA book study meetings, where each person reads a few paragraphs. I have heard both of your books read at least a dozen times in the last few days. What I found interesting was, each time I understood something that I had not before. It was actually quite interesting. I have a list of all your readers and it is over a hundred and twenty-five. I never felt the full power of your writing before. Each reader found tears at some point. It was very moving for me to witness the true impact you have on people.

I guess I'm like most of our friends and family, where we think we know you when in fact we hardly know you at all. I owe you a huge amends. Everything about you, your posture, your words and the way you're always smiling and kidding around is all a disguise! No one knows how deep your pain runs. You cheat us out of getting to know the real you by you always acting so cavalier and unflappable. Now for the worst of the worst. I honestly didn't think you were that good of a writer. Truthfully, I only breezed thru them. I didn't spend thirty minutes between the two books. Your low sales numbers don't reflect the power of your writing ability's. Baby I understand your desire to maintain your autonomy. But damn it David, you need help. Your work is too good and meaningful to just sell a dozen or so books a month. Hell, you give away three times that many every month.

Amanda is coming in tonight. She and the rest of the Robert's family have all but begged you to let them help you. Sweetheart, please know that I love you with every ounce of my being but I am done with your ego driven cadence of, "I'll do it myself."

Damn it to hell David, you can't do it yourself. It takes money and influence to bring a book forward to the masses. We don't have the money or the influence, the Roberts do. Hell they have enough money to retire half of the national debt and they are absolutely in love with you! It's time we ask for the help that has already been offered, multiple times!

I sat and watched Woody and Maddi Quinn standing and reading to you while balling their eyes out, than the Walker clan did the same thing, but what put it over the top for me was the Kivi couple. Remember when you sat with Marge Kivi for only twenty minutes and changed her and Axel's lives forever? This is a farm couple that have been married for forty years. You helped them find the love they had and lost for many, many of those years.

They saw the news story on you and have driven more than 60 miles every morning to bring you and me each a long stem red rose for the last five day's! There are ten long stem red roses in that vase over there. They stand in the hallway and peak in on you, they hold hands and softly say the, "Lord's Prayer." I can hear them sobbing as they turn to walk away to drive back to the farm. Yesterday they brought you that box over there. I think you need to open it now. Before I get it for you, I want to finish what I have to say. I watched these many tender hearts that would all trade places with you, so you could live, for just another day. I found my and I believe your deepest truths. For me, if you become famous I am afraid I will lose you. Not that I would ever think I would lose you or your love, but afraid I would have to share you.

As for you, I have come to the dead nuts realization that you are not holding back because of your ego. You are holding back because of your deep humility. Baby you are deserving of your hard fought success. You have overcome a tragic and lonely life. It is your time and it is God's will."

Heather got up from her chair and retrieved the gift wrapped box with ribbons and a bow. She untied the ribbons and lifted the box cover. She looked inside and turned her back to me as she cried. I felt frustrated that I couldn't stand to hold her or even take her in my arms. She turned back around and tipped the box down so I could see its contents. The contents of that box spoke a million words. Inside was Axel Kivi's John Deere baseball cap. He has worn that sweat stained, faded and tattered cap every day, for more than twenty years! He even wore it once with a white tuxedo on!

I couldn't touch the hat and risk contamination or infection. I now have the tears that Heather was having. After a few minutes, I knew it was time for me to surrender. I looked at heather and said, "You are right, all of you are right. Call Amanda and tell her to bring her check book. The big check book! Have her also bring along Father Martin.
There is a young lady who is also a Physician that could use an official blessing.

Chapter 33 THE CIRCUS RETURNS

I awoke with a start as I heard the band Alabama was playing. I didn't know who they were until I was at my first NASCAR race at Talladega. Those cats brought me to a whole new world of country pop music. I listen to them often, their music is good for the soul. Heather was facing me with her headphones on and was playing some kind of a pet rescue game on her iPhone. I snapped my fingers, her head came up fast with a start. Her eyes went wide as she said, "Holy shit you just snapped your fingers. I'm going to go get the doctor. I said, "No honey no, let's just have a few moments of, "us" time, just us. I want to thank you for loving me. Few women would stand watch over their husbands as you have done for me. You have shut down everything in your life just to be with me. I have just one question, just one question my dear. Who the hell do I have to sleep with to get a cup of coffee around this shithole?" Heather started to cry as she said, "Ten days ago I had to watch you die. One moment you were mowing the lawn, when you came by you looked up and blew me a kiss. Seconds after that, you instantly went down. You just didn't fall down, you were slammed down to the ground. At first, I didn't know what happened. I did see the lightning flash but that was of little ways away from us. I didn't think it hit you. I ran down off the deck and you were out cold. Your hair was smoldering and there was steam coming off of you. Your rings were laying next you on the ground. They were now just melted blobs of gold. I would have not even seen them if not for those tiny diamond chips winking at me, from your baby Saunders ring. You were still breathing with smoke coming out of your mouth. I brushed out the small flames from your hair with my fingers. I don't remember calling 911, but I heard the sirens and the rumbling engines of the big fire trucks. After that I just didn't see a lot. I just saw a lot of uniformed people and some man put his arm around my shoulder as they were wheeling you to the ambulance. Just before they were going to load you in, I saw them start to do chest compressions on you. That's all I can remember other than riding with a lady police officer. I found myself sitting in the emergency department waiting room all alone. It was the most alone I have ever felt in my entire life. It felt like I had been waiting for days, my belly was boiling with acid, waiting for someone to come out and tell me that they had done all that they could do.

Now you're laying here snapping your fingers like I'm your goddamn servant and I love it! The doctors told me you might have a permanent if not greatly diminished thinking, talking, and movement functions, and you snap your fucking fingers at me? You prick! I love you so much, I could just kiss your face like the dogs do when they want pets." I thanked her as I said, "Baby I'm sorry that you had to go through all of that, so let's get back to that coffee matter."

We were both laughing and crying at the same time. Heather said, "You have been burning (oops poor choice of words) through a full IV and a piggyback of electrolytes every hour. Your urine output is still well below normal, your body is sucking up all the fluids like a sponge. This is day ten and you've lost twenty-six pounds since you were struck. Yes you needed to lose some weight but I don't think this is the time or the right way to do it. You can only have ice chips and those have to be limited. No liquids or soft foods at all for at least another week. I said, "Bullshit, you gave me coffee yesterday with a straw in it!" She smiled as she said, "They told me to expect you to have hallucinations but no sweetheart, you have not had any coffee."

I started to feel grumpy, "God damn it, it's time I do! I want to have a cigarette now! Heather said, "The last time smoke came out of your mouth was because your insides were on fire and boiling. I don't ever want to see that ever again, you are done smoking and I mean it!" Yup, I've just lost another battle.

There was a tap on the door and in came the, Head Nurse with three other nurses pushing a machine that looked straight out of a porn, horror movie (not that I ever watched that kind of trash). The nurse said, "You're going to have company in about an hour. We're going to change your surgical bandages and wrap your hip and leg with waterproof dressings and we are going to use the cherry picker over here to lift you out of bed to give you a shower." I was surprised that I didn't feel any pain from being lifted, turned and bounced around a bit. Then I remembered Doctor Phillips did promise to manage my pain for me. I gritted my teeth as I thought, "I'll be dammed if I'm going to go to those NA meetings too. They better get me off of this shit pretty damn soon." I think I told the nurse who was washing my hair that I wanted to give her my babies maybe a dozen times or so. The shower was the absolute best in my entire life and I told them so! Heather was laughing as I heard her say, "Sorry ladies, I'm afraid that you have awoken the beast, I'm damn glad that I don't work here!"

They brought me back to my room. The hospital Barber was there and gave me a haircut and a shave. I could tell that he was a smoker the smell of him was sour and a bit repulsive. I thought about the last sixty years I've smoked, I have to wonder how many people I repulsed with stale cigarette smoke. I'm pretty sure that I'm a reformed smoker, starting today.

All during my haircut and shave the nurses and Heather were teasing me and cracking wise. It felt good in my heart to hear Heather laughing. She's has looked so serious, so drawn and drained that I was afraid I would never see a real smile from her ever again. I promised myself that I would make a 200% effort to get back to normal, in record times. Heather needs and deserves her comfort. I will work my ass off to heal and make us both whole again. I don't remember the nurses or Barber leaving.
I woke up to hearing the unforgettable and melodic voice of Paul Roberts and I felt myself smile.

Chapter 34 DEAD AWAKE

I looked at Paul as he said, "It's me, your buddy boy! I hear you've been slacking, just laying around and making people wait on you like you're some kind of a big deal. You've gotten so fucking lazy that you won't even feed yourself. Can they maybe jam a pork chop with mashed potatoes down that tube for you, ya lazy bastard!"

I was frustrated not to be able to shake Paul's hand. Paul continued with, "A few of the airlines had to put on extra flights to accommodate all the people who want to come and see, "His Majesty the Honorable, David J Brown!"

Me: Good to see you Paul, now shut the fuckup. I know you've been doing some of your sly power moves around this joint, while I've been loafing. Such as you buying me the best of care with that million dollar donation. And yes, fuck you! I don't want my name on any dedication plaques. I don't want anything that shows that I had anything to do with this. I do greatly appreciate your efforts. I understood that these digs that I'm enjoying at the moment are also of your hands. What the fuck else have you been up to, to embarrass me?" Paul grinned as he said, "Oh not much really, but I will tell you this, I'm taking this 'Little Hottie' sitting next to you, out for dinner tonight. You can't come because you're not even invited."

Me: How nice of you, 'Buddy Boy' you rotten prick! How is Jane and the rest of the crew?

Paul: Jane is at your house, we have been staying there for the last eight days, to care for the dogs, so this lovely young thing can swoon over your lazy ass.

I'm pretty sure your dogs like Jane a lot more than they like you, you grumpy old bastard! Jane is in great shape and she is anxious to see you. Edna and Amanda are coming in tonight. Since you shredded my passport and made me step down from my own corporation, I had to turn over my private jets to the company. So now I have to make reservations to use my own goddamn jets, you bastard. And what is the shit about my girls having to kidnap a Catholic Priest? You sarcastic, sanctimonious, sacrilegious, son of a bitch!

Me: Pauly boy, this is serious. Sit down, shut up and listen. This my show and I call the ball. *Capeesh*?

Paul we can't make any part of this about me. I've been thinking about those two paramedics that brought me back. Yes they saved my life with CPR and the drugs they administered. I just can't help think of the hundreds of people that laid on that very same stretcher, in that very same ambulance, who lost their lives with those very same two paramedics. The story, this story has to be about the men who saved my life. If you want to dedicate whatever you're million dollars will do, for the Burn Unit, do it in their names. Paramedics make less money than police officers, firefighters, nurses and postal carriers. If you have a few extra bucks to throw around, throw out a check to them for $10,000 each.

Paul: How many paramedics work for that company? Let's just say maybe twenty employee's times $10,000 is only $200,000. Is that all your life is worth, you cheap prick? Every employee of that company will get a "Good Citizen Award" plaque and a check from David Jay Brown books LLC for the amount of $25,000 each. Don't forget that those Paramedics also saved Jane's life! What else are you going to gouge me for? You, rotten bastard?

Me: I need you to run the show for me with the media. I'm not feeling all that swell at the moment. Will Amanda and Edna becoming with Father Martin and will they be arriving in time tonight for dinner?

Paul: Yes my lord, they will be wheels down at 5:42 this afternoon.

Me: Good you will have one more guest for dinner. Doctor Phillips will be joining your crew for dinner. I want her to sit next to Father Martin for reasons that are none of your fuckin business. Looking at Heather, "Will you take care of that sweetheart?" Heather nodded her head. "Doctor Phillips can't say no, understand?" Heather again nodded her head. Paul looked at Heather as he asked, "Doctor Philips has to sit next to Father Martin?" Heather smiled sweetly as she said, "None of your business, 'Buddy Boy!"

Paul: Jesus Christ David, now you've got her calling me, "Buddy boy?"

Heather again angelically smiled as she said, "Careful Paul, he will have the entire world calling you 'Buddy Boy' before the sun goes down tonight." Heather pointed at the grease board she said, "Read it." Paul started laughing as he said, "You asshole, you call your primary Physican, "Gwen?" I have to assume that neither her first nor middle names are Gwen. You call your Neurologist, "Ice man?" You my good man, are some kind of fucked up! I fully understand way they're calling you, "Wild thang!"

Me: OK you guys let's get serious now. I need your help with all this media bullshit. I don't have my full wits about me. I need you to speak for me. I only want to thank the paramedics and doctors and nurses.

Then came a light tap on the door but it didn't open. Paul got up and answered the door. There was the unit charge nurse and four suits, two men and two women. All wearing lanyards with hospital photo ID's. The charge nurse asked if they could come in. Paul glanced at me and I nodded my head. Heather stood up and said with a strong directing voice, "No one is to step within five feet of my husband. We must protect him from germs and any bacteria's. He has open wounds that must be guarded." she reached over and pulled the chair alongside my bed and firmly said, "No closer than the back of this chair!"

The charge nurse and the suits all nodded their heads. The players were; the Hospital Administrator of the 380 bed hospital, the Chief of Medicine, the Risk Management Officer and the fourth was a media, 'Pool Reporter,' for all the networks.

Paul introduced Heather, then me and finally himself as my personal emissary. "All questions will be directed to me. Mr. Brown is not to be directly addressed." Again, four heads all nodded.

The hospital administrator said she was there only to observe the interview and to protect the patient's rights with, "HIPAA privacy rules." The chief of medicine said nothing, the risk management guy said, "Yes, me as well." The pool reporter said he only wanted to make an outline for tomorrow's dedication and the one million dollar donation to the hospitals Burn Unit. Paul said, "The donation is from a private foundation that demands absolute anonymity. The dedication will be given in the names of the two paramedics who saved Mr. Brown's life. They will be present tomorrow so you can meet them in person." Paul smiled at the hospital administrator as he said, "Your doctors and nurses also saved my wife's life when we were visiting from Chicago a few months back. Paul turned to the reporter and said, "There has been a grave misunderstanding about the amount of the donation. The donation is not, one million dollars (he paused for the desired effect he then said) the donation is for ten million dollars." The group of five all collectively gasped as Paul casually smiled. After the group regained their composure, the reporter asked if he will be willing to speak to the Chicago affair with Mr. Brown and the grocery store projects. Paul paused and then said, "Father Martin and my wife Jane, will speak of that after tomorrow's ceremony." The reporter then asked, "Is it true that Mr. Brown's project has gone nationwide?" Paul said, "Yes only because of Mr. Brown's tenacity, many projects are currently being developed in several cities throughout the nation." The reporter asked, "Can you tell me about the poster board sign outside of this room that reads, "Wild Thang?"

The charge nurse asked Paul if she could answer. Paul nodded, she said, "Mr. Brown has won the hearts of the entire nursing staff. Due to Mr. Brown's warmth and kindness along with his quick and colorful humor he was dubbed as, "Wild Thang" as a term of endearment. Mr. Brown is a wonderful person, a wonderful patient and incredibly wonderful novelist." She pointed at my stack of books as she said, "Mr. Brown has saved many lives as both a Paramedic and a Police Officer. He now touches people's lives all around the world with his writings and helps damaged people turn away from their darkness. Now that's pretty wild, wouldn't you say? Hence, "Wild Thang!"

Reporter: "Thank you nurse, Mr. Brown's story goes much deeper than any of us reporters have realized."

Me: If I may sir, you of all people, should know that for every good story, there is a great, back story. The reporter was both blushing and gushing as he said, "I had no idea, I thought the story was simply just about some unknown author who was struck by lightning and was becoming famous for taking on the city of Chicago. Now I get the whole "Wild Thang" thing, yes Sir I surely do!"

I smiled as I said, "I think that's enough for today. I will see you all tomorrow, please remember that Mr. Roberts is my point man." They all thanked us and left the Room. I looked over at Paul and said, "Slick move in waiting for the 'Power heads' and reporter when you dropped the ten million dollar bomb. You're a good man, Buddy Boy." I asked him, "How many Bills did you drag along with you on this trip." Paul answered, "All of them, they all want to see you. I have six of them with me here now. You have had two Bill's outside your door as soon as Heather called about your accident. You have become rather famous of late. Your safety is important to all of us, we love you."

Me: You may want to hold off on the love stuff for a while. After dinner, I want to see the entire family and the Padre, back here. Heather, you take Jane to the house, you are officially off of night watch. I want you to sleep in our bed to get a restful night's sleep. Paul if you would not mind rounding up, "The Bills." I'd like to see them all, now if I can. I also want to check out their wardrobes!" Paul started to laugh as he gave me the finger and said, "Watch this," Paul took out a key fob and made a big display of him pushing the button. I'm laughing as I said, "Asshole, you can't auto-start your limo from here." Before I could give Paul the finger in return, in burst six very serious looking, rather large fellows all with their hands inside their suit coats and their heads on a swivel. Paul and I both laughed as everyone said hello. Heather put herself between them and my bed as she issued the now, 'standard warning and rules' of approaching me. The Bill's complemented Heather on her crowd control techniques.

Chapter 35 THIS AIN'T OVER

I remember Heather kissing me goodbye with her saying, "I am going home to shower and dress for dinner. Thank you for giving me the night off."

I woke up to the sound of laughter. There was the entire Chicago crew minus Jane. I asked what time it was and Gregory said, "It's 20:28." I had to think for a moment before I realized it was actually 8:28 p.m. That told me how slow my mind was, it was shockingly embarrassing. I have used military time for fifty years and now I have to think about it. I wonder how much of my other functions I have left or lost.

Gregory: You prick, you bust our asses about the, 'Bills' attire and here you lay in what, a 'one size fits all' hospital gown. Yeah you got style dude!

Amanda: That "Wild Thang" sign says it all doesn't it? You ever do this shit to us ever again and my 'Big Brother' will double tap your fucking skull! I have never felt so heartbroken when we got the news. Dad sent cell videos of you with all those machines you were hooked up to and all those wires. It just crushed me. Mother was so torn up that I thought we might have to hospitalize her. I just felt so damn defeated that I couldn't even comfort my own mother! That told me how much you mean to us. I was searching in my mind why I was so deeply affected. It took me a few days to get to the true guts of it all. I was putting on my makeup. I looked at myself in the mirror, when the answer came. I realized that you are the first person in my entire life to ever look at me, but you don't look at me you look in me! You did it the first time we ever met. You have always done that. I hate you and I love you at the same time. You scare the shit out of me and yet I feel perfectly safe with you. It took me this long to understand what your eyes were telling me. You are saying that I did not have to lie to you. You always knew the truth, you saw deep into my fears and told me that my fears are not real. You gave me approval without you ever saying a word. I'm beginning to think that I understand Father Martin's suspicions.

Me: I held up my hand to stop her babbling with saying, "Baby the only thing I ever look at when it comes to you is your butt. Now give me a kiss." Amanda leaned over and kissed my forehead and stepped back.

Next in line was Edna. "You are some kind of a bad ass. You take 50,000 volts, you died, and now you're laying here giving us shit? The only time I ever saw my husband cry was when Mother had her stroke. When we got the call on you going into cardiac arrest, Gregory broke down like a little kid. How in the hell does an uncouth, uneducated man that we hardly know, take over our hearts and life's?"

Me: Edna honey, I didn't and don't take over anyone's, anything. I didn't take your hearts or your life's. You gave them to me. Unbutton your blouse and show me that hard steel you're wearing.

Edna: Oh it's there, you know damn well it's there, you pervert! If I wouldn't have to go visit my darling Gregory in prison, I would ask him to shoot your ass, and yes condition one, as always!

The door opened and two hospital maintenance workers pushed in a cart stacked with chairs. As they were unloading the chairs, I noticed for the first time, the black and yellow tape on the floor. I asked a maintenance man about the tape. One guy said, "You're wife had us put it down a few hours ago. It runs all around the bed and is exactly five feet from all around the edge of your bed. She had us measure it twice, just to be sure!"

Paul: Well "Pajama Boy," kindly tell us why you called us altogether on this fine evening would you please?

Me: Kids have a seat. Before I start, I want to thank you for bringing Father Martin along. Padre I trust you found your mission with Doctor Phillips?

Father Martin: David, you may be temporarily out of commission but your intuition has not failed you, not at all. You are still able to follow, and do God's work. Doctor Phillips and I have plans for several sessions in the next few days."

I could see and feel the tilted heads and raised eyebrows. I smiled and said, "Buddy Boy, you want to tell em?" Paul grimaced as he said, "Excuse me Padre and ladies, but David would like us all to know that that's none of our fucking business. Did I get that right there, Pajama Boy?" I gave Paul the finger and we all laughed. I could feel the apprehension leave the room, obviously Paul knows how to put people's anxieties to rest, I was greatly proud of him.

Me: Guys, I wanna make this brief. But first tell me how dinner was. Did Heather eat a full meal?

Paul: When we got back to your house we all talked for a few minutes before Heather said she needed to take a twenty minute nap before her shower. Jane checked in on her and she was sleeping soundly with the three dogs wrapped all around her. We didn't have the heart to wake her. Jane stayed behind and I went to dinner with the crew.

Another tap at the door and in walked a middle aged, attractive, rather heavy set redheaded woman in a crisp white nurse's uniform with full cherub cheeks. She looked like she has been happy every moment of her life. She acted startled to see everyone in the Room. Paul jumped up and said, "Hello Ann, we're just having a brief family meeting and we will all get out of here in just a few minutes. The nurse nodded and said, "I will be at the nurse's station," She left the room.

I looked at Paul and asked, "Who is Ann?" Paul, said, "Oh shit, I'm sorry I should have introduced you to her." Father Martin got up and left the room.

Paul: Ann has been your, private duty night nurse, since they moved you from the ICCU and took you to, "The Burn Unit." She has sat up with you for nine straight nights. I told her four days ago to take a few nights off and I would have another nurse to come in to look after you. Ann flat out refused, she said she didn't need the money and she didn't want to leave you. Ann is from, Saint Cloud, Minnesota. She came to take care of you. It seems that she has been a Facebook friend and a fan of your writings for some time now. When she saw the TV news reports that you were hurt she drove here and found Heather and volunteered to care for you. Ann is a heavily credentialed and early retired R.N. She has worked in specialty trauma units her entire career. I checked her credentials and took her to the hospital admin for approval to place a private nurse with you. They were more than happy to oblige. She has refused any type of payment. One of the Bills followed her to her car and got her license number. One of Gregory's federal friends ran her license plates and found out where she had her car financed and we paid off her car loan. I don't think she knows it yet, let's keep this a secret. We also followed her to her hotel, we arranged for a refund of her credit card charges and we have her hotel stay covered for as long as she would like. I don't think she knows that either. I hope we can get out of town before she finds out.

It is obvious that she feels a deep kinship to you. She is not just a wacked out fan like, Kathy Bates in the movie, 'Misery.' She told me that she was a severely beaten child of alcoholics. Her parents were killed in a car crash and she was adopted by a very nice couple when she was eleven years old. Both of her adoptive parents were and still are sober alcoholics long before her adoption. I put our best two investigators on her and everything checks out. And asshole, you can wipe that look off your face and no she does not own a baseball bat. We have hidden cameras in this room to keep you safe.

Tomorrow morning you will have a private meeting with all of those twenty-three paramedics from that company that saved both Janes and your lives'. A bordering ambulance service will be running their calls during our get together. Each of the paramedics will receive the $25,000 certified checks along with Ann. It will be just our little secret. Paul took out his phone as he looked at Amanda and said, "Will someone wipe David's tears please as he said into his phone, "Father you may come in now, if you please."

Father Martin came back in escorting Ann. Father brought Ann to the edge of the tape line, and said, Ann Gifford, please meet Mr. David J. Brown. Ann blushed as she said, "I have already met Mr. Brown, I have changed his dressings and bathed him every night. We have just never talked." The room roared with laughter just like the old days of the drunkin bowling team of a time past. Ann said, "This is the first time that I've seen you awake. I've heard your voice when I first came to the door tonight, to start my shift. I have watched your TV interviews and listened to all of your Podcast interviews over and over. Your voice is even more smooth and melodic in person."

Paul said, "David, I think your friend Ann, should sit with us, as you tell us of your need for this meeting. I smiled at Ann as I asked her if she could handle some tough talk. Ann started to giggle as she said, "My husband died two years ago from cancer. He was a police officer, he was a filthy mouthed fellow much like yourself, remember that I've been sitting with you for eight nights. You Sir, talk in your sleep, you and my husband would have been great friends!"

Me: Ann honey, lean over here and give me a kiss on my cheek then have a seat.

Well kids you ain't gonna like this. None of you will like this but you need to hear me-out, before you hold a pillow over my face. We must slam on the brakes for the entire grocery store project! Right now, and I mean tonight, not tomorrow but now, tonight!

Father I have never come at you directly before, but I am coming at you now, head first! I need you to write a press release tonight. I need it to go out tonight. I want every person in the Greater Chicago Area and the National Networks to chip a tooth while eating breakfast in the morning. I want it to go to all of your Chicago area newspapers, the mayor's office, the school board, the archdiocese's daily paper, the unions and anyone else you can reach. Rather than me having to twist the lovely Roberts families' arms to get this done, I'm asking you to be the arm twister, you might even have to snap a few bones and possibly separate a few shoulders. It's just that important. So everyone listened tight, the grocery stores projects will absolutely fail! It will never work with Chicago's liquor laws. Do you know that a store can sell liquor only a hundred feet from a school, a playground, or a church?

You know God damn well that the minute these stores are open, that the pricks of commerce will be watching and doing feasibility studies. If they see any activity they will try to buy up the surrounding properties and put in a liquor store, a gas station and convenience stores. Those businesses do nothing but draw all the maggots of the streets. Gang bangers, junkies and drunks will set up camp and stay. We need to stop that now! It will ruin everything, those big money fucks don't care about the families, the kids or the elderly. I don't know if you have to have all of the buildings around our stores condemned or request a special 'hundred year moratorium' on the properties within two city blocks. Maybe we can build a P.A.L. gym, off duty police officers man those buildings and the street thugs know that. Maybe a boys and girls club, maybe a clinic, maybe a neighborhood skate park and playground. Hell I don't know but I do know what liquor stores and convenience stores do to neighborhoods.

Father Martin: That scares the holy hell out of me. You are absolutely right about all of that you have said. I will carry this ball to the end zone and I will use the Roberts family to block for me!" Father Martin stood up and said, "Kids, David Brown has spoken from, "Upon High," we better get to it. There is much to be done, we need to leave now so David can get a decent night's sleep.

I woke up to see Doctor Philips sitting in a chair next to my bed. I saw that she had my first book, "Daddy Had to Say Goodbye" in her hands. I asked what time it is and how was dinner? She smiled as she said, "Dinner was absolutely wonderful. The Roberts family are all very sweet people. I found Father Martin to be a delightful man, we are going to spend some time together after the dedication. Father said he has a story to tell me about you, but only if he has your permission. These people are all madly in love with you. Never mind what time it is, it's late.

Me: How nice for you and what the hell are you doing here and what the hell time is it?

Doctor Phillips: The hospital has reassigned my patients to other physicians. You are my only patient.

Me: Cool, I've never owned a Doctor before! Paul Roberts bought me my very own doctor! Do you hate me babe?

Doctor Phillips: No, I don't hate you but after tomorrow you will be hating me. Don't call me, "Babe", call me Gwen. Mr. Roberts is a wonderful man and $10,000,000 buys a lot of considerations. I will be spending some time tomorrow with one of the nation's leading burn specialists who will be doing your skin grafts, compliments of your friends of the, "Greater Chicago Area." Your first surgery will be in two days. Tomorrow is going to be your, 'free day'.

Heather has scheduled visits with your friends who are more than just a bit anxious to see you. I now have something to tell you. I should have told you sooner but I wanted you to have some time with Heather and your friends.

David, I know that you have asked about your increased blood draws and have been suspicious of the nurse's answers. There are times that I wish you didn't know so much. You know that you have had a low grade fever for the last two days, but you haven't asked about it, because you already know the answers. Your white blood cell count is rising, almost hourly. It is not through the roof but it is certainly cause to be concerned, especially with your family history. I have meet several times with a trusted and close personal friend who is a heavily experienced Hematologist. He has suggested a spinal tap and a bone marrow draw for a more accurate platelet count. It's your call but I personally advise against it.

Me: Excuse me Gwen, but do you have trouble with saying, Cancer or Leukemia? And don't bullshit me with that, "Trusted and close personal friend," garbage. Tell that cheap prick to buy you a decent engagement ring. I saw your eyes sparkling just now, and oh yah Gwen, nurses love to talk.

Doctor Phillips: Stay in your own lane, smart ass and yes I am terribly upset with your blood work. I have been a Physican for twelve years. I have never been so deeply moved by a patient. I have fallen in love with your kind and loving heart just like everyone else. My boyfriend tells me of his Leukemia patients suffering and how it breaks his heart, but he has to push his pain away, to treat his patients. I worry about him. I become blurred with yours and his two personalities, both strong, both kind and both elusive.

Me: Gwen, I think you're a swell gal but you don't have to protect me. I know my body, and my family history. If it's Leukemia I will deal with it later. What is important here and now, is that I recover to my maximum ability's. I can see the stress in Heathers eyes, she is losing weight which she can't afford to lose. Her posture tells me that she is feeling helpless and defeated. I'm sure she is having flashbacks of her brothers suffering and finally his death. I can't have that. Do not tell her about my blood work problem. I want your word Gwen. I know that you are bound by law with patient's rights but I have also seen your heart. I want you to promises me, right now!

Gwen: You son-of-a-bitch! You are determined to make me tougher than I am.

I know what you are doing. You are a sweet man. Yes it will be our secret.

    Me: God damn it Gwen, I only asked you what time it is, I didn't ask you how to build a fucking watch! What time is it?

    Doctor Phillips: It's 1:19 am. Ann and the hospital called me. They told me you were running a bit of a temp. I was just going to briefly stop by to check in on you. That was about 9:30pm. David, something strange happened at dinner that I can't put my finger on and I felt restless. I couldn't help but smile as I looked over at your dwindling stock of books, knowing of your generous heart. I sent Ann home for the night. I found a big part of my truths in your books. David I'm a speed reader, I read for enjoyment but not always for content. That is where you tripped me up. Every chapter caused me to pause, but I refused to get locked into it, so I pushed thru chapter after chapter tightening the building knot in my belly. I continued pushing forward but I knew I was lying to myself. Every chapter tore at my heart, but I couldn't let it seduce me. I just couldn't allow myself to feel that pain, but your pain became my pain and I couldn't allow myself to admit my deep sorrow that I was feeling for you. You were the entire topic at dinner tonight. When I came to check on you, I knew when I looked at you, that I had to get honest with myself. I have to let myself go and just ride the waves. I know I had to shut down my brain and read from my heart. So I picked up 'Daddy Had to Say Goodbye' and this time, I begin reading it as it is written and I was intrigued by the author. I daresay that you are a lovely and a very brave man.

Chapter 36   WITH DEEP APPRECIATION

The next thing I remember was that once again, morning came early. The bathing crew with the 'cherry picker' for the full body wash and hair shampoo came in the door.

After my bath the Barber was waiting with Heather, the Robert's clan and of course Father Martin. Heather, Jane and Ann were the only ones who looked well rested. Father Martin look like dried dog shit, the rest the clan didn't look much better.

As I was being shaved by the Barber, Edna said, "At 1:30 this morning we were about to draw straws to see which one of us gets to shoot you first. But like always, you are right. The mayor's office called on our way over here this morning and it seems that the papers Father sent has the Mayors ass in flames. I would never make any kind of a statement about you being charming but you sure do however, know how to get your way. Is there a chance that our daddy fathered you back in his days of extreme drink? You're just like him with a slight annoying brashness that I don't enjoy. I don't know if I hate loving you or I love to hate you. You are a good man and a total prick all at the same time."

After my shave, I was dressed in the clean hospital gown and they laid me into a high back, wide wheeled chair made from jell foam. They wheeled me and the carts full of the monitors that I was tied to, to a private, hospital employee dining room.

All twenty-three paramedics were there in uniform standing around on one side of the room. We were all on the other side of the room. It looked like a silly scrimmage line that you might see on Saturday Night Live. The Paramedics thought they were there for an appreciation breakfast and to see their two fellow workers receive their plaques of appreciation for saving my life. They had no idea about the $25,000.

Father Martin stepped into the center of the room to say a few words and give the blessing before breakfast. I said, (louder than I intended) "Ann, you are on the wrong side of the room, go stand with those people over there. Ann looked puzzled as Heather took her arm and escorted her to the group of paramedics.

After father gave the blessing, Jane and Heather crossed the room and stood in front of the group. Jane introduced herself, Heather, the family and me. Jane told the group about her stroke on-board of her aircraft and the paramedics who saved her life.

She asked them to step forward. Heather took out a fistful of envelopes from her shoulder bag and handed Jane two of them. It was as if Jane and Heather had rehearsed that routine a few times beforehand. Jane asked for a hug from each of them and handed them the envelopes. Heather than asked the two paramedics who treated me and saved my life to step forward. She hugged them both and gave them their envelopes.

Paul stepped up, took an envelope from Heather and the three of them walked to Ann and presented her with her envelope. Father Martin passed out the remaining envelopes to the other paramedics. Paul then said, "David is still at high risk of infection, please keep a five foot distance from him. We ask that you each keep silent about the contents of your envelopes. Please only share it with your immediate families. Your envelopes are all for the same amount. You may now open your envelopes. There were looks of bewilderment and tears, followed by celebration laughter and non-ending thank yous.

It was crazy making for me to have to sit there and smell their food with my having to look up at my IV standard hanging above me, with knowing that I had to wait for another week or more before I can eat anything.

I was tired and I had to fight to not nod-off. I thanked everyone and asked to be excused to return to my room. I begged off the early afternoon Burn Unit dedication donation or whatever the fuck it was. I was still tired and felt more than a bit embarrassed to be seen in the hospital gown and in a wheelchair by a bunch of strangers.

I was awoken by three people in full surgical garb. I recognized Doctor Phillips eyes. She introduced me to the Chicago surgeon and some other Doctor that was an Anesthesiologist. Dr. Phillips said, "David, we are going to open your dressings to exam your leg. I fear that your leg is infected and you may be on the edge of Gangrene. I am going to take a few samples for a lab test. As she was cutting the bandages away, the Anesthesiologist started to play thirty questions of my medical history. It was pissing me off because Gwen and the other Doctor were looking down at my leg and looking up at each other, talking in a whisper. I knew damn well that the, 'gas passer' was trying to distract me and talk loud enough to cover up the whispering.

After they were done with rewrapping my leg Gwen said, "I am going to personally deliver these samples to the lab. We should get the results back in a few hours." I saw Gwen stick a pre-drawn syringe into the IV port in my hand.

I woke to Heather nuzzling my ear. I was pretty groggy and it took me I few minutes to realize that I was looking at Heather standing in front of me but yet she was still nuzzling in my ear. What the fuck, am I back to hallucinating again? Have I just been having this colossal, mega dream? Am I spiking in my coma? Is this actually check out time? Is it over for me? How many levels of pre-death are there? I wonder if I will be able to watch my soul leaving my body.

I felt wet on my face and realized it was Heather with a cold wet washcloth. She smiled as she said, "You are fine baby. Every now and then you just drift away for a few seconds. The doctors say that it is a normal reaction for your condition."

I didn't dare tell her what my thoughts just were. Just then and lucky for me, the Roberts crew all came tromping in. They were actually very quiet. I looked at Amanda and said, "Either you are bare foot or you have tossed away those hooker heels and learned to walk like a lady."

Amanda: He's fine, fuck him, let's just go home. As she leaned over to kiss my forehead, I felt her tears spill on my neck.

Jane was patting my arm as she said, "The doctor said we could each kiss you before we leave. Of course the final decision is up to my third daughter here, Heather. Yes it is easy to fall in love with Heather."

Paul: Well 'Pajama Boy,' we came to say so long. We will be going wheels-up immediately following the dedication ceremony. Dr. Phillips told us that you had a slight fever and didn't think it would be a good idea to visit you after all the dignitary handshakes and risk germ transfers. David, I don't know how to say goodbye to you, none of us do.

We have been briefed on the procedures you are about to undergo. Our hearts hurt for you, deeper than we can even say. Doctor Phillips has assured us that she will be with you every step of the way. I know I can speak for us all in saying, friend fight the good fight, push through and win. You my darling man, have taught each of us how to truly fight, fight to win and then….win!

We had hardly finished with the kisses and air hugs when three people wheeled in a surgical cart with Doctor Phillips. Doctor Phillips said, "People, it's time, I must ask you to all leave now. Heather you can come with us to pre-op after you put these on."

Heather was handed a stack of what I could only think was the same clothes as the cart pushers were wearing. The door closed behind the last of the Roberts family filing out.

Doctor Phillips: David, you are in trouble, big trouble with your infection. We are going to do a complete three phase, split-thickness graft right now. We are going to use fresh donor skin from a younger person so the graft should heal quickly. I will give you a few minutes with Heather after we get you prepped. Sorry for the short notice, let's go ladies. There was a flurry of hands pulling monitor leads off of me. I felt like I was sliding down a steep, enclosed water slide.

Chapter 37 HURTING YOU TO HELP YOU

An unfamiliar male voice said, "Welcome back to the land of the living!"

Who the fuck was that? Who is talking? They are talking from far away and they sound like they are muffled. I can't get my eyes to open. I can see a shadow over me, but I can't get my eyes to adjust.

Male voice: How do you feel, are you warm enough?

Me: I don't know.

Male voice: Are you in pain?

Me: I don't know.

Male voice: Thank you for warning us.

Me: I'm getting cold. What warning? Who are you and where am I?

Male voice: You are in post-surgical recovery. I turned up the heat on your blanket. I am your Nurse Anesthesiologist my name is Ken. I can give you something for pain anytime you need it. Let me know.

Me: Ken, I think I could use something now, my leg is starting to burn and my back feels like I was kicked by a mule, what warning?

Ken: You might feel a little cold in your arm for a few seconds. You and your wife both warned us about your reaction to anesthesia. Neither of you understated the possibilities. We normally don't tell the patient's what happens in surgery but you gave us more than we could handle. I am sorry but we had to restrain you and you broke loose twice. I have never had to lay on top of a patient to keep the bed from tipping over. I'm sure you strained your back during your struggles. I have never witnessed the strength you displayed, not from any size man. Can I ask you something?

    Me: Sure Ken as long as you make my arm cold again, my back is killing me.

    Ken: David, your x-rays show that you have had a broken neck and arm, along with several broken ribs but no surgical scars. You also have several wicked looking deep knife or sharp object scars, only one scar shows that stitches were used to close the wound. Were you a P.O.W.?

    Me: No buddy, what you were looking at are the remnants of the life of a severely beaten child. Ken sucked in air as he said, "David I am so sorry, I have no business asking you these questions. During surgery, Doctor Phillips was telling us about you being an unrelenting advocate for abused children and recovering adults from child abuse. She told us about your two novels, that she said, "Those books will take you to your very core."

    Me: Take it easy Ken. You have done nothing to upset me. This is a subject that I must talk about, at every given opportunity. I understand that most, if not all patients that do become combative in surgery is all out of fear.

    Well, not with me pal. What you witnessed with me, was pure unadulterated and unbridled rage. I was fighting my demons. I had to fight because I knew nobody was coming to help me. Today I fight on two fronts. Every day I must choke the shit out of my inner demons. Every day I have to tell myself that I cannot run away. If I don't tell my truths, I will become my own victim. Now if that hasn't put you on your ass, I would like another taste of the cold stuff screaming into my veins, if you will.

    The cold came fast and I found myself laying deep into the bed.

    Me: Ken, how long have I been here, it seems like for fucking ever?

David, this is Doctor Phillips with Heather. You are in a sterile sealed room and you must remain here for the next four days. You can have no visitors. If all goes well we will start physical therapy then. It shouldn't take more than eight to ten days for you to be able to walk again.

Me: Bullshit Gwen, I'll be strolling in six days or less under my own power. I guess that's the only way I can get out of this chicken shit place for a smoke.

Doctor Phillips: Heather, now that you can see that you got your man back alive and he is still the same asshole as before, you have to wave goodbye and leave now.

I slept a lot. I kept hearing vacuum doors sliding back and forth. It reminded me of being in Paul's jets and Amanda's break away pod with all those vacuum doors and heavy locks.

Doctor Phillips: David, this is your third full day in this chamber. You have been a very good boy, mostly because of the drugs you have been given. Tomorrow evening you will be leaving this unit and going back to your solarium room. The burn specialist is quite proud of his work and of your recovery. He is going back to Chicago after he visits with you and me for his final exam and report in the morning. But for right now my dear friend, we are going to have dinner together!

I couldn't wrap my head around what she just said. I was even confused for a minute or two. Am I going to actually be able to eat food? Like real fucking food? I haven't even thought about food for a long time now.

Either I telegraphed it or I looked up at my IV bags as Gwen sharply said, "Don't you even fucking think about it. You still need IV fluids, you're not getting steak tonight.
We are starting on a soft diet. You will get unflavored Gelatin, and one very specially prepared soft boiled egg. And for desert my good man, Ice water!"

The next afternoon I was being slowly wheeled from the burn unit. The nurses were lined up on both sides of the hallway reaching out and touching my arms and wishing me well. I could feel their love and I remembered the painful looks in their eyes every time they had to turn me to change my dressings. We both understood that they had to hurt me to make me well. These ladies define the term, "Angels of Mercy."

    Heather and Doctor Phillips were standing in the hallway, the nurses stopped so we could have a kiss hello. The door to my room was open. As they were turning the bed to push me in my room I saw my, "Wild Thang" poster was missing. Heather read my mind and said, "It's ok, you'll see." Heather dialed her cell phone and I heard her say, "He is in his room now" as the nurses transferred me into my bed. Heather looked at Gwen and asked, "Now Doctor?" Gwen nodded her head and said, "Yes, he has been an awfully good boy!" I saw Heather pick up a carafe and poor a steaming cup of coffee. I almost pissed myself with joy! Gwen smiled as she said, "Go easy cowboy, you get only one cup three times a day. Not a tumbler but a cup. Now help me Heather, what's that word he likes to us so much when he is bullying someone? Yea, there it is, that's it….*CAPICHE?"*

    Those two women laughed and giggled all through my first cup of coffee in eighteen days.

    There was a tap on the door. It was Ann and Ken. It surprised me to see Ken, I didn't think I'd ever see him again. They had what looked to be a wrapped large sign.
They held it as they asked Heather to unwrap it. It was my, "Wild Thang" sign with an additional top sign that had two rocker lines that read, "The one and only" (on the top rocker) and "The original" (second rocker). The rockers were lettered like a circus sign would be with all those crazy colors. It was now one sign and framed in what looked to be teak wood with bright gilded edges. I saw Ken nod at Heather and her nod back. Heather announced, "Ladies sodas in the cafeteria are on me. We are going to let these two boys talk all about the biggest deer and fish that they never brought home." Heather kissed me and the three ladies giggled out the door.

Ken: I have something to tell you. I was way out of line in the recovery room the other day. It is understood in our industry, that we never engage our patients in personal conversations. I work for two different Anesthesiology groups. I have assisted in Doctor Phillips Surgical Suites many times. She was always quiet and all business. She didn't allow any cross-talk or joking. But with you, she was serious at first then as things went along so smoothly, she became someone that no one had ever seen before. When she started talking about you, we all kept looking at each other with WTF looks. I guess I foolishly thought that I had license to speak freely with you, from listening to Doctor Phillips.

Mr. Brown, I felt guilty as hell for bringing up your past pains with you. Even though you said it was a non-issue, I still felt that I violated you and my professional responsibilities. I went to Dr. Phillips the next day and told her of what I did to you.

She stood up from behind her desk and grinned with a hard set jaw and said, "If it were anyone else other than Mr. Brown, I would pull your dance card in the medical field and you would be trying to feed your family on fast food wages. I don't think you were foolish, unprofessional as hell but you, like the rest of us, have fallen to David's charms. David had his way with you. That man can seduce you when he is fully placed into a medically induced unconscious state. You gave David another soul to reach out to. Obviously he got to you. I won't belittle you with a scolding. Now I have work to do, see yourself out."

Mr. Brown Sir, my wife and I both downloaded your books and finished them late this morning. You showed us a world that we never knew existed. We worry about our children and the influences of other children. We always hope we are doing things right by our kids but you never know what they are thinking. Your statements about children's perceptions throughout your books certainly do support that. We have never taken a family vacation. Mostly just weekend visits at relatives cabins during the summer. We also were brought to the realization that neither of us have not spent any 'real time' with our parents or grandparents. Christmas and birthdays are pretty much it. I haven't sat down alone with my grandpa since I was a little boy. Not much different with my dad. We let life get in our way and miss out on what is really important. Family, family is everything.

    Me: Ken, shut the fuck up for a minute and catch your breath! Stop with that Mr. and Sir bullshit. You have earned the right to call me Dave. My name is Dave, call me Dave. *CAPICHE?*

    So you're leading up to telling me of some kind of wonderful vacation plans to far away locations, where your eight your old daughter will have tea with Cinderella and your seven year old son can hang out with some pirates and Buzz Lightyear right? Don't do that stupid shit. Your kids will be nuts, they will make you guys all nuts and your parents and grandparents will be exhausted and suffer from aching joints and feet.

    Now don't answer, I'm tired of listening to you. Just nod your head. Do you or your family own a cabin or property on a lake? Ken nodded his head. Good, now you listen up and listen hard. Little kids don't need or even want the cutesy shit we throw at them. Little kids want to be listened to, they want to be respected and to be treated as they are special. Not any different than big people.

    Do this, arrange a week with you guys, your kids, grandparents and great grandparents. Go buy a dozen of each or even more, of Birch and Pine tree seedlings. Plant two of each tree in a special place that the kid picks out. Special place and special trees for each kid, for each grandparent. Help them do it, don't you do it yourself. There will be a time my friend, when great grandparents, grandparents and even you and your wife will all be gone. You are building memories. Someday your children will have children and you will be a grandparent. And when you are gone your grandchildren will have a special place to visit with grandpa. It's a fuck of a lot better than going to a cemetery and a headstone to visit. Take the kids to Wal-Mart or somewhere so they can pick out cartoon character fishing poles and help them catch sunfish and tadpoles and other stuff. Sit and talk with your kids and grandparents, more importantly listen. Mostly listen!

So, Skippy, you done wasting my time? Hustle your ass out to the nurse's station before those nasty girls get back. Get yourself a fresh cup of hot coffee and keep your mouth shut. And no, you do not use cream or sugar.

The ladies returned from their soda party only a few minutes after the coffee disappeared.

Gwen: David, Heather will help you with your dinner before she goes home for the evening. Ann will sit with you tonight. I will check on you before 10:00pm.

Dinner consisted of unflavored gelatin and another soft boiled egg. I tried to feed myself but my hand was too unsteady. Heather finished feeding me, and told me she would come back in the morning before she went to work and left for the night. It made me smile to know that Heather was going back to work and trying to return to some sense of normalcy. I still didn't like the way she looked.

I looked at Ann and told her I needed to close my eyes for a bit but she was to wake me when Doctor Phillips came back. "Ann, it is very important that I speak with Doctor Phillips tonight, this cannot wait until tomorrow. Promise that you will wake me Ann?" Ann nodded her head and said, "I promise David, get some sleep now."

I woke to hear Doctor Phillips and Ann whispering. I startled them by saying, "You girls planning to do a bank job? There is no whispering allowed around me. Gwen have a seat, we are about to have our first fight." Ann started to get up as though she was about to leave the room.

"Ann, stay seated, we might need to have a referee. I trust you both to hold my confidence. We are all buddy's here right? I am growing damn tired of hearing of everyone else's plans for me but nobody asks me for, my impute. Well, here is my plan. First, Heather is barely able to keep her feet under her. I don't think that she has slept or eaten a decent meal since I've been here. Gwen,

Heather will be here at 7:00 am tomorrow. You must convince her to allow you to give her a high mega dose of, Vitamin B-12, IM. Please prescribe her a sleeping pill as well. I can't lay here and watch her crash. Either you do your best, "Loving friend" act or I'm going AMA. I trust your supreme ability's will not let us down. Secondly, I am starting to get the shakes from my high doses of pain meds. I could hardly hold a spoon in my hand at dinner. I want you to cut my meds by 75% starting now. I won't allow myself to become a god damn zombie. I had to watch my mother go through that shit all of my childhood, I fucking hate junkies."

    Gwen and Ann were both sitting back deep in their chairs and I realized that I must have been giving them my, 'thousand mile death stare'. I instantly felt like an asshole but they must realize that Heather is in trouble and they are our only hope. That's when I could feel my chest heaving as I said, "I am sorry to have frightened you ladies."

    Gwen: David, I greatly appreciate your passion and love for Heather. Yes, I very much agree with your assessment of Heather's condition. I will convince her of the need to give her a Vitamin B-12 shot tomorrow morning.

    As far as you demanding that I reduce your meds by 75% is not safe or realistic. I wanted to wait for a day or two longer before I have a discussion with you two on your current condition.

    David, you say you are a big boy and you can take it, no matter what. I am not telling you this to test your mettle, but since you brought on this conversation I have no choice but to respond as your Physican. Ann would you please call the nurses station and have them bring in three cups of coffee? I want you to be here for this.

    David, I am very pleased with your progress overall. Your surgeries went very well and I am quite happy with the results. David, we don't have a problem but we do have a situation. You are smart enough to know that most problems can be fixed, and most situations rarely can be fixed. We must learn a way to adopt to our situations. We must accept these conditions as our new normal. Only then can we move on."

I held up my hand to stop her as I said, "Gwen, do you mean this? As I held up my trembling hands. Yes, I know about lighting strike victims who often times develop Parkinson's type tremors. You read that to Heather and me several days ago. I think she was still in shock and didn't have the ability to listen, with all the fears dancing in her head. I have intentionally been keeping my hands under the covers when she is around. I think she might have caught me tonight, when I forgot and tried to feed myself. I tried to cover it up by saying that I can't wait to get off the pain meds as they were making me jittery. Guys look, I have been a liar most all of my life, there were times that I would lie when the truth would better serve me, I was just that self-conditioned. I stopped that shit twenty-eight years ago when I got sober. Now I am lying to protect Heather and it is becoming easier to lie to myself. I hate this shit, I hate every bit of it! I have to get my head right. I sure as hell wish Father Martin was still in town!

Gwen: David, good news on that front. Father Martin is still in town. He is coming buy to see you tomorrow.

Now about that lying business, you already know about that information that I had withheld from you. This afternoon when Heather said, "Now Doctor" as she poured you your first cup of coffee, was a set-up. Heather caught on a few days ago. I had her pour you that coffee and hand it to you to watch how you were going to grip and control the cup and hold it while you drank.

David it is too soon to tell if your hand trembles are temporary or permanent and if permanent, to what degree. David I know you are a high energy guy with no quit in you but you have to be realistic with all this. You have suffered from several, all but life ending injuries. David, you can't just brush this off and walk away. You still have some very serious injuries that we still don't know the full extent of. I am going to put this as straight to you as I possibly can, and I am most certain that Ann will agree with me.

David my friend, you fucked yourself! Ann has read your books several times and I am into my second re-reads. You're the guy that shouts from the mountain tops about trust and faith and dealing with life on life's terms. How we must take it head-on, no matter what. Where the hell is that guy now? Show us that fierce warrior who has so many times placed himself in great peril to save a total stranger, without ever expecting so much as a thanks. Bring that fighter to us, bring him hard and ready for battle. Bring him to fight, to fight for his own life.

You wrote in your last book about Sylvester Stallone, you showed a great deal of reverence as to his charictor as a man. I remember in one of his movies, where I think he was talking to his son about how life isn't fair. How life will put you down and keep you there, if you let it. How nobody will hit you harder than life will. How life is not about how hard you can hit, but about how hard you can get hit. You gotta be willing to get knocked down, get up and move forward and risk getting knocked down again. You can't blame anyone for your failures but yourself. Take your punches and hit back, keep hitting until you win. You have to be willing to win. I think my favorite line in that entire sequence of that movie was, "You're better than that!"

I know that I'm preaching to the choir but damn it David you have lost your focus. You fight for everyone, you teach them and you show them how to win. And you show them how to keep winning and even how to win for others.

Your readers, your people, need you and……'Skippy'……you need them!

Heather has stacks of 'Banker Boxes' full of copies of emails and letters from your readers. They all write how you have enlightened them and given them the hope that they couldn't find for themselves. Father Martin is coming in to sit and talk with you. I would pay money to sit in with that conversation and listen to him jack your ass!

Chapter 38 CLIMBING INTO THE RING

I woke up to being alone in my room. I was startled not to see Ann sitting there, but it felt kind of good to be alone. The sun was just starting to come up over Lake Superior. The sky was glimmering with a deep purple-salmon color that was shifting to a bright red hue. That would make a beautiful post-card, without question. It brought back the old saying that I have heard and repeated most all of my life.

"Red sky at night, Sailors delight. Red sky at morning Sailors take warning."
That little rhyme is a true statement. Well hell, I think there is another storm brewing, maybe even boiling at this very moment from my little tiff with Doctor Phillips last night. We went pretty hard at each other. I don't remember if I fell off to sleep or if the good doctor 'put me down' like ole Shep.

I know that she was trying to provoke me into getting honest with myself and deal with what I was facing in the future. I knew I was trying to minimize my fears of my greatly restricted future life. Knowing my sarcastic mouth and my drugged up mind, I'm thinking that I will have a few amends to make to at least two very kind and loving women. I chuckled as I asked out loud, "Which of these storms will break first, the lake or the ladies? I vote for a severe thunder storm that rattles the windows and floods the streets. It would be much less scary!"

A light tap at the door tightened my stomach muscles. It was a nurse that I had never seen before. She paused and looked at

me rather strangely before she said, "I have orders to disconnect your heart monitor and remove your electrode patches."
She removed the wires and said, "I will try to pull these off fast, so it won't hurt too bad." Before she started to pull off the patches, she said, "You have a very large collection of patches." Before she could start, in strolled Heather and Doctor Phillips. Heather looked a little better, but her eyes were still sunken and dull looking. As she approached me the nurse stepped back, as Heather leaned over to kiss me. The nurse said, "Excuse me, I can come back." Doctor Phillips held up her hand and said, "Nurse, stay where you are and do your job. Do not use a 'quick pull' technique. Take it slow and easy. Mr. Brown is a tough guy, let him show you how tough he is. He just loves to show-off!" Three women roared with laughter. Doctor Phillips placed her hands on her hips as she said, "No whimpering allowed, Skippy!"

Doctor Phillips: Well Rocky, are you done sparing? Are you ready to step into the ring? Are you actually ready to fight?

Me: Only if you step in the ring with me.

Doctor Phillips: Oh hell's yes I will! No more of that silly little girl shadow boxing you've been doing. I'm going to bring it to ya, let's just see how well you can take a punch.
We both laughed, but I saw her nostrils flair and I knew she is going to push hard to get me on my feet.

Heather: If you two are done with playing patty-cake, I have a man to feed and a job to go to!

Heather gave me a playful glairing look as she said, "I understand that my loving sweetheart has arranged for me to have a needle slammed in my ass on this fine summer morning. It would be a shame if I accidently spilled this tumbler of ice water on your chest."

More laughter as Doctor Phillips pulled a sealed vial and empty syringe from her lab coat pockets. She said to Heather, "Hike your skirt and pull em down" as she was drawing to load the syringe. I so much wanted to tell her to hike her skirt higher, but I knew that the whole, 'ice water thing all over my chest' was not an empty threat. I just sat and smiled. Heather read my mind as she said, "That grin on your face will earn you a cold bath, asshole!"

All during our exchanges, something felt strange, I guess I felt it right away when the nurse came in the room. But it just didn't register at the moment other than the nurse looked very young. But then again at my age everyone looks young. I would have picked up on it sooner, but those ladies had my head so twisted I couldn't focus.

Doctor Phillips: Don't get used to that bed you been laying up in like a king. From this point on, this bed is strictly for sleeping. When you're awake you can be sitting in the upright chair or in a wheelchair. We're going to start your physical therapy this afternoon, as soon as you're done with Father Martin. We are going to go for a stroll as soon as Heather finishes feeding you. You're going to meet some very interesting people who are even more interested in your health and well-being than you are. I'm sure they will change their minds about that, in a short period of time. So we're going to have several meetings. I'm going to introduce you to the physical therapy staff that you will be working with.

I said ok, and it sure as hell didn't take long to eat a soft boiled egg and some more that tasteless shit gelatin. Heather gave me to kiss and out the door she went to work. The nurse was still standing there and hadn't done anything. Doctor Phillips told the nurse that she could leave now and she will have someone take care of those leads. The nurse left the room and Doctor Phillips sat down. She had a grin on her face that made her look like a twelve-year-old naughty little girl. I'm thinking ok let's have it.

Me: So Doc, tell me about the game you're running on me. That nurse is far too young to be a nurse and it just so happens that she didn't do a damn thing and beyond that she is an exact copy of a younger you. So once again, what's up Doc?

Doctor Phillips: Excuse me for laughing but Heather told me that we would never pull it off. That young nurse is not a nurse, she is a second year college student who just so happens to be my niece. She is in love with writing, books and movies but mostly she likes script writers and now authors. She has gotten to meet a few authors but she thought they were very pious and standoffish. I wanted her to see what a real human being was, that just so happens to be an author. I think you've turned her around from what she thought she wanted to be. Originally she wanted to be a writer herself and maybe even going into movie script writing. You showed her the human side of life, not the best side, but she did get to see the human side of the author living as a human being.

    She of course read both of your books and now she got to see the man without all the props and fanfare. I promised her that if it would be alright with you, that I would schedule a meeting for her, to actually meet you. I hope you will talk with her about being an author and maybe help her with some of her career goals and David, I must surrender and admit that you are far quicker in observation than I am. I reduced your pain meds just last night and you show none of the fogginess as most patients do. Are you suspicious about everything and everyone in life? Rhetorical my good man, of course you are, you were a cop.

    Me: Doc, you know I will. I like young people who are smart enough to know that they need to learn before they can do. I find that quite refreshing and courageous.

    Doctor Phillips picked up her phone and dialed a number and said, "We're ready now." Then came in four official looking, real nurses. They said, "We're, going to help you to transfer from your bed to your wheel chair."

    Doctor Philips: You don't have any strength in your legs currently, you have heavily atrophied. We're going to assist you in everything you do, when it comes to standing, sitting or lying down. It's going to take several days for you to start to get your balance and get your muscles coordinated to work for you. In the meantime we will take care of you to prevent any further injuries.

    Me: "Several days" you say? Bullshit! I will be walking in three days. Let's get this party started!

The transfer felt a little awkward but they got me in the wheel chair and hung my IV bottle to the standard mounted on the back of the chair. The good doctor said, "We are going for a spin. First stop, I want you to meet that, "Cheap Prick" you took a couple of swipes at. I think you'll like him, he's a very nice man." She wheeled me down several different hallways, took the elevator down a few floors and down a few more hallways and came to an office that read, Doctor Leonardo Armstrong, Chief of Hematology.

He got up from his desk and came around and we shook hands. He went back to sit down behind his desk, he had a very light hearted smile on his face as he said, "David you did not break into the leukemia arena, you were very close, scary close, but your fever's would drive your white cell counts. Those weren't false reports, just indicators that you have the same genetic blood make-up as your family does. I'm sure that's not a surprise for you, so you're in the clear.

Now about that statement you made of me being a, 'cheap prick' with my fiancée's engagement ring. In my defense I gave Doctor Phillips, (who I understand you like to call Gwen) the choice of either having a very nice and expensive engagement ring or she could have a new engine for her race car. "Gwen," chose the new engine. So I hope this explains the, 'cheap prick boyfriend' myth. We both race midget dirt track cars and snowmobiles and it's a very expensive hobby.

We chatted for a couple more minutes and Gwen said, we had to be on our way, as we were leaving his office, I looked back and waved and muttered just loud enough for him to hear me, "Cheap prick!"

The next stop was Doctor Fisk's office, aka "The Ice Man." He was very cordial as he said, "You're too early in your recovery to be able to measure what is damaged and what needs to be revitalized. Keep in mind that the human body consists of mostly water. The brain and heart are at approximately at 73%, lungs 83%, skin 64% and muscles and kidneys are 79% and bones 31%.

Your overall water level is only at 65%, that's why we are pushing ice water and the IV's. Remember how I told you, that you could trick the body and not the brain. Well the body can trick you too. Part of your physical therapy is to find out what you might need if anything, as to repairs. Much of that is up to you and how hard you are willing to work. I understand your pain meds have been greatly reduced, you will find muscle and nerve groups that you have always taken for granted. You pushing hard through all of your physical therapy exercise will help those nerve endings reconnect. We have to see how far you can bring them before we can come up with a plan, that is, if in fact we even do need a plan.

Some patients although rarely, will not require another surgery. We will just have to see how it goes. So again, a lot of it has to do with your own dedication. So at this point, we won't be seeing each other until after all of your physical therapy. One word of caution, I know that you are a hard driven fellow, but find a balance so that you won't hurt yourself further. The number one injury in people that are recovering from muscle and nerve damage comes from patients that push too hard without assistance. Patients who haven't walked for a lengthy period of time, such as yourself want to think that they have their full ability's and end up further hurting themselves. Don't think that you can rise from your bed or wheelchair without help. You will do a face plant that you will never forget, I promise. Any questions?

Me: Yes Doctor, not a question but rather an observation. I have a corner room at eight stories high with a full view of Lake Superior and the bay. You're camped out in a fucking dungeon. Do you need some help in getting an upgrade? You do know that I'm kinda a big deal around this joint, right?

Next was the physical therapy staff. Gwen introduce me to five people. Four women and one man. This is where Gwen started strutting like she was an army general with a riding crop in her hand slapping her high-calf black riding boots. She said, "Folks this man's future lies clearly in your hands. What you do with and for him will determine and define the rest of his life. Not just as to his ability to have free movement, but also his mental, emotional, and even spiritual structures. You have a large job in front of you, our patient, Mr. Brown here is more than just a bit of a smart ass and he will try to work you over. At some point you will want to tell him to go reproduce himself. Here is what I want you five young people to think about when it comes to Mr. Brown's caustic, sarcastic mouth. Think back about when you were bullied as a little kid in school. There was always that one bully. Remember what you thought you would like to do to that person but you weren't big enough and you weren't strong enough to fight back? Remember how you wished that you could tell him exactly what you think of him? Remember? We all have had those meanies in our life's that still bothers us in our minds today. Well right before you at this very moment, sits your bully. And now you have power over him!

Mr. Brown does not get any relief from anyone, it's too dangerous. Mr. Brown oftentimes looks at kindness as weakness and if he sees it, he'll take advantage and will think he can hedge any corners he can. Don't let him do it. My goal is to discharge Mr. Brown in fourteen days from this day. Don't let me down!

I thanked them all with a big grin and said, "We'll just see how tough you guys really are."

I said, "Gwen take me to lunch." She said, "I can do better than that, I'm taking you outside for a stroll around the hospital and we can visit all the flower gardens."

The first thing I did was reach for my cigarettes which of course I didn't have.

Doctor Phillips: "Skippy, you are so damn habitual, no you're not going to smoke. You can enjoy some fresh air and this beautiful scenery. Fill your nostrils because it's going to be awhile before you get to do this again.

Me: Where did you pick up that, 'Skippy' bullshit from?

Doctor Phillips: Your friend Amanda suggested I call you 'Skippy' back when you were unconscious, so you would know that she was here with you.

You should know that after tonight, Ann will no longer be with us. She's going back home, she knows that you don't need her help any longer and she's just hanging out now. She wants to go back and see her family. She has grandchildren and two grown adult kids. We're having a little going-away party for Ann tonight. It will be held in the large Doctors conference room. There will be a number of people stopping in. Ann has touched a lot of people's hearts. She's a wonderful person and she has made a lot of friends around here. She is highly respected with all of her credentials and her sweet kindness. You got lucky when you found her or she found you. I think it was just one of those things that was meant to be. But you didn't you hear me say that, because I'm a professional scientist, so just leave it right there!

If you haven't figured it out yet, all of this pampering bullshit is going to go away rather quickly. So, I can tell my niece that you will meet with her?

Me: Yup, anytime my schedules free I'll be happy to sit down with her.

Doctor Phillips: Father Martin will be by to see you this afternoon. You do recall given him permission to tell me about something rather private? After Father meets with you he will meet with me.

Me: I've got a pretty good idea what the 'private matter' is, as a matter of fact honey, it's written right in my second book.

Doctor Phillips: Yes I know it is, I just couldn't believe that it was all true. I just thought I was reading a very knowledgeable writers works, when it comes to the spiritual life. I had no idea that you actually had that true conversation. I only have fourteen more days to enjoy this freak show that you brought to me. I'm certainly going to miss you when you go. And don't call me honey!

Me: Gwen, I've got plans for your niece. Tell her she must attend Ann's party tonight. If by chance she is busy, tell her the deal is over.

The meeting with Father Martin went quite well. He just quietly listened and told me I was doing the honorable thing but not the smart thing. He said, "You can't protect everybody you care for, you used to try to protect the entire world. How did that go for you? The world is still there and it's still a mess. I understand that whole thing about feeling vulnerable and weak and pathetic looking, but you're not looking at the fight you have fought just to remain alive. That in itself is an incredible story. Allow yourself some room for your own humanism and show the people that care for you and have to look after you some respect. They are tough enough to love you and they deserve to be told the truth. You always push yourself off as their healer, allow them to help you heal. It is time that you champion yourself."

We had some light chat about how the program with the Girls and Boys Town went. He gave me an update on the grocery store arm twisting. Now the stores are going to be deemed a part of the school curriculum so it actually has a classroom in each grocery store so that gives us a larger distance buffer. The mayor and his council have quite seriously taking on your recommendation as to a moratorium on building in that area. I think it's going to fly. Speaking of flying, I've got a flight to catch and I still have another very special person to visit with.

I smiled as I said, "That 'very special person,' thinks I'm fibbin about a conversation you and I shared and I wrote about. Oh and, Padre, she likes to be called 'Gwen' when she's not wearing that silly hospital coat."

Chapter 39   HARD TO THE BONE

    I requested another bath and shave to attend Ann's going away party. I was more than just a bit surprised to see the number of people that came into the room. Of course, Heather bought some beautiful gifts for Ann, as well as a number of the nursing staff brought gifts. There was a catered Mexican food lay-out along with a beautiful chocolate cake that I knew I wasn't going to get near, and it was killing me!
    When Heather took me back to my room there were two more of those plastic USPS totes full of letters. Heather said, "Looks like Ann will have something to do tonight." I looked at her as to ask what she was talking about and she said, "Ask your babysitter."
    Annand I talked for several hours back in my room that night. She had made a list of every topic or name that I mumbled in my weeks of sleep. She told me that she did that for both Heather and the Quinn's but she herself was quite curious as to some other names. She asked me if those names were real or those were characters names I was developing for my new book. I said, "I don't remember what I said while I was sleeping, will you read them off to me?" It seemed like she read those off for several minutes. I said, "Well who wants to know about this, you or the Quinn's. Ann said, "Well I'm quite curious and you know I have nothing to do all day long since I've retired and I'm thinking this

maybe the time to take a stab at writing now that I've have seen how easy it is!"

We laughed as I smiled and said, "Anny girl, you wanna party, I mean really party?" She looked at me with a quizzical look as I said, "I know it's coming with the Quinn's, I know they're going to be up both of my nostrils wanting to know everything about everything about everything. I know they were here during the early days and they stayed with Heather most all day and well into the late evening. Part of it was they were doing it from their own hearts. I have no questions or qualms with that.
The other part is, they're gathering data. I am certain that we will be having some extensive meetings, reference to all my meanderings while I was either unconscious or asleep. How would you like to join in that little party? And if you would like, we could put you up in the Corker Hotel. You can stay there all during this time at no charge, that's the dining room as well as room service. I owe a huge debt of gratitude and I want to repay the Quinn's for all they've done for Heather and for me. I will repay you as well, so if you're up to the challenge to join our little club, you are more than welcome. I'll let you know when we are going to start. It won't be for probably a couple of weeks yet, but I think you'll get a kick out of it all. Ann said, "Well, I've already met the Quinn's and they filled me in about you, to quite an extent. You really are an incredible person, and those two little farm people, Marge and Axel. I just adore them, I just wanna hug him every time I see him. I don't leave in the morning until after they come-by to say hello."

Me: Then we got a deal, I will let you know when I blow this pop-stand and catch my breath. I want to spend some home time for a couple days then we will get after it.

Ann: I feel funny about bringing this up because I feel so undeserving. David, I came here to care for you because you filled my heart. I did not expect anything in return. What you did for me in your writing is something I can never repay. When you guys gave me that check I was absolutely stunned. My daughter called me this morning to tell me that she opened the mail (she picks up and opens my mail for me every day) and she said, "Mom, it's the title for your car with a 'paid in full' receipt from your bank!"

David, I just bought that car four months ago. I took out a six year loan so I wouldn't have to worry about making a late payment in case I have a financial emergency. I did well with my 401k and I have modest savings account that should carry to the age of 80.

Then I did an early check out at my hotel this afternoon and packed my car so when I leave here in the morning, I can drive straight back home to Saint Cloud. My knees trembled when the desk clerk slid my credit card back to me and smiled as he said, "Your stay has already been taken care of." He wouldn't tell me who paid for my room. David, these things, these kind of things, aren't supposed to happen for people like me. I don't even know who to thank!

Me: Slow down sweet sister Ann. You want to know who did these things for you. I will tell you, hell I'll even show you! But would you mind getting me a warm wet washcloth first?

Ann went into the bathroom for the warm washcloth. When I heard her turn on the water I said loudly, "Ann look up at the mirror. That's who you have to thank." Ann spent some time in the bathroom. When she did come out she was teary eyed. She started to walk towards me with the warm washcloth and I held up my hand with, "Ann honey, the washcloth is for you, now sit down. You are deserving and that's all you need to know. Tell me about what Heather meant about you would have something to do tonight with those two post office totes.

Ann: I hope you don't mind but I alphabetized and sorted all the cards and letters you received with return address. I have put together a master list of them and sent them to you and Heathers email. I will be happy to do these new ones tonight.

Me: Don't you fucking dare to sneak out in the morning without saying goodbye to me. No, you don't get to whisper, by-by. Wake me up, I want a morning hug and a hot cup of coffee with you before you leave.

I woke up to the smell of fresh coffee. Heather and Ann were talking softly. I laid there quietly to eavesdrop on their conversations. I still have a nagging feeling that there are some things that no one wants to tell me about. It makes me grateful that they want to protect me but it also pisses me off that they don't think I'm strong enough to handle it. If you want to piss me off and watch my blood boil, all you have to do is underestimate me. You will see a wall of blinding, rolling flames that will not burn out, it will grow and take on a life of its own!

I coughed and opened my eyes. Heather smiled and said, "Good morning, 'Sleeping Beauty,' how do you feel?" My voice was a bit croaky when I smiled and said, "Good Babe's, doing good."

Me: Thanks for hanging around Ann, I was almost certain that you'd be burning gas by now, on your way back to your life.

Ann: Not a chance big boy, you promised me a hug. Besides you gave me a look last night that told me I didn't have a choice. It reminded me of Sister Kelly, my first year nursing instructor. She was a tyrant and you just knew that you would burn in hell if you ever crossed her.

Me: Cute. Sister Kelly, a catholic nun, 'burn in hell', 'crossed her'? I see what you did there.

Ann: You looked like you were planning my demise or some other kind of evil in your sleep. David I have watched you sleep for almost three weeks. I watched, (studied is a better word) your sleep monitor and of course the other machines you were wired to. What I find so interesting is that you had absolutely no facial muscle movement, all of your vital signs showed steady-normal but your brain monitor would scream activity. There were times that you would spike so sharply that I thought you were going to launch into outer space. The doctors would just shake their heads and say, "There is no explanation for this. We have never seen this before."

I'm not a fan of Sci-Fi but it was like your brain was running a marathon and your body was in a totally different room sleeping. You freaked everyone out.

You my dear man, are your own television network. I sorted your new boxes of mail, you have some letter reading to do. I have a hug to collect from you, and a 144 mile jaunt to get home to love up on my grandbabies.

Chapter 40   BUSTIN BALLS

Well, as advertised, physical therapy was a total bitch. They had me hanging from a trolley kind of contraption from the ceiling that looked like one of those sex swings. My feet were just barely touching the ground and there is this overhead mini crane that would part walk me and move my body forward to make my feet keep up with it. I had to have a couple shots in my knees of cortisone because they just didn't want to loosen up. I wish I would have kept my mouth shut with reducing my pain meds by 50% but I will be damned if I will tell anybody. I was really feeling that pain from physical therapy and I was exhausted. I slept fitfully every night. After the fourth night I came to realize that this may be part of that, "New Normal," bullshit.

I felt that I needed a distraction, maybe more like a greater purpose to offset this grind. I told Doctor Phillips to, "Send me your niece after my physical therapy tomorrow and I'll be happy to sit with her for as long as she would like, or until I fall asleep from this ass bustin you've been giving me. You better know that I will tell her the truths about life and the industry she thinks she wants to dive into. Oh and yes, I don't want her showing up in 'Jammie pants' or tie dyed anything. She will present herself as a lady or the deal is off.

Doctor Phillips: She has lived a pampered and sheltered life. I think you woke her up with your books. I was hoping that college would bring her around but she is still insulating herself with all the, smiley-giggle groups. I would much rather you snapped her out of it before life has its way with her. She is in no way prepared for the fucking life will give her. Please be gentle but firm, if that's even possible for an asshole like you!

Little Miss Carrie Lynn Phillips, was sitting outside my door when I was being wheeled down the hall from physical therapy to my room. She's a very pleasant young lady who seemed to have her wits about her, I already knew that I would like her. I intentionally didn't offer her a seat. I started with, "So Miss Carrie Lynn Phillips, here is my first question. How do you feel about dashing down the hallway to the nurses station and getting me a hot cup of black coffee, am I asking too much of you?"

Carrie Lynn: Oh no sir, not at all. I'll be right back. Carrie Lynn launched out of the room like an Olympic runner and was back in a flash. She was a bit wide eyed as she said, "The head nurse at the desk showed my where your coffee maker was, in the meds room. Did you know that you have your very own coffee maker? That's pretty cool." I smiled as I said, "Yup, it's amazing what $10,000,000 will get you!"

I motioned to her as to where to sit down. I said to her, "Carrie Lynn, I will lead our conversations. Is that clear? So my first question to you young lady, is what's in it for you? The time you're willing to spend with me begs me to ask, what's in it for you, and what do you think you're going to get from me? I want specifics, Carrie Lynn and I want to get to know everything about you that I possibly can. I want to know all about your writing, how you write and more importantly why you write.

Carrie Lynn: Well Sir, I've thought a lot about it. After reading your books I realize that I don't have the skills or the style to do anything like you do.

Me: You are right young lady, you may come close but neither you nor anyone else can write like me. I wrote about my life, the life I lived. My pain, my fear, my hate and my blood, it all belongs to me and to no one else.

You can try to copy me, but readers can smell and taste a faker from miles away. You will commit suicide by literature. Once you lose your creditability in this world you might as well become a politician. I would never tell anyone that they can't be a writer. Who knows, you could very well be the next Agatha Christie or Sue Grafton.

As long as I'm pushing you around, knock that shit off! I am not a Sir or Mr. Brown, I am Dave. Furthermore, don't make the fatal mistake of judging yourself against anyone else. That is a dream killer!

There is an entire world out there that will be more than happy to stomp your ass and destroy you, without even knowing your name. You don't need to do it yourself. Now continue young lady.

Carrie Lynn: Why do people have to be so mean?

Me: Baby Girl, understand this. Water's wet, rocks are hard and fuckin people are mean. The reasons are many, but to boil it all down, brings you to the very same conclusion each and every time. Jealously is your answer, jealously is always the answer. People are jealous because they want to be you and they know they can't be you. It tells them that they are less than you, so they want to, and will go to great lengths to destroy you so you can be at their level and feel their pain. That's some pathetic shit all right but that little girl, is our world. The only people that will cheer for you is your family. Don't make the mistake of thinking the world loves you because you love the world. You got that? Let's move on.

Carrie Lynn: But sir, look at you. Ah, I'm sorry. Let me start over. But Dave, look at you. The world does love you! Everyone is in love with you. The nurses are a little jealous of me because they have to work and I get to sit with you. I guess I get your point now about how others want to be you. I sure hope nobody here hates me.

Me: People, some people, more like just a few people, do love me. Most people accept me without prejudice because I gave them everything that I have of who I am. Don't expect that to happen for you and just so you know, love don't pay the bills.

Now, Carrie Lynn, it is time for your renaming. Have you ever watched the old cartoons of, "The Jetsons?" Well sweetheart you remind me of the Jetsons daughter Judy. Check it out when you get time. Judy Jetson is a total babe and very sweet and respectful. So, hello Judy!

Carrie Lynn: This is so cool! My Auntie told me that if you give me a nickname it means you really do like me. Like, really like me. Thank you so much! Please do call me Judy from now on.

Me: You're welcome Judy. And Judy, you have just broken a major rule with me. You let me run out of coffee!

Judy bolted from her chair and was off to the races. With a fresh cup of hot coffee I smiled as I was about to pull Judy's covers.

Me: Judy you asked earlier why people have to be so mean. Don't confuse being mean with being honest. You may think I'm being mean now, but I'm being honest with what I'm about to say to you.

Judy, you are a hider. You hang out with a group of geeks thinking you're safe. You act like a geek to be accepted, but you are not a geek. I agree with you as to what you said earlier about not fitting in. Here is what I see in you.

You are embarrassed with your intellect. You challenged and tested out of the eleventh and twelfth grades of high school. You started collage when your classmates weren't even old enough to get a driver's license. Your GPA has always been a four point plus and you will graduate collage before you turn twenty years old. You geek it up and you dumb yourself down just to try to fit in.

Follow me with this; Say you break your arm and you just wrap it in an ace bandage. We both know your arm won't mend properly without it being properly set by a Physican. But we just decide to call it good enough. A few months later you are having pain and have limited use of your arm. If it had been cared for properly, you would have no pain and a full range of motion. Now your pain brings you to a Doctor who refers you to an, Orthopedic surgeon who tells you that he will have to re-break your arm to set it properly but there is some nerve and muscle damage, that he may not be able to repair. So now you may have a lifetime of discomfort and limited motion in your arm and shoulder. All of this bullshit could have been avoided but because you were afraid of the initial pain of the surgery and you are now permanently fucked!

You are a bright girl Judy. Finish up to what I'm driving at.

Judy: I think you just told me that I make my own misery, right?

Me: Yes my dear child, you are right. And that sweetheart is how you tell the truth without being mean. You don't fit in with those people because you don't belong there or with those people. You are in the wrong place, for you. In the real world of shakers and movers you will be a superstar!

But even superstars are not loved by everyone either. Check this out, There are thirty-two teams in professional football. Training camp has at least twice if not more than the fifty-five player roster to start the season. The teams only keep the very best of the best. You don't think the tryout and veteran players that are released don't carry a grudge? So now you have the starting players, the second and third string (who are not good enough to be starters), right. The second and third string player's only hopes to become starters are if the first stringer gets injured or arrested. So more than half of the team players are praying that more than half of their teammates get fucked-up so they can play ball.

Then first string players all hate the coaches and the quarterbacks for not giving or passing the ball to them. The jealously amongst players being favored is rampant.

So there are roughly 1,760 professional football players who all secretly hate each other. Isn't that cute? Oh yes, they do those dumb-ass, end zone dances and ass patting after a good play but at the same time, their guts boil because they didn't get to make that play.

All completive sports are the same. There is only one winner. Do you think you can win a NASCAR race from the rear of the pack on the final lap? Of course not, but nobody pulls their car off the track fully knowing that they have no chance of winning. Why do they stay on the track? Because they hope the entire field crashes out, they pray that all the other drivers fail so they can win. School and amateur sports are the same. Winning, oftentimes has to do with someone else loosing.

Honey, that shit is no different in any work place. People get hired when others don't. People get promoted when others don't. People get fired and their co-workers go into a feeding frenzy to get their job and they descend on their desk to pick the bones clean before you leave the parking lot! Let go of that "We are one-we are the world" bullshit. You are a party of, 'One' young lady.

Yes, there are a lot of hospital staff here to help me. They are good people that get paid to help me. Remove the pay and there would be no one to help me!

No one except, for that lovely creature Ann! I never meet Ann before but she does love me. Ann put her life on hold and at a great financial loss to help me. She sat with me for twelve hours every night. She changed my IV bags every hour, she monitored all of the machines that were keeping me alive. She changed my bandages, she gave me sponge baths during those several days that I was in a coma and I had no idea that she was even there and what she did for me. No grandstands, No cheering, No trophies, No awards. Nothing but heart, total heart.

If you want to study a real hero, if you want meet and admire a true champion? Spend some time with Ann! Ann is my hero!

Tomorrow I need you to go to Service Printers Company and pick up some packages for me and bring them here tomorrow for your 7:00 pm shift.

For now, I am tired and I need to sleep. Go to the nurse's station and tell them that you are ready to leave. I have arranged for hospital security to meet you at the nurse's station to escort you to your car. Do not leave this floor without an armed escort, this is a dangerous area, I don't think you would enjoy being robbed and raped in the parking ramp. Do as I tell you! *CAPICHE?*

Chapter 41 WORKING FOR DREAMS

The next morning I felt like a needed a day off. Everything hurt, I think even my hair hurt! At the same time I knew I needed to keep pushing myself. I enjoyed the looks on the faces of the physical therapists when they said, "Time is up for today." I grinned and responded, "Time may be up for you, but I have a body to rebuild and I'm not done yet!"

I was getting stronger but I still couldn't walk of stand-up by myself. I looked at the wheelchair and knew it was too far away from me to take a chance. I buzzed for a nurse. I didn't get a nurse. I got Heather. She saw me leaning towards the edge of the bed as she said, "Don't even think about it. All you're going to do is fall and hurt yourself. You don't want to fall and end up in a cast, unless you are enjoying all this attention you're getting." I laid back and took a breath then said, "Yes dear, you're right dear, good morning dear." We both laughed and kissed good morning. I came to terms with my palsy condition and leveled with Heather a few days ago. I decided last night that I was going to feed myself from now on. Breakfast arrived and it was a bit different menu then the last two weeks. Today it was scrambled eggs, bacon, whole wheat toast and a blueberry muffin. Heather smiled as she said, "I ordered this for you last night, it's time you get a reward for all your hard work. I hope it agrees with you." I smiled as I told her to sit down because I was going to feed myself. She smiled as she said, "It's about time you start to take care of yourself, as soon as you can walk with a cane I can take you home. The dogs are missing their daddy."

Well that sure as hell got me off my ass. No day off or slacking for me. I really haven't thought about going home, I couldn't even see beyond the next few minutes. I guess that this is how easy it is to become institutionalized.

The P.T. tech came to get me. She is someone I haven't seen before. She helped me transfer from the chair to my wheelchair. She got behind me as I said, "No dice sweetheart, I will drive this buggy myself. I'm trying to get healthy not to be an invalid." I still had a ways to go with my arm and hand development. I bounced off a few walls on the way to PT but I made it. I told the other tech that I was done with the trapeze act and I wanted to walk on the treadmill. The tech said, "I don't know if you're ready for that, I will have to check with your Doctor first." I said, "Ok, I will wait right here, go give her a call." I wheeled out the door and into the hallway, locked the brakes on the wheelchair and pulled myself to my feet with the handrail. I was putting all of my trust into that handrail would hold me. I made it to my feet and I was no more wobbly than anyone else that just drank a quart of whiskey. Now I'm facing the wall but can't pivot my hips to face forward. I started to break a sweat as I thought, "Fuck it, I will just side step down this God Damn hall. I was pretty proud of myself with making it maybe fifty or sixty feet. Until all hell broke loose.

I heard an overhead page for, "Mr. David Brown, please return to your room." I was giggling so hard I almost lost my balance and fell down. I heard pounding footsteps coming towards me from the cross hall. I didn't realize that I was a, "High-risk protected patient." Someone brought my wheelchair and I sat down as I was getting my ass reamed by three, plain cloths cops with badges swinging from necklaces and a handful of security guards.

I didn't realize that I had a protection detail. These cops were pretty slick about hiding out in plain sight. One was wearing a matching work shirt and pants with a large name tag that read 'Maintenance' and a tool belt. One was a female in a nurse's uniform and the other one was wearing surgical scrubs. Doctor Phillips came running up with terror in her eyes.

Doctor Phillips: David, I am so sorry, we should have told you. I should have told you. I will take you back to your room and these officers will fill you in.

Me: Not without a cup of coffee you won't, as a matter of fact you better bring the entire pot.

The ranking officer, (the nurse) said, "We had picked up some intel from the streets that there may be a plot to kidnap you and hold you for ransom. We arrested two men this morning at 1:13am on this floor, heading in the direction of your room. They were pushing a laundry cart with bed spreads. Both had hand guns along with plastic cuffs and duct tape. They are both wanted felons for parole violations. When you came up missing a little while ago we of course thought the worse. I apologize if we frightened you. Please understand that there was $10,000,000 donated in your name to this hospital. There has been 24 hour police protection for you since Mr. Roberts put in the request. From this time forward we will provide a uniformed police officer to escort you and we will post an officer outside your door 24/7." I looked at Doctor Phillips and said, "Honey, call for a few extra chairs, we are all going to have us a little sit down."

Me: I am talking so don't anyone interrupt me. You motherfuckers set me up as bait. S.O.P. calls for security at the door and at times in the room with a 'high-risk patient.' I've done this dance since before you all were born.

You would rather risk my life to further your position within the department by making the arrest. What the fuck would have happened if they would have gotten to me? I will tell you what would have happened. There would have been a hell of a shootout and I would have killed those fuckers. Think how your personnel file would read about how you three caused several hospital patient's to be wounded and killed because you had a plan! I may still be a bit frail but I keep a 9mm Kimber under my pillow, I'm an excellent shot and I'm a very light sleeper.

You three should know and I am certain that you all do know, that Kidnapping is a federal offense. Part of the federal kidnapping law states that any and all jurisdictions must report any and all threats of kidnappings to the FBI immediately. Don't any of you bullshit me about making a report to the FBI or that your supervisors approved your cute little operation. Do you realize that I could have you three and the rest of your merry little band all charged with criminal negligence?

FYI sweethearts, before you puff out you chests and tell me who you all are, and what a big stick you carry, know this. Mr. Roberts has a son that is a very close friend of mine. He is the Section Chief in the Chicago office of the FBI. Now before I decide your fates, let's all of us have a cup of coffee and relax for a bit.

I then turned to Doctor Phillips. "Gwen, I am sure that you didn't tell me or Heather as you were trying to protect us from worry. You are a Doctor, you are not a cop, so you get a pass. The reason I left PT was because they wouldn't let me use the treadmill. I am not here to be babied, I am here to gain strength so I can go home and have my life back!

Me: Officers, I am sure that you are all good people and serve our community to the best of your ability's. How about we just all call this a non-issue, shake hands and we all go on our ways with no further mention.

Three heads nodded in unison as they stood and we shook hands. They left quickly. Doctor Phillips had a drawn and cautionary look on her face as she said, "I never thought of the ramifications of what could have so easily happened. I almost threw up when you talked about wounded and dead patients. I saw your power and I saw your mercy in a matter of just a few minutes. No one has ever taught me more about life as you have. You called me, "Honey" when you told me to order coffee and chairs for the police officers. I kind of liked that. Don't you ever fucking do that again!"

Me: Admit it Gwen, if there wasn't a Heather and a 'Cheap Prick' in our lives you would be sitting on my lap right now.

Gwen: Not that it hasn't been a thought but you are way too much for me. I think we both got lucky with who we have. On another note, my Niece absolutely adores you.
How in the hell did you come up with 'Judy' from the Jetsons? Her mouth ran a hundred miles an hour about how you make her feel normal and important to you. She is excited to be running a personal errand for you. Do you want to enlighten me on said errand?

I started to laugh as I pointed to the four USPS totes full of letters. I told Gwen that Judy was going to pick up 5,000 4 1/4 x 5 1/2 printed 'Thank You' cards and envelopes from the printers and she was going to respond to each letter sender that wrote a return address on the envelope.

Gwen almost spit out her coffee with laughter as she said, "You sure do know how to get the most out of people."

Judy came to my room pushing a cart with five sizeable boxes. The time was 6:58 pm. I welcomed her and told her to sit. I went on to tell her that I knew that she had more to say when she left last night. I smiled and said, "I would like to listen to what you have to say to me, Judy." She giggled at the Judy part.

Judy: You kinda know that I'm thinking about going into the entertainment field. I'm not sure what avenue I want to pursue yet. I know I don't have the skills to become a writer but I think I want to help independent authors like you. I wanna help people get noticed and recognized. I wanna help build people's careers. I whole heartedly agree that your books should be turned into a movie. I would like to be that kind of person that arranges those things for people without finances or agents.

Me: Judy there is more to it, what is your true agenda and don't bullshit me.

Judy: Well this didn't take long now did it? I was told by some other people that you don't play around, you get right to it.

Well I've never lived the kind of life you had to live, but I somehow feel that I have. I don't feel like I fit in. I know people think I have a lot of friends and I do a lot of things with a lot of the girls but I kind of feel like I don't really have a place in life. Please don't tell anyone about this especially my Aunt. I'm working on it and I'm not in trouble' but I am struggling with some depression. I know you'll understand that, but I also want to do something for you. I just don't know how to go about it. Could you give me some direction as to what I could do for you?

 Me: Yes sweetheart there are a few things. But there are a few things that you have to understand about me. I am very direct and at times very demanding, it's not personal it is just what I want. If you back slide I'm going to bring you up short, real quick. It's not that I'm angry with you, it's that I'm just disappointed in your efforts and that has no measure about who you are or what you're trying to do. So just keep that in your mind. You needn't be afraid of me and I'm not here to crush you.

 Now do you see those four plastic totes over there from the United States Post Office? Those are your first assignments, and here's what you're going to do. First open one of those boxes you just brought in here. Pull one of those cards out. Those are "thank you" cards. You are going to open and write every person who wrote me a get well card and letters. Introduce yourself as my personal assistant and just state that I'm not currently in a position to personally respond as to a temporally lack of abilities with my hands, but I felt that I wanted to recognize their kindness. You up for that kiddo?

 My dear friend Ann, who you met last week, took on the painstaking process of alphabetizing every letter and putting them in packs of twenty. Don't mess those up, keep them in alphabetical order just as you found them. You will open a letter and read it. Write your response, put the letter back in the envelope and back in the box. When you finish the pack of 20 letters, rubber band them, place them back in the box and take out the next pack of 20 and continue until you are done. You're going to read to me what's in each card and letter. Also, you must address each person by name. Is all that clear?

Judy: Yes sir, that looks like a lot of work. Can I take some of this home?

I smiled as I said, "Nope, I'm going to sit and watch you do it for however long it takes. I want you to run down to the nurse's station and asked them where the business offices are. Dash down there, tell them I need to borrow a letter opener, be sure that you tell them it's for me. You shouldn't have a problem. Hot foot it back here, swing by the nurse's station for my coffee and we will get down to business. Ten minutes later that sweet girl, with her letter opener and coffee smoothly sailed back into her chair.

Judy said, "They wanted to bring it up to you themselves, so they could meet you!" I just laughed and said, "Yeah there are a lot of people here that think I'm somebody that I'm absolutely not. I'm just a regular guy that just so happens to have written a book, two books actually and almost completing my third, but I'm just a man. I'm nobody's hero, I'm nobody's champion, I am just me.

I nodded to Judy with saying, "You better get to it baby girl, unless you want to spend your entire summer sitting here." She hesitantly reached for the first rubber band bound stack of letters.

Judy was trembling as she slid the letter opener into the first letter. She pulled out a two page, hand written letter. A $20 bill fell out. Judy said, "David there's money in here!" I smiled and I said, "Yes, set it aside, write $20 on the top right side of the letter, now read the letter." Judy started to read the letter to herself. I smiled as I said, "Sweetheart, read the letter out loud." Judy started to read, she didn't make it past the fifth sentence when her tears started to form. She gave me a confused and pleading look. I smiled as I said, "Yes, there will be money in a number of those letters, there will be tears in each of those letters. Each letter tells of a broken heart, some will be of a broken life. Look at each of those letters and as you open and read them, take a moment and realize that you are not alone.

You have just found your true purpose. Your purpose is to allow your heart to feel the heartbeat of each letter writer. You have just became an adult! You are now the adult that I can proudly call my friend. Wipe your tears and get busy.

Chapter 42   JUDY… JUDY… JUDY

Judy finished the third pack of twenty cards and letters and looked spent.

Some of the cards were simply signed get well cards. Some were brief notes and others yet, were hand written or typed letters. There was a stack of cash of all denominations and checks. Poor little Judy looked more puzzled than before.

Me: Well what was this like for you? Did you figure it out yet?

Judy: I found two things so far. I never realized how many people that probably look perfectly normal, can go through life in such deep pain and nobody knows it, not even their families, friends and co-workers. So many of these people never believed there was a way out, they just surrendered to it. A lot of these letters talk about depression and excessive drinking along with broken marriages and estranged children.

Almost every one of them thanked you for giving them hope and showing them that there is a way out. I still don't understand the whole money thing. I just finished sixty letters and there must be seven or eight hundred dollars in checks and cash in this pile. Why?

Me: Not so fast pretty girl. I want to know what you felt as you were reading those letters. I don't care what you think about your experience, I want to know what you felt in your belly!

Judy: I am not really sure yet. I am sad for those people having to live all their lives with the pain of feeling unwanted and even hated by their moms and dads. Two letters talked about always being sad and feeling all alone.

Me: Baby girl, look in that mirror there. Those two letters you just talked about, are who is standing directly in front of you. Those are your people, you may not be near them, but you are with them. Being together even at a distance helps with your loneliness when you share a common bond. There is still one more thing, I can see it in your eyes. Say it Judy, you need to say it, say it out loud.

Judy: Please don't get angry and take this the wrong way. I can see you sitting here right now, I can see that you're a living man but you don't seem real. I read chapter#30, from your book, "Flesh of a Fraud" more than ten times. I didn't even know who you were or that you wrote books until I saw my Aunt on TV being interviewed by, FOX, CNN, MSNBC and a bunch of other networks, even the BBC!

I read your books on my Kindle and saw you on TV when you were being taken out of the ambulance, you looked dead. My Aunt was on TV almost every day talking about your condition and you still being in a coma. My aunt would only say that you were stable and your condition was guarded. It's embarrassing to admit this, but I came to the hospital to try to sneak a peek at you almost every day. They wouldn't tell me your room number, so I took the stairs to each floor and walked by every room checking the patient's names on the doors to find you. I could never find your name. I saw a policeman sitting in the hallway on the eighth floor each time I went there. I figured that it had to be you. There was not a name on the door where the policeman was sitting but I was afraid to look too hard because they looked at me and it scared me. My aunt caught me when she was coming out of the elevator one night. She took me by the arm and made me get in the elevator and she took me outside. She told me to go home and that you were trying to wake up.

Every time I walked by your room the door was closed but I felt something strange. I don't really know what it was but it gave me the chills so bad that when I got home and under the covers I still couldn't warm up. It was a different kind of chills, but it was warm outside. I think the chills came from inside of me and not because it was cold.

Me: Honey come back. You were talking about chapter #30 before you went off on this side trip. Stay focused. What is it about chapter #30 that you read it ten times or more?

Judy: It all belongs together. I got the chills every time I read that chapter and I couldn't figure it out, so I would reread it. Those chills and the walking by your room chills were the same. The very same! I had those chills yesterday when I actually got to meet you and again today, right up until you told me to open the first letter. I felt like it wasn't even my hand that used the letter opener. But the second it was open, I felt the chills go away and it was almost like sitting on the beach in the sun with a warm breeze.

I feel like what Father Martin was talking about in chapter #30. You are a real person but you are not real. You are more like a spirit than a person. Almost like an apparition. I hope I haven't offended you, but Father Martin said it first.

Me: I got nothing for all that. I am just a man. Those people wrote those notes from their hearts. All they needed to be told was that it is ok to feel their pain and to let it go. They just simply needed to feel their own hearts and understand that they have purpose and they have the right to heal. I don't know anything about that mystic temperature stuff. Maybe you are a bit anemic?

Sweet little Judy jumped from her chair, smiled and kissed my cheek. She said, "I am going home and I am going to bed. I am going to sleep with the covers on the floor and my windows wide open." She opened the door and turned back with, "Anemic, you asshole?" As she gave me the finger and left the room.

My favorite barber, Bob Oliver came in for my morning shave. Bob was a real nice guy who loved to fish and talk about fishing. I am guessing Bob to be in his mid-fifty's. Bob had worked in his grandpas and dads barber shop when he was nine years old. Bob's job was to shine shoes, pour and serve the customer a shot of Jameson Irish Whiskey, and sweep the floor after every haircut. His other job was to pour a $3.00 bottle of 'Ten High Whiskey' into an empty bottle of Jameson Irish Whiskey. Bob laughed when he was telling me that no soul in the barber shop ever got near anything like Jameson Irish Whiskey other than the label.

Bob liked to rib me. He would ask me every morning, "Hey Bucko, what did you have for dinner last night" as he flicked my IV line. I would smile as I said, "Why don't you take a pail of worms for swimming lessons you no fish catching ass-buggy."

Doctor Phillips came into my room just as my, 'Blue Shirt' (police officer) was about to escort me to physical therapy. Doctor Phillips asked the officer to wait outside and closed the door. As she was about to speak I almost said, "What's up Doc" as she said, "If you say, "What's up Doc" I am going to kick you right square in the balls! This is going to hard enough, without your smart assed remarks."

Doctor Phillips: God I hate having this discussion with you. Please try to act like an adult for just five minutes would you?

Well here it is. Leo and I are going to be married eight days from now, a week from Saturday. My Daddy passed away three years ago. My Uncle (daddy's brother) was going to walk me down the aisle. My Uncle fell and broke his hip yesterday afternoon, so he's out. If you can act like an adult, Leo and I would like to ask you, if you would mind walking me down the aisle. I'm asking you to walk me down the aisle. As in WALK not some asshole in a wheelchair or using a cane for sympathy. I want a man to walk like a man. But there is something I also have to tell you and it breaks my heart because I've never really talked about it to anyone. My father, who was a wonderful Daddy was also a good man, but David he was an alcoholic and he never tried to find his way out of the bottle. When I would confront him about his drinking he would just smile and say, "You're not old enough to tell me how to live." My daddy was a very successful businessman and we wanted for absolutely nothing, as a matter of fact I never applied for any loans or grants for all my years of college. Mom and Dad footed the entire bill for all of my educational and living costs. I never had to have a job, I just went to school. Daddy was a very nice man, he wasn't mean at all. He was never cross with anyone and he never said harsh words to anyone. He mostly just stayed quiet, drank and read. My dad read all of the greats, many times over. He loved literature but he loved his booze equally as much. Daddy died from cirrhosis of the liver. He died as what you people would call, "A wet alcoholic." My Daddy would have loved your books and would mostly have loved your writing style.

David I've never met anyone like you, hell no one has ever met anyone like you. You have shown me that people that want to live sober can live sober.

You really have reached into my belief system and given me a true understanding of the human endeavor. I am so proud of who you are and what you have become. Today I look at you like it wish that you were my dad. It hurts me as a physician to have to stand away from you and look at you as a patient. But when I look at your eyes and listen to your voice I know I'm looking at a form that is far greater than just the standard, average Joe. You carry a gifted grace that is so rare, so uncommon that I too get the chills, the same as Judy. Yes I've been talking to Judy about her shivers. As a matter of fact, I understand you gave my niece reason to flip you off last night.

Well here I am, standing in front of you feeling like a little high school girl just before her first date. So now I have to ask you. Will you please walk me down the aisle? I smiled as I said, "Sweetheart, it would be my extreme honor to walk you down the aisle and when I bring you to Leo and I join your hand over the top of his, I will not kiss your cheek. I'm taking you full on the mouth, and who knows, if I'm feeling a bit giddy I just might give you a little slap on the ass!

Now get the fuck outta here, I've got some physical therapy stuff to do because some 'snot nose' wants me to do some kind of a walking thing in eight days from now, so I need to get busy!

Well the good doctor must have gotten to the people in the physical therapy department because this morning they were absolutely fuckin ruthless! I was wanting to throw-down on those mean, nasty girls. When I finally got through with physical therapy, my 'blue shirt' escort came to meet me as I wheeled myself out of the physical therapy rooms.

When we got out to the hallway I looked at him as I said, "Partner, I need you to drive. I got nothing left to turn these fuckin wheels today, would you mind?" He laughed and he goes, "Yeah I'll be happy to, I couldn't help listening to you and Bob going at it this morning." I said, "Do you know Bob, that barbering soulless dick head that tries to cut my fucking ears off every time he shaves me?" Blue shirt smiled as he said, "Bob and I are fishing buddies and actually, we are best buddies!" I said, "Oh please tell me about all of his fishing success." Blue shirt told me, "If Bob has invited you to go fishing he has put you in the, 'high regards category' and you should be flattered. He turns down a lot of requests. I suggest you go with him, I don't know how you fish but I'll tell you what, he knows more than most when it comes to catching quality fish. That and he is a lot of fun. Personally I would not let that shaky son of a bitch get near me with a scissors or a razor, but you don't have many options!"

After my beating in PT, I woke from my nap and thought I've got to get ahold of that kid. I called Judy and I said, "I want you down here now! I don't give a fuck what you're doing, you get your ass down here now. Make sure to dress like a lady, I don't want to see those Jammy pants from Walmart bullshit."

It was less than an hour and there was a tap on my door. Judy had a look of concern, maybe even a bit of fear on her face as she said, "You wanted to see me, right?"

I said, "Yeah baby, sit down. We have a lot more to talk about but first of all, you don't have enough time in the next eight days to go through all of these letters. I want you to take these letters home with you, as you suggested earlier. Just like before write a response and bring them back. I'll be having some postage stamps delivered tomorrow or the next day and you're probably going to have some ragged fingers from peeling those sticky fuckers off the sticky backings.

Late this afternoon you're going to have an early dinner with two pals of mine. They are very sweet young ladies who are quite precious to me. They will be more than happy to reinforce your anger towards this dink who is sitting across from you right now. I'm thinking there's a great possibility that the three of you can become swell pals. I am sure that they will be telling you some stories about how they got knocked around by this mean nasty bastard. They will tell you their own stories about how they got their own chills. This doesn't mean you get a pass you are still going to be here at 7 o'clock tonight and you're going to do three times what you did last night. I'm going to watch re-runs of 'Gun Smoke' while you do your paperwork, are we good with that?"

Judy: As long as I am here now, can I just stay and do my work. Would it be ok if I have dinner with you and Heather tonight? I would really like to get to know her. My aunt calls her, "Saint Heather!"

Me: Are you still freaking out about the money in those envelopes? Here is what this money deal is all about.

I have received many requests to offer an audiobook and iTunes version of my first book, "Daddy had to say Goodbye."

Judy: I thought you already did that. I read some of your face book posts about how excited you were to complete the reading of your book.

Me: Well honey here's your first adult lesson in life. Some people in some cases, many people in most cases, don't care about you and they will just flat out fuck you, anyway they can. On the other side of that, some people want so much to please you that they over extend themselves and promise results that they have no possible way of completing. So at the end of the day you end up greatly disappointed. A case in point young lady.

To have a printed book turned into an audio book it must be read, recorded and edited. The editing is the most time consuming and of course the most expensive. Just one hour of reading can take an average of four hours of editing. The average cost to have a book recorded by a top professional can easily cost between eight to ten thousand dollars or even more. I live on my social security and the very few dollars of my book sales. I only make $1.82 on a $17.95 book and I wrote it! The bulk goes to the publisher. With an audio book, I will only receive 30% of retail price and I have to pay for the production costs. There is of course no guarantee that I will ever recover my production costs let alone ever see a profit. Keep in mind sweetheart that a freak lightning strike brought you here. You or most of this city along with the rest of the country would never have heard of me. Only my friends knew that I was a writer and have published two novels. I guess there are a few people in the 'Greater Chicago Area,' who know or heard of a hard talking nobody author who bitch slapped the Chicago shakers and movers. But I digress.

So I think I've established with you that I'm a broke joker who has been a failing author from the very first day that I picked up an ink pen.

I wanted more than anything in the world to have my books go into audio books but I didn't have the money and I knew that I never would. Contrary to my own council, not all dreams come true.

After a few months of trying to shake off my disappointment (if not depression) I still couldn't let it go. I had to find a way to bring my work to the world. Keep in mind that my only goal from the first day that I began writing was to help people. Profit was not even a thought and it still is not. I want to help people like me. That's all I ever wanted.

I know that I have a deep and smooth voice that people seem to enjoy. I decided that I will have to find a small local studio and use my voice to make an audio book. I did a few face book posts asking if anyone would be interested. I was given the name of a young fellow by some dear friends of mine. They told me that he is a musician who has recorded several records for his band and a few other groups. I phoned the gentleman and left a message. He didn't return my call. I phoned him twice in the next two weeks. He never returned my call. My friend that recommended him contacted him and the guy finally called me back. He said that he had excellent equipment and the quality of the recording would be top notch. I thought this guy could be the real deal so we made an appointment to meet in person. He didn't have a professional studio but said he had a portable recording studio so we could either do it in my home or his. We met and discussed cost and time lines for release. Our first meeting was in April of last year. I made it clear that I wanted to have this audio book to be listed and for sale no later than mid-November of last year. He agreed to the timeline and said he would have it wrapped up and listed by the end of September. We agreed on three, two hour sessions a week. I paid him half down on the agreed price.

 We recorded at his home on the third story (attic) in a very old house on a busy street. The windows rattled in the least bit of wind so when I was recording reading my books, any outside noise would be picked up into the recording mix. This was not by any means a recording booth with acoustic panels and a glass enclosed control room like we all have seen on TV. There was a single light bulb covered in dust from the J.F.K. era. The microphone was a boom mic that he had so close to my mouth that it kept brushing against my nose. All he had was a single control panel that looked like a kid's toy and about the size of a New York style pizza box. There was a button to pause the recording and to flag that part for edit. It sat on a 1950's coffee table that looked like someone had been playing Ice hockey on it. I couldn't reach the button from the 'rocking horse' stool. So he said, "I got something that will work, I'll be right back." He came back in the room with a wicker laundry flip-top basket that he must have pulled out of a dumpster from a demolition site.

 Our three times a week recording session only lasted for one week. Due to his demanding job with mandatory over-time, we went to twice a week schedule. That only lasted for two weeks.

Then he claimed that he had to work double shifts due to staff shortages. It ended up being a hit and miss one session a week. I still finished the book in the first week of November. He said he could easily have it all together before the 3rd week of November. I wanted the book to be released and available on Audiobook and iTunes the very first day of December for the holiday season. Well, month after month went by excuse after excuse, challenge after challenge, according to him and suddenly, six months had gone by and no audio book. A professional studio could easily have a finished project in less than a month!

    I don't think he has the ability, I think he over sold himself, I think he is a decent guy he just doesn't have the moxie to say, "Geez dude I'm not capable, I'm sorry I failed you." So instead he just ignores me. Well I don't fucking have time for people like that and yes he's a decent enough guy but there's nothing fucking decent about doing what he did to me, because he couldn't deal with his own failures.

    I did a brief Facebook post to tell my readers and friends that there would not be an audiobook release due to production problems which are out of my control. I stated that I always sign my books, "Dreams are worth Dreaming, dare to Dream and Dream Big!" What I failed to tell myself was to dream with reason!

    How's that for a sweetheart story, and that's why you saw that $20 with the note and all the money that followed. My readers want me to have my books professionally recorded. Questions?

    Judy: That is just horrible! This breaks my heart! Who does that to someone! I want to go kill that fucker myself! How can you sit there looking so calm? Yes I can see in your eyes that this makes you sad but if I were you, I would go to war with that slimy bastard!

    Judy was on fire for sure. Her fists were clenched, her neck muscles were twitching and her eyes were wide and bulging. All I could do is smile and nod my head.

Me: Honey, here is one of my secrets that I share with almost no one, so listen-up. Prisons are full of killers, killers much like myself. No I never committed a murder but I have wanted to. I even developed plans to kill people, lots of people. Lots and lots of people actually. I was never like those psycho mass shooters. No these were bad guys, people that harmed me and others. What kept me from pulling the trigger?

God's grace my dear child, is the name of that tune. God saved me from myself when I didn't even ask him to. Honey, I lived a great deal of my life as a controlled ragger. Think of it as a bowling ball rolling inside of a wooden railroad car. Never in control, always slamming around not caring about the damage I was causing to others or even myself. At some point, either the wooden sides of that boxcar would be destroyed or the bowling ball would fatigue and shatter into dust. When I stopped drinking and got sober I knew that I had to climb out of that boxcar. An old pal of mine who has long passed, would look at me when my guts were in flames and softly say, "Calm wins." The statement of, "Calm wins" must always be far out in front of my emotions.

Sure I could go and punch the motherfucker out of him, give him a swell nose job, reset his jaw and crush his larynx so he could never lie and fuck over anyone ever again. Do you think that would magically make my audio book appear? How do I draw satisfaction from slapping the snot out of him when I'm sitting in a jail cell?

So now I may not even get to bail-out of jail because I was legally carrying a gun while committing an assault which is a felony in most all states. Now I get to hire an attorney that I can't afford, and you already know of my deep distrust of lawyers. The court will try to put me away deep into the darkest corner of the jail because they hate cops both past and present. If the prosecutor or judge read my second book I would be shot for escape when locked in my cell while being chained to the wall. Then of course comes the medical bills for repairing the little weasels face and let's not forget his lifetime of pain and suffering. Oh yea, I sure

fucked him up. I extracted my pound of flesh and he will never try to pull that shit on anyone else ever again!
And to think that it only cost me all of the money I have or will ever have. That …… and my fucking freedom!

    Baby girl, learn from me. Nobody cares how you may feel or do they give any part of a fuck about what you think. Calm wins! Now you say it, say calm wins, say it again, say it again. Do you say you're bed time prayers? (Head nod) good girl. Here is your wake-up prayer: Calm wins!

    Judy: You sure do have a way to tell it true. How did you become so wise?

    Me: A lifetime of fear that boiled into hatred that stole my soul. Get busy with your letters, I need a nap.

Chapter 43   GIRLS MAKE ME CRY

I woke from my nap and looked over at Judy. She had a letter in her lap and she was crying.

Me: You stub your toe?

Judy: This is so sad. This women's Husband and son were both volunteer firefighters. They both killed themselves a week apart. What do I say to her? What can anybody say to help her? I feel so inadequate, so helpless. I've written out sixteen cards. They are all different but all the same. How do these people keep going?

Me: Honey under their conditions they are all doing pretty good. Stop with that look of horror and listen to me. I don't have to read every card or letter to know what is in them. The mere fact that they are writing means they are trying to heal. When I glance at those totes it makes me smile. You may see sorrow and loss, I see hope with action. We are looking at the same thing but we see two widely separate views.
Which one do you want to see?

Judy: How do you do that? I would have never thought that.

Me: Honey, I have experience that was born from the horror you were wearing on your face a minute ago. Hurt is hurt, sorrow is sorrow, loss is loss. You don't have to personally experience these people's pains to understand. What you have to do is open your heart to feel their hearts. Those people's letters are their therapy. They are reaching beyond their misery to help. In short, it helps…..to help!

Baby, help me slide into that chair. We are going outside for some fresh air and touch some grass, some leaves, some flowers, we are going to look at birds and if we are lucky we might even get to see a squirrel. We are both going to put our hands on our hearts and then we will place our hands on each other's hearts. Touch your own heart, feel your heartbeat and know that you are alive because you have purpose. When we touch each other's hearts, we find the strength to give action to our purpose.

Judy: I love how you make everything make sense for me. They never teach these kinds of things in school. I love my mom and dad and they are really nice to me. My parents have never raised their voice to me. I'm a spoiled kid and I've gotten everything I've ever wanted. My parents are very kind and loving and affectionate. It's embarrassing to admit this and I know that I have no right to, but I have felt like I was that little boy in your first book. I felt that loneliness and that sadness, am I wrong for doing that?

Me: No baby, you are not wrong, we must never apologize for our feelings. We oftentimes must apologize for our actions however. But our feelings are our own. Feelings are private property. If we deny our feelings we are then denying ourselves the experience of our purpose and our place in this world. Judy you were singing the song of my people. Now let's get outside.

Judy opened the door. Before it was full open, the entire doorway was blocked by a wall of flesh. Two well dressed, very large men were standing with toothy grins as the both said, "Hello Skippy!"

It was two of the Bills! They seemed genuinely happy to see me. Their handshakes were very gentle but quite sincere.

Judy almost craped her pants as she ran to the far end of the room. The Bills grinned as they said, "It's ok young lady, we are friends of David.

David we need a few minutes with you." I looked at Judy and I could tell that she still wasn't sure if we were safe. I put my arms out to her and told her to come to me. I put my arm around her waist and she leaned into me like a small child. I said, "Sweetheart, do you remember reading my second book, and reading about Mr. Robert's security people, these are two of the gentlemen that I was writing about. These fine gentlemen are some of the Bills. We call them all Bill so as not to tip off bad guys by calling them Agent. These Bills are the top security agents in the nation. I felt Judy start to go limp, a Bill scooped her up and laid her into my bed. I reached over and pressed the emergency button hanging from my bed rail. Two nurses were there in just a few seconds followed by several uniformed police officers. When I saw a K-9 officer with a large German Shepard, the bells went off. The nurses got Judy to come around and took her out of the room. I looked at the K-9 officer and asked, "Bomb threat?" He nodded, I nodded and asked, "This is not the first one is it?" He again nodded. He then nodded at a police Lieutenant. The Lieutenant smiled as she said, "The FBI is tracking two IP addresses which are linked with cross-communications so we suspect that they are teenagers playing around, we hope to have them in custody in the next hour. We hope this will end it." I looked at the group of officers and asked, "Any of you folks in this room that were here two days ago?" One hand went up. I looked at him and asked, "Am I bait again?" His answer was, "No sir, and never again, you have my word!"

One of the Bills whispered something like, "Lieutenant you may stand down." The police officers left much quicker than they came in.

One of the Bills said, "We have a Bill at your home with Heather. She is packing a couple of bags, you and Heather will be sleeping in your office/suite at the Corker Hotel. You will have two nurses from the federal prison and a nurse named Ann that Heather has requested. We have a plane ten minutes out of the Saint Cloud airport to pick up the nurse, Ann. I hope this suits you.

We are going to have a live news conference with all the local stations for the six o'clock news. You will be taken on a stretcher past the reporters and cameras and be loaded into a waiting ambulance. The hospital's Chief of Medicine will be addressing the reporters and tell them that you are being flown to a hospital in Minneapolis for further testing. You will be driven by us two and two of our other Bills, in Paramedic uniforms. We will drive into the county jail sally port. You will get into a civilian van and put on civilian clothing and be driven out of the sally port and be taken to the Corker Hotel. We will drive into the, 'vender-show' garage and we will take you to your suite. Any questions or concerns?"

Me: "You guys are fucking amazing, thank you! Would you please go to the nurse's station and bring Judy back here? I have to make sure that she is ok.

Judy came in the room with a nurse and still appeared a bit shaky. I told her that I was going to a medical center in Minneapolis for testing for a few days. I assured her that I was ok and not in any medical trouble. I told her that the two ladies she was going to dine with tonight are going to help her with opening and replying to the cards and letters. Hospital security will carry the boxes to her car. The Corker Hotel will give you girls a room to work in. Honey, I need these done in the next three days. I will get the postage stamps to you guys. You will be paid for your time, paid rather handsomely!

Judy threw her arms around my neck, kissed my face and said, 'I love you so much." I smiled and said, "Baby I love you too, see you in a couple of days."

On the way to the jail the Bills told me that they got the delayed report of the botched kidnapping this morning. Which was followed within the hour of the bomb threats. They couldn't get in the air right away because of severe thunderstorms and tornados in the area. There are now twelve Bills along with Gregory and Edna, on the ground. Gregory is with the FBI Agent in Charge, Edna is with Homeland Security. We will not let anyone get near you or Heather. Your nurses are federal employees and have been well vetted, we have honored Heathers request for your friend Ann to attend to you and she was given the standard briefing on secrecy and warnings of prosecutions. You're Physican is the only other civilian that will be able to visit with you. The only thing that could potentially expose your location, is if you order Dinty Moore Beef Stew from room service.

We had a good laugh with that. I asked about the seriousness of the bomb threats. Bill smiled as he said, "I'm not going to give you the standard bullshit of how all threats are taken serious and are fully investigated and prosecuted. We are pretty sure that these are kids sitting at their keyboards in their bedroom while mom and dad are too busy to look in on them. We are about to snatch them up.

The media is hungry and the hospital is scared shitless. We are going to feed the media the finest meal that they have ever been served. We are going to enter two homes without as much as a knock on the door. We will be using FBI Bearcats to take out the entire front of the houses. The entire families will be taken into custody. We will be using Drones to capture the action of entry and the arrests for the media, they will have seats on the 50 yard line and the 'Perp Walk' will be slow and showy. There will be more fully suited SWAT teams then animals in a pet store.

We will put a stop to this bullshit real quick. If parents are not willing to raise their children with the basic standards of decency, then we are here to give them a nudge.

Mom and dad will have to burn through little Tommy's and Billy's collage funds to keep them from doing life terms. This will be the biggest one-time event in the history of this city. It will be the, Opening of Fishing season, Deer season, Grandmas Marathon, Tall Ships, Fourth of July, and the Blues Festival, all rolled into one and all the other things that makes this city great.

We know of your deep affections for the Duluth Police Department and their officers, both past and present. We will protect them and their jobs from, "The Voodoo Women," who hates cops and only wants to hang flower baskets, promotes panhandling and of course wants to be known as the, "Queen of the Universe of Bicycle Paths."

This is a federal operation and we will keep Duluth P.D. out of it. Did we miss anything?

Me: P.T. Barnum would scrape and bow to your marketing genius. I love the message that will resonate throughout the land. It will send the keyboard warriors back to discovering their pathetic little wieners and popping zits.

It was nice to be riding in a vehicle again. I hadn't realized how much I have missed in the last few weeks with all this coma and recovery stuff. I felt real hope for the first time since all this began. No dread no worry, I'm just going to smile and take care of my sweetheart.

When the van pulled into the hotels vender garage, I saw Doctor Phillips and Heather standing together along with two uniformed nurses and of course two other Bills. Heather looked weary and Doctor Phillips looked to be stunned with amazement. A nurse wheeled a wheelchair to the van as they opened the door.

We all went to my suite. Doctor Phillips was so off her game with all this, 'made for movies stuff,' that a nurse asked, "Doctor, would you like us to connect Mr. Brown's IVs, would you like us to take his vitals?" It still took a minute or two for sweet sister, Gwen to regain her wits.

Doctor Phillips: Yes, thank you nurse.

As the nurses were doing their thing, Gwen's head was on a swivel. Everyone else stayed in the kitchen/dining area. I reached to Gwen and asked, "Something on your mind sweetheart?" Heather gave me a scolding look. The nurse said, "The IV's are running and the patients vital signs are all normal. Would you like an EKG Doctor?" I guess Gwen wasn't the only one stunned from the day's events, as for the first time I noticed the exact replica of all the machines in my hospital room right down to the oxygen and defibrillator. Gwen sent the nurses to the dining room and there was just her, Heather and me.

Doctor Phillips: Don't call me sweetheart and just who the hell are you, I have to sit down!

Gwen sat on a couch along with Heather, I wheeled over to the wall panel switch hidden behind the drapes and pushed the open button. The entire room opened to nothing but glass for walls.

Gwen sucked in her breath and quietly said, "Jesus Christ, David what the fuck is all of this. I smiled as I said, "What you haven't read my books?"

Gwen: Yes, I read your books but I thought that it was all fiction. I know this is the Corker Hotel but I didn't think that this was real.

Me: You mean like chapter #30? You know the one that drove you to visit with Father Martin? Oh yes, speaking of Father Martin, I understand that he will be officiating over your wedding. I am not sure that you will remain in favor with the Roberts family for hijacking their Private Priest!

Gwen: Damn it David, what don't you know, and what is all this cloak and dagger stuff all about?

Me: I guess that you have come to realize that I'm not just another pretty face?
Its 10 minutes until the 6 o'clock news. You may find a few answers then. I looked at Heather as I asked, "Honey would you mind making us some popcorn? Let's watch.

They both started to throw couch pillows at me. It was the first time in quite a while that I heard Heather have a playful laugh. Gwen smiled as she said, "I would love to fill your IV line with popcorn kernels!"

The news showed the Bearcats breach the front walls of both houses. The drones showed some killer overhead photos, and as promised, every family member in both homes over twelve years old, were escorted in handcuffs to homeland security cars and vans. Heather looked at me with wide eyes as she said, "You knew that this was going to happen? I am about to ask you who the hell are you!"

Me: Guys take it easy. The Bills briefed me as you were home packing your bags. I can't comment on anything they told me but I bet hospital administration just took a big gulp of delicious fresh air. The danger is over and there are two young pimple farmers, who will never be allowed in any government buildings and will rise to the top of the 'no-fly' list and remain there for the rest of their lives.

Doctor Phillips: Damn it David, you are so elusive that I am never quite sure who I am talking to. You don't have multiple personalities, you have multiple lives! Does anyone, do you Heather really know who this guy is? You never tell anyone the same thing, you hide behind those gorgeous eyes and disarm everyone with those same warm eyes. You seduce women with your warm and sensual voice and later that same man with that same voice can cut your heart out of your body. I thank that you might have come from the dark side. The dark side that never sees light, just muted shades of gray, very dark gray!

You are so loveable but you dance away when others want to do for you, what you have done for them. It hurts me to care for and about you but you close the door on me and everyone else. You love everyone but won't let anyone in, to love you back. It just gets so frustrating. It hurts me to know that you have been so deeply hurt and you won't accept my attempts to comfort you. I am beginning to understand the whys of your failed marriages. Like them, I feel that I have failed you too. Am I wrong to feel this way?

Heather: Doctor, I will take this one. I have loved this man since I was 11 years old. I wasn't infatuated with David, I loved him. Today I realize how and why I loved him. Like you and like me, David tells us that we matter, we count, we are worthwhile and we are deserving. David deals out validation like Las Vegas card dealers at a Black Jack Table. His reasons are obvious if you are lucky enough to break down his walls. David knows an entire lifetime of loneliness, not just his childhood as he would like you to think but his entire lifetime, right up until this very moment. You have marveled at his many scars, sadly his invisible scars are many, many more and much, much deeper. I knew two of his wives. They were nice women and as David said in his first book where he gave thanks with; "To the women that loved me....for as long as they could."

David is deeply mistrusting in the love and friendship arenas, because of a past that he still can't come to terms with. The fact that he was beaten daily and starved told him that nobody loved him or cared about him. Doctor, where would you be today, with that kind of childhood?

As much as I wish I could change all of that, I know I can't. As David has taught me and has told thousands of others, "We are powerless to change anyone, we can only change ourselves!"

In my case and in yours as well, all we can do is let him love us, until he can find his way to love himself. If I were to quit on David I will be quitting on myself.

I know that you will understand this Doctor. David has always been a scab picker. Just when his wounds are about to heal he picks his scabs and re-opens his wounds. Of course I'm talking about his emotional wounds. David opens himself to help others. After a period of time they seem to get what they need and move on and leave him with nothing more than an infection that takes him a great deal of time to recover from. David helps people by telling them their truths which are often times his truths, his truths of his pain. Some mean people use their demented twist of the truth to harm others. They weld others truths as a weapon of ego driven superiority. David doesn't do that, he never has.

Yes David is a rare if not strange cat. He asks for very little from others and gives all that he has. He always wants more for others than he wants for himself. It always takes me back to chapter #30 and Father Martin. David is on a mission for a much higher authority, than most of us mortals.

Me: I want a pizza and a coke. You guys talk too much, I'm going to see the nice people in the kitchen.

Chapter 44   BREAKING FREE

The front desk rang the room and announced that Ann was in the lobby. One of the Bills said he would go get her. I said, "I will come with you, as I stood from my wheelchair. Ann has never seen me walk, I want to surprise her."
 Both Heather and Doctor Phillips all but lunged for me as I began to wobble. I held them off with my patented, "Back the fuck off look." I asked no one in particular, "What the fuck good is physical therapy if you can't use it. I have to stroll down the aisle in a few days, I'm in training god damn it! Besides if I can't stay on my feet Bill will give me a piggy back. Nurse, unplug me from this water pipe in my hand. I've got an old nurse friend to go hug on!"
 Ann looked like she had been pulled thru a knot hole as she scolded me for being on my feet. I collected my hug and introduced Bill to Ann. She looked him up and down as she slyly said, "David, this lovely man looks like he is in dire need of bed rest, can I keep him?"
 When we got back to the suite, Ann was warmly welcomed by everyone. When Heather asked her how she enjoyed her flight. Ann responded with, "Well I almost didn't come, I thought that someone might be trying to kidnap me, like they did David!"
 I dropped into my wheelchair and waited, as Heather started to levitate with rockets blazing.
 Heather: What…what…. kidnaped? Somebody better start talking right about fucking now! See Doctor, this is the kind of shit that David just brushes off. Nothing is ever a big deal!
 Me: Baby it was just a couple of crack heads that wanted to take me for a ride in a laundry basket.

Everyone cracked up, everyone except Heather.

Me: Jesus Christ, I'm sitting here with a top Physican and three veteran nurses and nobody can see that your patient is in distress? I am in need of an emergency nap!

This time Heather smiled as she said, "See Doctor, like I was telling you, he could have been murdered and it just somehow must have slipped his mind to tell me.

Heather kissed my forehead as she stepped aside for Ann and the other two nurses to wheel me into the master bedroom to put me in bed for my nap.

Heather woke me two hours later. She laid down next to me and put her head on my chest. She apologized for her acting out with saying, "I know that you were trying to protect me so I wouldn't worry, I love you too. I don't want to live in fear like that. This one time you get a pass for intentionally lying to me. You are the one that always says, "A half-truth is a whole lie, a little white lie or any color lie is still a lie, that an omission of the truth, is still a lie." And you still lie to me, if there is such a thing as an honorable liar you would win a trophy. Because I know you so well, I won't bother to ask you to never lie to me again."

I obviously fell back asleep and felt pretty good when I woke up. This time I was all alone.

Because the bed was on a raised platform I didn't dare to try to get to my feet alone. I looked around for a 'nurse button' but nothing was there. I heard movement and turned to see a bright eyed Amanda Roberts. She smiled and said, "You sleep pretty. Now if you are willing to get up off your ass, I'll take you down to the Lounge for dinner. I can't believe that we are all alone, with you in a bed and all I can think of is going down stairs for dinner! Everyone is in the lounge, let's go!"

Amanda helped me into the wheelchair and kissed my cheek with saying, "Only you my love, can stomp a mud hole in the Grim Reapers ass!"

When we entered the lounge the group was eating. I looked at Heather and said, "Look at what I found trying to climb into my bed!" Amanda drew back her arm to hit me, but caught herself and asked, "Doctor Phillips, Is there a safe place to punch him?"

Doctor Phillips smiled and playfully said, "Try the head, everything in there is already broken!" It was laughter all around. Doctor Phillips said, "Hey Skippy, you hungry, you are officially off of IV's. Go easy unless you want to puke your spleen up. No spices, pizza or fast foods. The trout is delicious!"

Me: Hells yes, I will eat a fish, and don't call me 'Skippy', only my baby sister Amanda gets to call me 'Skippy'!

Amanda: David you always call me, "Satins Little Sister." That means that you have finally identified yourself! We all thought you were a 'Sky Pilot,' you just told us that you are a Subterranean, you little devil you!

That meal turned everything around for me. I didn't realize that I had a headache until it was gone. I actually felt good. We all sat in the living room for a bit before my bed time. At some point it struck me. Amanda is here. I looked at her and asked her what the hell she was doing in Duluth. "You on the lamb baby, the heat looking for you?"

Amanda: No smart ass, we got a swell deal on jet fuel so I thought I'd burn some up! In truth, I couldn't stand the way you looked when you were in a coma. It haunted me every moment of every day. I felt like you had already died. I dove into a heavy depression and having a drink seemed like a hell of a good idea. I sat down with Daddy and cried my eyes out. I haven't gone to Daddy since I was a young lady. I was the reality checker for him, I steered him through all the business deals. I became the parent and he became the child.

Dad has done so well in his sobriety that I see him as the Daddy I had when I was just a little girl and before he developed his alcoholism. Daddy has become my rock. Daddy picked me up this morning for an AA meeting. We were almost to the meeting hall and dad told the driver to turn around, "We are going to the airport."

Dad said that I needed to see you and put my last sight of you away. I love my Daddy's new wisdom, I love the way he cares about me, Mother and everyone else. You two are so much alike! If it wasn't for you, my Daddy would be at the bottom of Lake Superior!

I had to see you, I just had to see you awake, I needed to hear your voice and I needed to hear you talking shit to me. I needed to fill my heart!

Me: And the rest, you little fibber? There is more, let's have it, all of it.

Glancing looks between Heather and Amanda told me that I was sniffin up the right tree.

Heather: Damn you, why can't you ever allow us to surprise you, and no smart ass, I am not going to buy you a pony! You will be discharged from the hospital tomorrow. The staff is planning a 'victory walk' for you and the Bills will secure all the doors so you can't go out a back door. These hospital people deserve to celebrate and you will comply as a grateful and humble gentleman. No bullshit, understand?

Me: Yes my love. Amanda, your turn.

Amanda: We are having a small gathering on Friday afternoon for less than twenty people. I see that look, I promises no more than twenty. Quit looking at me like that! I am not lying.

Me: You miss read my look. I was looking at your butt! Doctor Phillips do you have anything to add? If not I do. Gwen where is your reception being held on Saturday?

Gwen: In the ballroom downstairs. We took the bridal suite here for our wedding night.

Me: Not acceptable, not acceptable at all. Do you like this joint Gwen? Of course you do! You and that blood sucker, 'Cheap Prick' will spend your wedding night right here in this room. You can have it for as long as you two want it. It's a hard no, as to your Bachelorette Party here. I don't want a bunch of wine and girly drinks spilled on my carpet.

You girl's go ahead and chat it up, I need to go to sleep.

The following morning I woke to having heather next to me. I smelled her before I saw her. She doesn't wear perfume or hairspray. I smelled her honeydew skin. Today is the best day of my entire life.

Ann put a kitchen chair in the shower and it was the first time I bathed myself since the accident. I needed help dressing but when it was time to leave the suite, I intentionally left the wheelchair behind. I walked into the hospital with the help of two Bills. We didn't quite make it to the elevators before I needed a wheelchair. I guess word got out, before I could get to my room to pack my stuff and sign the discharge papers.

The entire Roberts family was sitting in the hallway. I collected kisses and handshakes as we all wiped our eyes. I opened my door and the room was packed with balloons and flowers. I could not see a bare spot on the ceiling, it was wall to wall balloons. I went into the bathroom, closed and locked the door. I took a few minutes to reflect on god's grace and mankind's loving hearts. I did not feel that I deserved this kind of attention. All I did was survive, there is nothing heroic about that.

Hospital Admissions brought my discharge papers to me. I signed and was given my copies. As the clerk turned to leave she stopped and asked, "Can I ask you for a hug?" We had a hug, and I walked her to the door. I looked at the Roberts family, Doctor Phillips and Heather as I said, "Everyone please come in." I sat on the bed and patted both sides of me and said, "Jane, Heather, come and sit with me." I told everyone that I felt undeserving and almost ashamed to get all this attention. "All I did was not die!"

It was one of the Bills that stepped in front of me and smiled, as he said,

"David you are right about not dying is not heroic. These people in this hospital and us here with you now, are not celebrating that you are living. What we and they are celebrating is the way you live. You speak of hope quite often, you leaving here today shows these people what hope can do, not just for you but

what hope can do for them. We are all here to celebrate the power of hope! You are the center of hope and God's witness to believing. We all need to see God's powers and affections at work. God told you directly, to "Teach them well."
Come along teacher, we have a parade to attend!
 We all held hands and Jane led us in the 'Lord's Prayer.'

THE END

To my friends, my readers and my family.

This book brings my writing career to a bittersweet end. I have two emotions bouncing in my belly.
#1.I have just watched my best friend being lowered into the ground.
#2.I have just buried my worst enemy.
I don't enjoy writing. Most often times, I hate it. Many people think my writing is cathartic. It is however the exact opposite. I will always be broken but I am no longer shattered. I write in hopes to reach people like me. I also write as a living amends to those I have harmed. All three of my novels are much more truth than fiction.
I can no longer carry the torch. It is now the time that I focus on being the mate my sweetheart deserves. I have been selfish with my time and have neglected my household responsibilities. I was gifted a new open top kayak, a life jacket, a fly rod, reel and line with several hand tied flies by my family. Now is the time to enjoy the life that God has so graciously blessed me with. I will leave you with this:
"It is not so much about the paths you choose, as it is about the grace you carry along your travels."

Wishing you all the best.

Be well.

Dave

To contact the author, David J. Brown:
djbrownbooks@gmail.com

To order signed copies of David's three novels:
"Daddy Had to Say Goodbye"
"Flesh of a Fraud"
"Harvest Season"
Please visit David J. Brown's website
@www.davidjbrownbooks.com

You may also request to schedule David J. Brown to speak (80 minutes) for your upcoming events.

Printed in the United States of America

God Bless America

Made in the USA
Monee, IL
28 June 2020